Blaze of Glory

Blaze of Glory

AGATHA YOUNG

RANDOM HOUSE · NEW YORK

Blaze of Glory

Chapter One

SARATOGA lay quiet at the hour of dinner. The streets, which all through the afternoon had been crowded with carriages moving in slow procession to the springs or the shops or the race tracks, were almost deserted. On the open roads, no more light traps raced each other in clouds of dust and no stylish ladies in big bustles, with their little dogs on bright-colored leashes, promenaded in the parks. The dust had settled and the noise had subsided.

On the piazza of the United States Hotel most of the rockers in the block-long row were empty, and in the quiet of this evening of 1885 the huge white building looked as lifeless and as imposing as a picture on a circular, for at dinner time all the animation and the sparkle of the great establishment were shut inside. The hotel was built around a central court which had a fountain in the middle and triangular flower beds between cross walks, and all of the rooms of the court opened onto long galleries. This was the fashionable part of the hotel, the expensive part. Here lights glowed behind drawn blinds in every window and a hush hung over everything, for people were engaged in the solemn, nightly ritual of dressing for dinner.

Inside one of these rooms a young woman sat at her dressing table, submitting with catlike pleasure while a maid in a shiny black silk uniform brushed her hair. The hair was long and golden and, after each stroke of the brush, it sprang back into deep waves which caught the light and glistened. The brush rose and fell with a mesmeric rhythm and with each outward sweep Willoughby's head went back. Her eyes were half closed and she was lulled into a trancelike state by soft whisperings, as the maid counted each stroke under her breath. *"Quatre-vingt-dix-sept, quatre-vingt-dix-huit."* The whispering sounded like the faint rustling of dry leaves and there was no other sound in the room but the steady hiss of the jets in the gasolier.

"Cent!" The brush swooped down with extra force and then made a parabolic gesture in the air. *"Voilà,* Madame."

Willoughby shook back her hair, liking the live feeling in it which always followed a long brushing. The maid's compact figure, with its severely restrained bulges, bent forward and her naturally grasping, yellowish fingers gathered up a handful of shell pins from the dressing table. She began with rapid, deft movements and an air of confidence to twist and pin the blond hair.

Idly, Willoughby stretched out her hand for a gold-backed nail buffer and as she did so she caught an unpremeditated glimpse of herself in the glass. It startled her. The hand which held the buffer sank slowly while she studied herself. She was careful not to change in any way the expression which she had caught and she was cool and objective about her scrutiny, but this had turned into one of those devastating moments which happen occasionally to everyone, in which she saw herself, not as she thought she looked, but as the world actually saw her. The beauty which she knew she had was marred, it seemed to her, by a look of too much willfulness and the expression in her blue eyes was too cold. She knew that too much determination showed in her mouth and in the long, smooth curve of her chin.

These faults disturbed, rather than spoiled, her beauty but they were italicized by a vitality of both body and spirit, which gave every expression of her face, and every motion of her tall, beautifully proportioned figure, an extra vividness. She was quite aware that she possessed this vividness and aware, too, that her abundant capacity for life had an effect on other people, jarring them, almost, into a greater aliveness.

She was beginning to learn how to make use of this and she was working to learn the actress's art of guarding her expression always without ever seeming to do so. Now, still studying her reflection, she changed the line of her mouth slightly until it looked soft, the under lip full and provocative. She made her eyes bright and challenging, and she tipped her head a trifle to hide the force in the curve of her chin. She examined this new effect carefully and, liking it, she smiled, telling herself she *must* remember. This way there was no longer anything but softness and appeal in her loveliness and the smile added a last touch of radiance. Then her attention was caught by the coils and puffs of hair which were evolving under the maid's capable fingers.

"Suzanne, what on earth are you doing?"

The little yellow fingers did not pause. "Something new. Something ver-ee new, Madame. I see Madame's coiffure is just the ver-ee littlest bit old style. So I change it."

"I want it to be becoming."

"*Assurément*, Madame!"

A gleam of light came into Suzanne's small, black eyes and she leaned down close to Willoughby. She lowered her harsh voice to a harsher whisper. "Besides, Madame, it is necessary to do honor to a new man by a beautiful new appearance, *n'est-ce pas?*"

"How do you know there's a new man? You're incorrigible, Suzanne!"

"Because Madame walks with a new lightness and sings little songs to herself while she walks. This you have not done since you left your husband. Besides, I have seen him."

"You've seen him?"

"Handsome, Madame. Ver-ee distinguished."

After that they were silent and Willoughby watched in the mirror the movement of Suzanne's hands. They looked avaricious. Suzanne's top-heavy body in its glistening black satin uniform, which fitted so smoothly over her curves, made her look wet, like something dredged up out of a pond—a tadpole stood on its tail.

"I watch a great deal here at Saratoga and I see many things. The ladies' maids wear no little aprons, Madame. So I wear no little aprons. And I must have a little black purse that I carry in front of me—*so*—when I follow Madame on her walks. And a new black bonnet with ver-ee long, black streamers. *Voilà*, Madame. It is finished."

Willoughby picked up the hand glass and studied herself from all angles. Then she said, "Good," laid the glass down and rose. Suzanne spread a sheet on the floor in front of the cheval glass and Willoughby stood on it, holding her arms up so that Suzanne could fasten the ribbon-trimmed bustle around her waist. A petticoat with lace ruffles and more ribbon bows went on next. It fitted Willoughby's figure closely in front, and in the back it was cut to lie smoothly over the horsehair bustle. When the petticoat was adjusted, Suzanne went to the bed and picked up with care a yellow-gold gown which had a satin underskirt and draperies of tulle and a very low neck with shirrings of the tulle around the shoulders. Willoughby bent to let Suzanne lift the gown over her head, protecting her coiffure with both hands.

"The exact color of Madame's hair. It takes a perfect complexion to wear yellow. Nobody else will dare. They'll all look at Madame."

Willoughby laughed at the smug self-satisfaction in the tone. "I believe you think you created me!"

Suzanne looked puzzled. Then she said, "*Oui*, Madame," and began to adjust the gown over the shelflike bustle. While Suzanne hooked up first the boned China-silk lining and then the dress itself, Willoughby's eyes wandered around the room. Like everything else in the United States Hotel, it was elegant, if not quite in the latest fashion. Willoughby was a good judge of fashion. She would, for example, have preferred curtains with horizontal stripes made of one of the new materials which looked hand-woven, instead of the looped-back red velvet ones. She would have discarded the elaborate pressed-brass cornices which nowadays made you think of stodgy, middle-class England, and had the curtains hung by big brass rings run over a thick pole—perhaps from the handle of an imitation Moorish spear.

Everything was going Moorish. It was a different sort of elegance altogether that the smart world was striving for today—more sensuous, and so both more stimulating and more relaxing. You couldn't recline on the horsehair-covered settee in this room the way you could on a divan and a pile of Moorish pillows, even though, with bustles growing larger and larger, you had to do your reclining on one hip. But the Moorish style was new, even in New York, where most people still thought of it as shocking and bohemian, so perhaps the United States Hotel was wise to cling to its white marble mantels and the chandeliers and ornamental plaster which dripped from its high ceilings. There was something about a hotel room, though, which always betrayed its elegance. Perhaps it was the faint smell of dust and china slop-jars. Suddenly she was sick of it all. Suzanne, on her knees, was pulling on the tapes which drew the gown close to Willoughby's body in front.

"That's too tight!"

Suzanne looked up in surprise at the sudden flare of anger, and Willoughby said in a different tone, "Suzanne, I've never been happy or had what I wanted. If only I didn't want things so much."

Suzanne arose with a matter-of-fact patience. She had in her hand a loop of ribbon attached to the train of the gown, and she held it out in silence. Willoughby took it and slipped it over her arm. She always knew when Suzanne was angry because she blinked and then her lids looked a little like a parrot's. Suzanne turned away and Willoughby watched, in the mirror, the hard little back retreating eloquently. Servants had so many subtle ways of making you feel uncomfortable!

Willoughby stepped off the sheet and went to one of the two French doors. These were curtained like windows with lace under the red velvet. She pushed the lace aside and the smell of dust grew more pronounced. The doors stuck a little, but her hands were strong. She stepped out on the gallery which enclosed each floor of the court. The September night was soft, but had a hint of fall in the air. The darkness of the court was misty with the light from many windows. The fountain in the center plashed rhythmically, and the breeze bore sounds of voices and laughter. She stood by the ornate iron railing. It was like being on the edge of a stage, but it was more like the romantic color of her daydreams than the real stage had turned out to be. So far, the stage was hard work, dust and glaring lights, the smell of gas and a shouting director. No admiration, no excitement, and a constant threat of failure.

She sighed and turned back into the room. Suzanne was unfolding the tissue paper in a florist's box which lay on the bed. As Willoughby watched, she reached in and lifted out an American Beauty rose, held it away from her, and clucked approvingly at the length of stem. Willoughby's voice at her side startled her.

"Who sent these?"

Suzanne's hand dove into the box and proffered a small envelope. *Mr. Stuyvesant Lailey* was engraved on the card and under it was written, *For a great beauty. S. L.* She held the card a moment, trying to read something about the man's character from his writing. The scrawl looked forceful and authoritative, but it had been easy to see these qualities in him during their one meeting. She tossed the card on the bed and leaned over the box.

A small bouquet lay on the stems of the roses. It was the size and shape to be carried in the hand—round, the flowers tightly packed— and the frill which surrounded it was real lace. Willoughby lifted it out and Suzanne sucked in her breath in a hiss of approval.

"See, Madame, small orchids! Ver-ee rare."

The other flowers in the bouquet were pointed yellow rosebuds.

"Monsieur asked me what would be the color of Madame's gown."

"It's time to go. Give me my gloves."

Willoughby held out first one arm and then the other while
8

Suzanne pulled on the long, white gloves. Then Suzanne stepped back to survey her handiwork. Suddenly she laughed and the unfamiliar sound startled Willoughby.

"Have a good evening, Madame!"

Out in the wide, deserted corridor Willoughby walked with the lightness which Suzanne had remarked, and the carpet of straw matting rustled softly under her feet. She had a trick of leaning forward when she walked—not bending, because her body was perfectly straight and her head held high. This walk was another thing she had taught herself and it heightened greatly the impression of her unusual aliveness. It was a beautiful carriage, just short of imperious, and she was in complete possession of it. Because of it she dominated her huge bustle easily and it lent grace to the stiff, boxlike fashion which gave most women a look of rigidity.

As she approached the drawing room where she was to meet Lailey, she walked more slowly. She wanted to be a little late. He was not in the crowd just inside the archway, and she stepped behind some potted palms so that she could look for him without being seen. The palms made her feel as though she were in the wings of a stage and she liked the thought. She liked to act even when she was not on the stage. At first she thought Lailey wasn't there, but when the crowd in the archway thinned a little she saw him standing in front of the fireplace at one end of the room. His back was toward her and he was examining a painting which hung over the mantel. As she watched he made a slight movement of disparagement with his shoulders, glanced with contempt at the mantel ornaments of Japanese fans and dried grasses and turned to watch the other archway, obviously expecting her to make her entrance from there.

If he had looked in her direction he would have seen her, but she stayed behind the palms, estimating him. She was curious about him, having met him only once and then briefly. She liked the way he looked. He was tall, but built in such good proportions that you wouldn't be apt to think about it. His tailoring was perfect, and he seemed unconscious of it. His hair was more predominantly black

9

than gray, and his eyes were gray. The light eyes were arresting and they were alert and restless. The restlessness had a touch of impatience in it which she thought might be characteristic, or might have to do with her lateness. He stood in front of the fireplace as though, in a room filled with people, the most commanding place in it was the natural place for him to stand.

There was something about him which filled her with excitement. She leaned forward eagerly and parted the fronds of the palm as far as she dared. She was enjoying the moment thoroughly, the more because there was some risk in it. Ordinarily, she never looked twice to see what was in a person's face and she never attempted to read other peoples' thoughts except to find out how she was affecting them. She was not in the least an analytical person. She was looking at Stuyvesant Lailey in much the same spirit in which she might look at the cover of a book to see if it promised to give her a thrilling afternoon. Willoughby never read books, however, if there were anything else to do, for people were always more absorbing to her than books could possibly be.

Stuyvesant Lailey promised well. The gray eyes had a way of filling with fire suddenly. She saw it happen twice when some woman came through the entrance he was watching, and she saw it die out again when he discovered that the woman was not herself. When the fire was not in them, his eyes looked cold and assured and capable of anger. She liked that, too.

There had to be something more than anger, of course. The trouble was, there never had been anything else between herself and Sam, except the passion which so often had followed the anger. But Sam was back in Cleveland now and her wedding ring was in her jewel box upstairs.

Certainly Stuyvesant Lailey looked sure of himself, an attitude which she could understand because she felt that way herself. It showed when he raised his hand to acknowledge the greeting of a friend across the room. His gesture was a trifle perfunctory, as though he intended to keep his acqaintance from crossing the room to join him, and she looked to see for whom the gesture was intended. She saw a rather stout man with an "imperial" who she felt fairly certain was Ward McAllister, coming social arbiter, a man very few had the assurance to snub.

Lailey had retired into his own thoughts again and she thought that now his face looked sensitive and rather moody. A slantwise furrow had appeared between his brows. His changing expressions made her suspect that he was capable of a wide range of emotions and this excited her, too, because staid people, placid people, bored her and boredom was always threatening her.

She was afraid to stay where she was any longer for fear he would see her lurking there. She dropped the ribbon off her arm and stooped to arrange the flounced yellow train behind her carefully. Then she straightened up, moved her hips the way women do when they want to settle their clothes around them, and put her hands on either side of her tight waist, forcing her corset down. She took a deep breath, which made her stand up straight and tall, and her eyes began to sparkle. She stood there a moment longer, breathing fast, until she was sure that the vitality in her was all turned on.

When she and Lailey entered the dining room together, heads turned and the whispers made a sound like a breeze in the room. She loved it. Their table was small and lace-covered. A champagne bucket on a pedestal stood nearby. There was a mat of flowers in the center of the table, more yellow rosebuds and pale, gray-blue violets. She flushed because she had let her eyes widen in surprise at the sight of violets in September. To hide the flush she bent her head and began tucking the hands of her gloves into neat rolls on the backs of her wrists. When she looked up, she found that Lailey had been watching her. His gray eyes were almost insulting in their directness. The look made her angry and she showed it. He laughed. She put her hands on the edge of the table and pushed back her spindly gilt chair.

He said, "I'm sorry. Please forgive me. You're so *damn* good looking."

The spark died out of her blue eyes, and suddenly they were both laughing. The laughter made the diners at nearby tables turn to look at them. Feeling their stares, her heart began to beat more swiftly.

He pushed his plate away and leaned on his folded arms, as near to her as he could, and she raised her bouquet to her face and sniffed the rosebuds.

"You're on the stage, I understand. Why haven't I ever seen you?"

"I'm not on the stage yet. My first play opens soon." She said it primly because his gray eyes, which were at the same time cold and very hot, were resting on her breast just above the low-cut bodice of her gown.

"What a star you'll make! Your show opens in New York, I hope?"

"No. Philadelphia—then New York. And I'm not the star."

"*You*—not the star?"

"No—but I want to be a star. Because I want to be famous and have people look at me and whisper, 'That's Willow Cleveland.' I want to hear people applaud me and I want to make my life exciting."

He laughed. "You want a lot. It's exhilarating to listen to you, though. I like it. But I still think it's an extraordinary thing for you to do since—judging by appearances—you don't have to earn a living. How did you happen to start?"

"Because I want to make my own sort of life and I think I can, in the theater."

"I'd bet you won't be playing small parts long. Your attitude's unusual in a woman. Where do you come from? Is Willow Cleveland your real name or a stage name? It doesn't sound quite real."

"I don't very often talk about myself," Willoughby said.

He raised his eyebrows and his mouth tightened. The snub obviously annoyed him. Then he asked in a somewhat distant way, "If you're in a play, how do you happen to be in Saratoga? I'd think you'd have to be rehearsing."

"We have been rehearsing. Rita Délice, the star, has been in Paris and we've been rehearsing with what they call a stand-in.

They do that sometimes, and the star just rehearses for a week or two. She cabled Mr. Dubinsky—he's the producer-manager—that she'd be a week late getting home. I don't think he liked it very well, but he gave us a week off so we wouldn't be what he calls 'over-rehearsed,' and I came up here. Most of the cast is pretty angry with her because, of course, you don't get paid while you rehearse. They say she does things like that all the time. I suppose I would, too, if I were a star."

Lailey moved restlessly, as though his fine, compact body resented the limitations of the gilt chair. A waiter substituted turtle soup for the half-eaten caviar. He glanced at it and hitched his chair a little closer.

"Nobody in this place knows a thing about you," he said.

"I told you I seldom talk about myself."

He smiled, and she thought his smile made him look very friendly and pleasant.

"I even bribed your maid to find out about you. She took my money but she wouldn't tell me a thing except that you'd wear yellow tonight."

The waiter at her elbow said, "Sherry, Madam?" and she started slightly. "Please," she said, and watched as the pale gold sherry was poured into her soup.

"I'm going to call you Willow. Do you mind?"

"No. But don't let's talk about me any more. Tell me about you."

"Well, my name's Stuyvesant. . . . Hold on. Not too much—it cools the soup. . . . They called me 'Stu' at Yale."

"Stuyvesant."

"You make it sound nice. Call me that."

"Go on."

"All right—let's see. I'm a widower and I live in New York . . ."

She wondered whether he really thought that facts like these weren't generally known about Stuyvesant Lailey.

". . . I don't have any family except a niece who is coming from California to live with me."

"What are you doing in Saratoga? Races?"

"No. I came because I knew that the most beautiful woman in America would be here."

"Nonsense. You never heard of me before."

"Well, as a matter of fact, I came to make a deal. You know how it is in Wall Street—the reporters watch every breath you take, and they think they can tell by the way you tip your hat whether the Market's going up or down. I had a deal to work out with some Market operators and so I fixed it to come up here. They brought their families to make the meeting look accidental. Deal's closed now and I'm going home. But I might find I had some business in Philadelphia pretty soon."

She smiled and flushed. Then she said, "You're what they call a Market operator?"

"Well, yes and no. My father made iron in Pittsburgh, and I still own the mill. We made a little steel, too, of a special kind. Then a short while ago our chief competitor converted a hundred percent to steel. We couldn't let him get away with that, so we did the same thing. We would have done it before, only I've never been very keen about running the mill. It's the Market that interests me."

"That niece of yours," she said. "The one that's coming to live with you—what's she like?"

"I don't know. I've never laid eyes on her. To hell with her. It's you I'm interested in."

He leaned across the table and, grasping her hand, dragged it toward him through the violets and rosebuds. The thorns scratched her and an angry light came into her eyes. She said, "Let go!" She tried to pull her hand away, but he held it. He was watching her, and when he saw that she was perfectly capable of making a disturbance which would make other diners turn and look at them, he released her.

He said, "I'm sorry. I couldn't help it. You're the most attractive woman I ever saw. We're going to mean a lot to each other from now on, Willow."

"The theater comes first. I'm going to put everything I have into that. It won't leave time for much else."

14

"You have to have some social life."

"Perhaps."

"Why did you get so angry when I tried to hold your hand?"

"Because I hate to be forced to do things."

They were silent and after a moment he said, "I like your spirit—damned if I don't. Will you forgive me?"

"Certainly. If you will just let me do things my own way."

"Wouldn't you have been insulted if I hadn't tried?"

"Probably!"

They both laughed and after that they both enjoyed themselves until, at the end of the meal, he said, "How about having our brandy upstairs in my suite?"

"No!"

They looked straight at each other. Then, suddenly, he was on the verge of being angry, too. He said, "Maybe you'd like to take a walk on the piazza."

"That would be nice."

He was not sure from the way she said it whether she was aware of the sarcasm in his words or not.

The piazza of the United States Hotel was broad and long. A strip of red carpet ran its entire length and rocking chairs, in a single row, were backed against the wall. In spite of the gusts of fall wind which were tossing the trees, a great many people had come out of doors, some to sit in the rocking chairs, others to promenade slowly. He steered her toward the end of the piazza which was the darker, but if she understood this maneuver, she did not seem to mind. She walked slowly down the strip of red carpet, apparently expecting other people to make way for her, and Lailey was both amused and impressed because, for the most part, they did. He knew that he and she were attracting a great deal of attention, and he wondered if she knew it too. She had style. She walked well. She made him think of the figurehead of a stately ship.

When they reached the end of the piazza, he took her arm and turned her toward the railing. They leaned on it side by side, and she put up a hand to brush back the blond curls which the wind had loosened. Her other hand was resting on the railing and he put his over it. This time she made no effort to pull away. Her hand felt strong, and it gave him the impression that there was more of her character in it than in her face. It was not a particularly feminine hand, and though it was shapely and well cared for, it was not really beautiful. He ran his thumb and finger along its contour and then covered it with his own.

He said, "I swear I don't understand you, Willow."

"Why not?"

"You got really angry when I suggested brandy up in my place, didn't you?"

She laughed and he repeated, "Didn't you?"

"Well—yes, I did."

"Why should you? You look like a woman of the world. You know how to handle yourself—you know what things are all about."

"Maybe that's why."

"But still . . . Forgive me, will you? You *are* a woman of the world. You're on the stage, though I must say you don't look in the least like the average actress. You're not afraid to come to a big hotel like this with nobody with you but your maid and—don't get angry with me again—you're not afraid to have dinner with a man you only met once, and about whom you really don't know anything. Naturally, I'd suppose . . . And then you get angry. I don't understand you and you interest me. I like you a lot or I wouldn't be saying these things, so take it like that, will you? I wish you'd tell me about yourself."

She pulled her hand away and faced him.

"All right—you've been frank with me, so I'll be frank with you. It isn't often a woman says what she really thinks, and it's a relief once in a while. When a woman lives alone there are always men, and . . ."

"An attractive woman."

"And they all want the same thing. It's exciting at first. At first I loved it. It's a game, a competition. Each new one is a new adventure. But after a while you get awfully sick of it. You go on playing

16

the game because it *is* amusing, but in your heart you're awfully sick of it. And you get lonely. Not one of them cares anything about you really—it's a game to them too. Oh, some of them fall in love with you, or think they do, but they don't know what you're really like, and they don't even try to find out. It's themselves they're thinking about."

"I want to find out what you're like."

She gave him a swift look, but she did not acknowledge the interruption in any other way.

"It's a dreadful thing to wake up alone at night and realize that there isn't anybody in the world you care about or who cares about you—really cares about you enough to take you the way you are—faults and all. I'm not going to live like that any more. I'm going to get what I want out of life."

"I like you, Willow. I like the things you've just said."

"I like you too, or I wouldn't be talking like this. I haven't really said what I thought about things for a long time. It's queer to be saying these things to a stranger. I don't know what's got into me."

"Go on saying them."

"All right. What I'm getting at is this—I don't doubt at all that you and I could have a wonderful time together."

"Of course we could."

"But it would be just the same thing all over again."

"How do you know?"

"Stuyvesant, I said I seldom talk about myself, and I'm not going to—not, anyway, until my future is a lot clearer and a lot more settled than it is now. But since I'm telling the truth for once, I'll say this much. I let my happiness depend on someone else once. It didn't work. I was miserable. I'm never again going to let myself be in a position where my happiness depends on any one person or on a lot of chance acquaintances. I'm going to make my life over and I'm going to depend on myself."

"That's a hard thing to try to do."

"I know it is, but I'm going to have the kind of life I want, and I'm not going to let anything deflect me from it. You asked me to dinner and I've enjoyed it, but I've made up my mind it's going to stop there. I'm not going to complicate my life any further. You can get angry if you like. You have every right to."

"I'm not angry."

"But you don't believe I'm going to do it."

"I don't think you know how hard it is to make a success in the theater—or in anything else, for that matter." He was amused, and he was smiling. He put his hand around her arm, and he stopped smiling. "You're trembling," he said.

"I want so much to be a success and to have a life of my own."

"You don't have to shut me out entirely."

"No, not entirely." She held out her hand to him and he took it. She pressed his fingers. "I do like you, Stuyvesant. You're an easy person to talk to. I guess I've needed someone to talk to. And it's a relief to be yourself and say what you think. I don't believe I've said what I think about anything at all for a long time. I don't know why, but it's upsetting to do it. I feel sort of shaken. If you understand, then we can be friends. I'd like to be friends. If you don't, all right. I don't want you to say anything. I'm going upstairs now."

She started to move away but he took hold of her arms and turned her around to face him.

"Willow!"

They stood like that, he holding her arms tightly and she with her chin up, looking straight at each other. A light came into her eyes.

"The theater comes first!"

"We'll see about that. *I'm coming to Philadelphia.*"

Chapter Two

STUYVESANT LAILEY left Saratoga early the next morning, spent the week-end at home becoming acquainted with his niece, who had arrived from California in his absence, and Sunday night he was again on the train, bound for Pittsburgh and the steel mill. He stayed there for three busy and distasteful days and on Thursday night he was standing in a queue at one end of the railroad car, waiting for the train to pull into the station at Philadelphia.

Willow was not expecting him and that was part of his plan. He thought that by arriving in the middle of the evening he could, with luck, see some of the rehearsal and take her with him for a late supper afterward. He left his bag at the hotel and went directly to the theater, but when he got there, he was at a loss. No lights showed. It had the dirty and deserted look common to all theaters when no audience is present. Papers and street debris were caught in the corners of the doors. He looked up at the marquee to make sure that this was the right place and smiled because it seemed to him amusing that so many producers tried to circumvent puritanical prejudices by calling their theaters Academies, Lycea, Opera Houses, Athenaea—anything, in short, but theaters. This was no exception. The marquee bore a notice, in removable letters, announcing the opening of *The Rungs of the Ladder* the following week.

He crossed the sidewalk and tried one of the doors and, as he expected, found it locked. Passers-by were beginning to glance at him curiously. He looked about him and discovered an alley at one side of the building, a villainous-looking cavern of blackness. He entered it cautiously and saw, at the far end, some cracks of light which seemed to be coming from a door in the wall of the theater.

Inside was a wide corridor, deserted save for an old man sitting in a chair which was tipped back against the dirty wall. His hat was over his face and he had obviously been asleep, but when Lailey stepped inside the chair legs came down with a crash and he rose belligerently.

"You can't come in here, Mister."

"I want to see Miss Cleveland."

"Rehearsal's on. Can't see nobody till it's over."

"I won't disturb the rehearsal." Smiling, Lailey drew out his wallet, extracted a greenback and held it out. The old fellow blinked in astonishment and reached out a shaky hand. With the bill safely in his possession, he retreated.

"All right, Mister. I didn't see you come in. But you better be quiet while rehearsal's on—understand? Nobody's allowed in no dressing rooms except Miss Délice's, so you better wait in the greenroom till it's over. It's upstairs to the front. Don't let Dubinsky see you. I shouldn't do this, but I don't get to see one of these things often." He began folding the bill with care.

Lailey found himself in labyrinthine passages which were badly lit and had a curious odor. He had no intention of waiting in the greenroom, whatever that might be. With a rehearsal in progress he intended to see it. He walked rapidly with a swinging stride and, more by luck than a sense of direction, came at last into the dusty lobby.

A row of curtained glass doors seemed to indicate the auditorium. He pushed through one of these and found himself in a darkness made deeper by the brilliant lighting of the stage. A scene was in progress but Willow was not in it. He stood still and gave his eyes a chance to accustom themselves to the darkness. Gradually aisles and stalls became discernible. The boxes and most of the seats were under green dust-covers, but the whole center section was open and a lone man, who had the round, thick shoulders of a Buddha, was sitting about halfway between Lailey and the stage. As nearly as Lailey could make out, he was hunched over in a position of mortal agony. Doubting the reality of the agony, Lailey made his way down the aisle and took a seat directly behind.

Lailey's plan was to wait for a propitious moment and ask this person, whom he took to be Dubinsky, to release Miss Cleveland promptly so that they might have supper together. That anyone might object seriously to his presence never occurred to Lailey but, even to a nature as self-confident as his, the moment did not seem propitious. Dubinsky cast a quick look over his shoulder, saw Lailey and started to speak, but he was distracted by something which was happening on the stage. He began to beat the seat in front of him with his fists and said in tones of deep distress, "Look at them. Holy Moses, look at them!"

Dubinsky's voice startled Lailey, who had been expecting, without thinking about it, an accent to match the swarthy, rotund figure. In spite of the expletive, the voice was cultured, almost scholarly, in its inflections. He shifted his attention to the stage. The play seemed to be of the English drawing-room type and a number of well-mannered people were moving and speaking in a civilized way. He could see nothing wrong with it.

"What's the trouble?" he asked.

"Trouble!" Dubinsky pulled out a handkerchief and passed it over his eyes and around the back of his neck. Then the fact that he was talking to a stranger, whose presence in the dark house was unauthorized, seemed to penetrate his consciousness for the first time. He twisted with difficulty around in his seat.

"Who are you?"

"My name's Lailey."

"What are you doing . . . ?"

Again he sensed or heard something on the stage and it brought him to his feet shouting, "Hold it! Hold it!" He began with practiced rapidity to edge crabwise out of the row of seats.

There was a sudden silence on the stage. No one moved. The actors stood, in fact, as though they were frozen in a tableau, and then Lailey became aware of a furious thing. The illusion of the theater was beginning to dissolve before his eyes. Watching that moment was like watching something fall apart. In subtle ways that Lailey could not have described, the characters of the play faded away and the stage was mysteriously full of personalities which had not been there an instant before. Lailey was a trifle awed.

Dubinsky had reached the railing which separated the orchestra pit from the first row of seats. He grasped it in both hands, leaning as far over it as his short stature would allow. He spoke in tones of agonized pleading.

"Rita darling!"

The name evidently brought assurance to the rest of the cast that the lightning would not strike them, for they relaxed visibly. An actress came slowly downstage to stand just out of the glare of the footlights. She was small and possessed of no great beauty. She walked with infinite grace and stood as though her body weighed nothing at all. It was obvious to Lailey that she was the star, and he wondered what were the qualities which made this fact plain. Nothing tangible. That she was older than the others had nothing to do with it, but she appeared to be, in a sense, a more complicated mechanism, or at least the others seemed blunt and shallow by comparison. Older than she seemed, probably, and he remembered that he had been seeing her name on billboards for a good many years.

Her voice was startlingly rich and musical.

"Yes, Ike?"

Lailey thought she spoke timidly, like a guilty child.

"Listen, darling." The pleading was still in Dubinsky's voice. "What's the matter?"

"Nothing, Ike."

"Yes there is. You do it every time."

"What, Ike? I don't know what you mean."

"Yes you do, Rita. You begin to go to pieces right here in the same place every time. You get stiff and edgy—even your voice. I should think you could hear it yourself. Holy cow, Rita, the opening's next week! It's right here you do it, just before Miss Cleveland's entrance. Now let's take it over again."

A head with disheveled hair appeared from the wings with the suddenness of a Jack-in-the-box.

"From where?"

Dubinsky, now plodding wearily back up the aisle, said over his shoulder, "From the beginning of the scene, Burt."

"All right, folks. Places."

Burt withdrew and a youth whom Lailey had not noticed before, because he was slumped so far down in his seat under the first box, turned around and said, "You want me to cue them, sir?" Dubinsky said "Yes," and the youth turned up a light, put his finger on a page and said with no inflection at all, "Act-Two-Scene-Two-John-'She-fooled-you-all'," and slid down out of sight. The actors, who had reshuffled themselves and once more miraculously become the characters in the play, began to speak their lines. They assumed the emotional pitch of the scene as though there had been no interruption.

When they were launched, Dubinsky squirmed around in his seat and Lailey thought he was going to be asked to leave, but Dubinsky said, "Damned if I understand her. She was all right the first couple of rehearsals. I thought she'd got over it but she seems to be getting worse, if anything."

"What is it that's wrong?"

"I wish I knew. She's taken a dislike to this Cleveland girl. She's new in the cast and Rita wants me to fire her. I would if it weren't so close to opening. It's queer, because Rita never felt so strongly about anybody in the cast before—they're too far beneath her. Wait! Watch this scene now. Watch it! Rita can't do it to me again. Holy Moses, she *can't*."

23

Dubinsky's back was turned to Lailey. The play seemed to be building to some sort of climax, and Lailey could hear Dubinsky breathing heavily. Miss Délice was obviously making a real effort and, to Lailey's eyes at least, all traces of her nervous *crise* had vanished. Her voice was flowing out in mellow beauty. It seemed wonderfully full and strong for so plain and small a body. Then she no longer seemed either small or plain. A light glowed in her, and her sensitive personality reached out to him over the footlights. "She's an artist," he whispered to Dubinsky's back. "By God, she's a real artist."

Dubinsky did not hear him. The monologue had begun and her wonderful voice filled the theater. She was approaching the footlights slowly, as though drawn by invisible chains, her graceful body swaying.

Dubinsky rose quietly. He stood with his hands resting lightly on the seat in front of him. His head was up. At first Lailey thought it was a kind of tribute, and then he knew that this was not wholly true but that Dubinsky, in a sense, was sustaining her. She came closer, pouring out the beautiful voice. She was drawing strength from him, but there was more than that between them. They were creating something together. Lailey felt it with a growing excitement. Then he was swept into one of those rare moments for which the theater exists, when the stage becomes, not reality, but the transfiguration of reality.

Quietly, at the back of the stage, Willow made her entrance. The tenseness was no longer there. Lailey slumped back in his seat.

Rita's thin body quivered. Dubinsky sat down—but on the edge of his seat. Rita could not see Willow, but her voice was no longer filling the theater. Then she faltered. Dubinsky half rose, and sank back. Rita looked behind her. The swift look took her, for that fraction of a second, completely out of the part she was playing. There was nothing more in the theater than two women looking at each other.

The look was brief. It scarcely disturbed the flow of Rita's words at all, but it was as shocking to the nerves as though a dancer in a swift passage had stumbled. Dubinsky was on his feet at once; Lailey grasped the back of the seat in front of him. But like a good dancer, Délice recovered herself. The words flowed on, and there was a long sigh of relief that seemed to come from everywhere. Dubinsky sat down and Lailey saw the rumpled handkerchief pass over the thick, short neck. Lailey himself leaned back, crossed his legs and raised the knee of his trouser leg carefully between thumb and finger.

Willoughby stood now with bent head, and she looked almost meek, but Lailey realized with a start the power that vibrant quality of hers had on the stage. Even with her head down like that, hers was the presence you felt. There was something dominating about it, and the quality of Rita's which had made her stand out as the star paled before it.

Rita's words flowed on, but they were empty and expressionless. Dubinsky was bowed forward with his head in his hands, as though he had given up all hope of the play. Délice seemed to have diminished. She looked shrunken and her bones looked nearer the surface. The soft, fluttery gestures were meaningless, and this skeleton quality mocked real grace so that once or twice Lailey had to suppress a nervous desire to laugh. Only the sight of the bowed shoulders of the little man in front restrained him, and restrained him, too, from asking what in the name of all mystification was really happening on the stage.

A sharp edge had come into Rita's voice, and Dubinsky had begun to pound with his fists on the arms of his seat. Her voice went up and up, and a note crept into it that bordered on hysteria. Suddenly Lailey had the sensation of being precipitated into crisis. He wanted no more of it. He was about to get to his feet, when her voice went horribly out of control. He felt the shock of it all through his body. The jangled words ended in a sound that felt like a long cut of a very thin knife. She took one step toward the footlights.

"Ike, I can't go on!"

Silence. Lailey found himself half standing, and he sat down again on the edge of his seat. Dubinsky shoved himself out of his, and ran down the aisle, his arms over his head, shouting. Before he reached the orchestra pit Délice whirled around, pointing with her whole arm at Willow.

"It's *her* fault. Get her out of here. Get her out of here." Délice began to cry. "I can't stand it. I won't stand it, I tell you." Her face was contorted. The rest of the words merged in a long scream of grief.

Dubinsky was yelling, "Clear the stage. Clear the stage. Somebody get her maid." Burt came out of the wings and tried to put his arm around her to lead her off. She pulled away from him. Her high-pitched stream of words was completely unintelligible.

They ended in stormy sobbing and Lailey looked for Willow. She was still standing by the table at the back and she was watching Rita with an expression of amazed interest. Lailey was about to get up, to do he didn't know what, but something about Willow's expression deterred him and he stayed where he was. Then Willow glanced swiftly toward the house, lowered her eyes and bowed her head and he thought, she *does* have sympathy for the poor woman. Why did I think she didn't?

He picked up his hat and stood. Burt was shouting. Dubinsky was saying, "Rita, Rita," over and over again. A woman in a white apron ran out on the stage and took the sobbing little figure in her arms. Willow straightened herself and walked toward the wings. She passed Délice without looking at her, holding her head high. She was flushed with emotion and suddenly all Lailey's sympathy was with her. She had done nothing at all, and she had been humiliated and made conspicuous. He started to run up the aisle. He wanted to catch her, if he could, as she came off the stage.

He missed her because he lost his way, and when he reached the dressing-room corridor, all the doors were shut. A thin stream of agonized sound was coming from behind a door which had a white star painted on it. The sound was punctuated by Dubinsky's voice, earnest and pleading. There were voices behind the other doors, but Lailey could not hear Willow. Most of these voices betrayed a pleasure in the excitement, which he found exceedingly repugnant. Not

26

knowing where to turn, he went up a short flight of steps, pulled open a fire door and found himself, to his amazement, in the semi-darkness behind the scenes. The man called Burt appeared suddenly and said, "You can't come in here, Mister. This is the stage."

"I was just trying to find Miss Cleveland."

"She's off." Burt took his arm as though he were afraid to leave him for an instant among the ropes and gas pipes, and propelled him through the door. The fingers of his thin hand felt strong. "See that?" he said, pointing to faded letters on the door which said, "No Admittance."

"I'm very sorry. Where do I find Miss Cleveland?"

"Third door down there. I wouldn't look her up just now, though."

As Lailey was going down the stairs, the door with the star on it banged open and Délice came flying out. She was wearing a long, black cloak which made her appearance strikingly dramatic. Dubinsky was right behind her, calling, "Rita, Rita, come back here!" They both disappeared into Willow's dressing room.

Even from where he stood Lailey could hear Rita's shrill words.

"No, no, Ike. *I'll* tell her. Get out of my way. *I'll* tell her."

Then Dubinsky's voice, "If you'll come to my office, Miss Cleveland."

"No, Ike. She's going to hear it from *me.*"

Lailey approached Willow's door. He was walking on tiptoe, though he did not know it.

"Rita, for heaven's sake, she hasn't done a thing to you."

"Oh, hasn't she! She watches me and laughs. She makes fun of me behind my back. I turn around and catch her smiling that nasty smile . . ."

The whole theater, all the shut doors seemed suddenly to be listening.

"I've never been anything but perfectly polite to you." Willow's voice sounded sullen. "It's you who think . . ."

"Oh, haven't you! It's 'Yes, Miss Délice. No, Miss Délice. Thank you, Miss Délice'—sweet as sugar and all the time your eyes are laughing. There on the stage I can feel the things you're thinking like little knives in my back!"

"Rita!"

"She thinks she's better than I am, Ike. She thinks she's an actress—better than Rita Délice. Actress! Why you—you're nothing but a society girl out for a thrill—you and your grand airs and your French maid. You shouldn't be *allowed* on the stage."

"Rita, stop it."

"Keep still, Ike. You're fired, do you hear? Fired! Ike promised me!"

"Mr. Dubinsky . . ."

"If you'll come to my office, Miss Cleveland."

"Mr. Dubinsky, there's not a word of it that's true. I haven't done a thing to her." Willow's voice was loud and angry. "She hates me because I'm young and she's not. She's afraid to be on the same stage with me for fear people will see . . ."

The rest was drowned in Rita's scream. A chair fell over. Something crashed into the wall. As Lailey grabbed the door knob, he saw doors all down the corridor flying open.

When he went in, Willoughby was still backing away. Fragments of a cold cream jar and a white smear of cream lay on the floor behind her. The maid was clutching a garment like a shield, and Délice was in Dubinsky's arms, sobbing wildly.

Chapter Three

THE next day, after lunch, Willoughby and Lailey went to New York together. They had dinner together that night and he wanted to come up to her suite afterward, but she said, "No, it's too late and tomorrow I'm going to start 'doing the agencies.' If I got one job I can get another, even if it is late in the season."

He felt sure she was not as confident as she sounded.

At dinner the next night he thought she was looking pale and he was sure she was beginning to feel the strain of going from one agency to another, looking for a part. He noticed that she ate very little and that the hand which held her champagne glass was shaky, and these things made him realize that she was taking the loss of her part harder than she was willing to let him see.

He said, "You're what our governess used to call 'peaked looking.' I think I'll come for you early tomorrow and take you for a drive in the park. The air will do you good."

"It makes such a change in you when you talk like that."

"Like what?"

"Like just now. Kind. I thought you were only, well, predatory. No, I didn't, either. I knew in Saratoga that you could be a dear if you wanted to, but it makes a different person of you. You even *look* different."

He patted the back of her hand, and then he closed his fingers around it. She clung to them a minute.

He came to take her for a drive in a dogcart with a black body and red trim. It was a beauty and the chestnut mare in the shafts was a beauty, too. The carriage starter was holding her by the bridle, and when she turned her head to look at them, he had to move with her. She jerked her head and widened her nostrils and rolled her eyes until the whites showed. Lailey said, "She's got spirit but she's perfectly safe." The footmens' shelf on the Lailey carriage was empty. Lailey saw Willow glance at it. "I always want to be alone with you," he said. He knew that, when they reached the park, they were sure to meet other carriages full of people with whom he was acquainted and that the absence of a footman while he was driving so beautiful a lady was sure to start gossip. He wondered if she realized this. For his part, he did not mind the gossip, and he didn't think she would.

He handed her up and she negotiated the high step with grace. He pulled on his chamois gloves, held the reins at the prescribed height and the whip at the prescribed angle across the back of his hand, and said to the carriage starter, "All right. Thanks." The starter let go of the bridle, the mare tossed her head and they started off at a brisk pace. When they were rolling along the avenue he turned to her.

"Warm enough?"

"Perfect. This is a wonderful idea."

"I thought that it might be nice to drive out somewhere for dinner, but now I find I can't. Something's come up." That sounded abrupt to him and he said, "A man I know is here in town. I met him down on Wall Street today. He's from the Middle West—a competitor, but a fine fellow. Seems he's here to get his stock listed on the Exchange. I have a friend—a classmate—who's a broker—

Maurice Herrick. He handles some of my business, the routine stuff. Anyway, I saw a chance of possibly doing Maurice a good turn by getting them together. I've asked them both to dinner tonight. I *owe* Herrick a good turn," Lailey said, thinking of Vera Herrick.

A watering cart was coming toward them, hugging the curb on their right. The water was turned off and the dripping pipes were leaving two trails of wetness on the Belgian blocks. Just as they came abreast, the driver pulled a lever and a small fan of water squirted out. It was as though the driver of the cart were making a derisive comment on their style. There was not much water but it made the chestnut fling up her head and dance. It took all Lailey's attention for a moment.

"Damn the fellow. Did that frighten you?"

"Not a bit."

"What were we talking about? Oh, yes—about dinner. I'd have made it lunch downtown, but this friend couldn't. Anyway, it's about time I had dinner at home on account of my niece Claire. I'm afraid she's still pretty broken up about her father's death. I'm awfully sorry, darling. Tomorrow, though! Now, about this part you're trying to find. I think you've been trying too hard and tiring yourself out. I wish you'd give up looking. You say yourself it's late in the season."

"I *have* to find another."

"No, you don't—not since you and I have found out how much we like each other."

"Stuyvesant, you don't understand. I've simply *got* to get back into the theater."

"Don't be angry with *me,* darling."

"I'm not. I didn't mean to be."

"All right. Let's not talk about it any more until we get into the park. We'll find a quiet side road and then we can talk all we want to. There's something I want to say to you."

They entered the park by the "Scholar's Gate" at Fifty-ninth

Street and as they slowed to make the turn, the sparrow cop, so called because he wore the gray uniform of the park police, stepped out of his sentry box and greeted them.

"Good afternoon, Mr. Lailey. Fine day for a drive."

"Good afternoon, Pat."

"Don't see much of you any more, sir."

He was looking at Willoughby as he said it and Lailey knew that he was thinking about the days when Mrs. Lailey used to drive here.

"No, not any more."

Cornelia Lailey would never let herself be driven in the dogcart. She preferred the dignity of the big, open carriage and the two grays that had grown plump because she would never let herself be driven fast. She had come here every fine day when they were not abroad or at the house in Tarrytown, and sometimes, as infrequently as possible, Lailey drove with her. On these occasions he sat stiffly beside her, his hands on his knees, while she gave her whole attention to bowing graciously to her friends. Lailey glanced at Willow. The crisp air had brought color to her face and a loosened curl was blowing across her cheek.

"I feel like driving fast, very fast. There's a stretch of road . . . Want to?"

"Oh, *yes!*"

"All right. After we get out of this crowd."

The park was full of turn-outs of all descriptions. Even the children had carriages, tiny replicas of the big ones, drawn by teams of goats with red harnesses and led by grooms in uniform. There were people on horseback, too, following the bridle path which wound along beside the road. Several times Lailey raised his whip to salute a friend.

One of these horseback riders was a woman. She came toward them riding fast and her groom was having trouble keeping up with her. The way she sat her horse showed that she enjoyed being reckless. Her horse was big and she was small; she rode well forward and she carried her crop down along the animal's side, like a jockey.

32

When she was nearly abreast she saw them. A startled look came into her face, and the hand which held the reins jerked suddenly. It threw the big horse off his stride. He began to prance, and then his forefeet left the ground and he reared. There were a few seconds of struggle and the groom tried to get alongside to reach her bridle. Her crop flashed and came down on the horse's flank. He leaped forward and they were gone. The last impression Willoughby had of the woman was that her face had become very red.

Willoughby turned to look at Stuyvesant. He was paying close attention to his driving but he seemed to know she was looking at him. He said, "That was Vera Herrick. Wife of the fellow I was telling you about. Good horsewoman."

Willoughby continued to study his profile a moment longer. Then she snuggled her chin down into the fur collar of her cloak and she, too, watched the road ahead.

When they reached the speedway, they had their fast drive. It left them feeling exhilarated and, in some roundabout way which he could not explain, it increased his liking for her. Afterwards they found a winding side road which was bordered by weeping willows. The leaves had turned to gold-yellow, and when a breeze rustled the trees, some of them floated down. The mare, tired after her run, no longer needed attention. Lailey put his arm around Willow and drew her close.

"Darling, you've come to mean a lot to me—did you know that?"

"Have I, Stuyvesant? I hope so."

"How about you?"

"You know about me."

"I think I do, but I like to hear you say it. Your eyes are so dark today, Willow. I've never seen you so serious."

"I'm getting troubled about things."

"Anything else but the theater?"

"No."

"You don't sound convincing. It isn't money, is it?"

"No, but—Stuyvesant, I'm beginning to get worried. Really worried. All the agencies say it's too late."

33

She had been leaning against him, but now she pushed him away from her and sat up straight.

"When I think of what that Délice woman did to me, I could kill her. She had no right. Absolutely no right."

"Don't get yourself worked up over that *now*. That's past. That's water over the dam. I want to talk about us."

"I can't help getting worked up—whenever I think about it, I get so angry. It isn't only what she did to me. Stuyvesant, listen to me. I didn't do anything to her—you know that. Oh, I didn't like her and maybe she read my thoughts, but I didn't *do* anything to her. It was just that she *knew* she was getting old—she *knew* she wasn't up to this part, and she was trying to shove the blame off on me. She was trying to make me a—what do you call it?"

"Scapegoat? Yes, I think you're probably right."

"But what I'm trying to say is, she isn't up to the part and in her heart she knows it."

"Dubinsky wouldn't have put her in it unless he was pretty sure . . ."

"She's afraid."

"Then feel sorry for her, Willow, not angry at her."

"But Stuyvesant, she's going to ruin that play. It's a wonderful part. But Hester is sure of herself—she's arrogant, and Délice—she's old and *afraid*. She won't be able to disguise that. Oh God, when I think what *I* could do with that part."

"Willow."

"*I* could play Hester! Oh how I could play Hester!"

"I think you could. Willow, listen to me." He tried to pull her close to him again, but she was too full of her own emotions to be conscious of his, and she held him off.

"Willow, darling. All that's over now. I wish you'd try to forget it. Perhaps some day we could have a play put on especially for you. I should think something like that might be done. Would you like that?"

"Would I? Oh, Stuyvesant!" She threw her arms around him and hugged him and he laughed with pleasure in her spontaneous gesture. He was discovering more warmth in her every day and he had not been wholly sure she was capable of real warmth.

She was saying, "If I had a *real* part, a *star* part, I *know* I could be a success. I suppose that's just what every actress thinks, but I *know* I could. Would you really do that for me, darling?"

"Well, we could look into it. I haven't the faintest idea how you go about such things. That would certainly be a new venture for me!" The idea made him laugh and then he grew serious. "That would be a partnership and we would be very close. How close would we be, Willow?"

"Of course we'd be close—and, Stuyvesant, Dubinsky could tell you how to go about things—finding a play, and so on. He must know exactly how it's done . . ."

She said it fast, and he knew that she did it because she wanted to ignore his question. He tried to interrupt her but she went on.

"Stuyvesant, let's go to Philadelphia for the opening and we could see him then."

Lailey stooped down and looped the reins around the whip, which was standing in its socket; then he turned sidewise to face her, but she wouldn't give him a chance to get back to the subject he wanted to talk about.

". . . and he's a nice person, really, and he probably feels sorry about me, so he'd talk to us. Maybe . . ."

"Willow!"

He put his hands on either side of her face and held her so she would have to look at him. Her eyes weren't dark any longer, but brilliant with excitement.

"Willow, wait a minute. Not so fast. I asked you a question. I asked you how close you and I are going to be?"

"I've never felt closer to anyone in my life—and I hardly know you, really. I think it's wonderful. But listen, Stuyvesant . . ."

He laughed, kissed her on the cheek swiftly and let her go. "I guess we've got to talk about one thing at a time. All right. I think it's a good plan to see what Dubinsky has to say—but all this is a sudden idea, you know, and it would probably turn out not to be at all practical. There isn't any great hurry, either. Whatever we might do would certainly have to wait for another season. We can talk to Dubinsky when he gets to New York."

She was silent a moment and when she spoke again the urgency had gone out of her voice. "I'd still like to go to Philadelphia for the opening. If I'm going to do things I always like to do them and not put them off."

"When is the opening?"

"Saturday. What's today? Thursday? Was it only day before yesterday we got here? It seems like weeks."

"What sort of fellow is he?"

"Dubinsky? I don't really know. He's reserved. But he tries to do the right thing and I think he's fair—I do know that about him. That's why I think he'd talk to us—because he let something happen to me which wasn't fair, and he's probably sorry. I'm sure he'd be glad to talk to us—he'd probably think he owed me that much. We could see him Friday."

"I don't think it would be very wise to see him before the opening, do you? Isn't he pretty busy?"

"There's no rehearsal Friday night. There never is—night before opening—not in his company. He lets the actors have that last night to rest."

"Still, I don't think . . ."

"Stuyvesant."

"What, dear?"

The horse had come to a standstill under one of the willow trees. Patches of wet still showed along his flank from his fast run. Lailey picked up the reins. "We'd better keep him moving. What were you going to say, dear?"

"Suppose she isn't doing Hester well enough. Suppose she'd had a breakdown or something. We don't know *what's* happened. Let's not wait till after the opening."

"You're not thinking . . . ?"

"I suppose it's a wild idea."

36

"She's not sick. Anyway, hasn't she an understudy?"

"No—not a star like Délice. People don't want to see any-body else. If she's sick for a day or two, they just don't play those nights."

"Part of your answer's right there, dear. Even if she isn't quite up to her parts any more, people will still go to see her. And she certainly wasn't sick. It's a very wild idea, darling."

"I know. I know. I didn't mean it, really. But let's go on Saturday then. We'll see the opening and we'll talk to Dubinsky next morning."

"Sunday? He won't be at the theater, will he?"

"You don't know him! There'll be two rehearsals Sunday to fix things that weren't right in the opening."

"It's a hard sort of life."

"It's a glorious life!"

They were moving along slowly, and Lailey let the reins go slack. The gold-yellow leaves sprinkled the roadway in front of them, and the late sun felt warm where it touched their faces. For a while they were silent and then he put his arm around her again.

"Kiss me!"

They kissed, and it was stirring and at the same time tender. When it was over, they were both deeply shaken. They did not try to speak. She picked up his hand and laid the back of it against her cheek. Then she turned it over and kissed the palm. He pulled her to him and kissed her again. This time he was rough, and the kiss was searching.

"Don't, Stuyvesant. Not like that. Don't."

"You're going to be my mistress."

"Mistress! Do you know what that means to me? It means some cheap creature who's just a little bit too good to be a prostitute . . ."

"Willow!"

"Living in a flat, with nothing to do all day but sleep off the effects of the night and get ready for the next time the man wants her . . ."

37

"Willow, how can you!"

"Making herself agreeable because she's dependent. Making love when she doesn't want to, because she's *dependent*. And afraid, all the time, that she's going to lose the man and have to hunt around for another to be dependent on."

"The answer is, you want a theater career, and all you want of me is help."

"All I'm saying is, that I'm going to get back into the theater somehow. And Stuyvesant, I don't think you want me to say, 'If you help me to do that, I'll be so grateful I'll reward you by being your mistress.' That's what it comes down to, isn't it? I like you too much to believe you want it that way. If there were ever to be anything between us, I don't think you'd want it to be like a payment to you. Not if you stopped to think. You'd rather have me say, 'I want you because I can't be happy without you.' Isn't that the way you'd really like to have it, Stuyvesant?"

"Do you think you'd want me after you were in the theater? If you had your own life to occupy you?"

"How can I be sure? How can *you* be sure?"

"What would you say if I said to you I wouldn't help you unless you wanted me enough to be my mistress now?"

"I don't think you'd ask that question."

"What if I did?"

"Do you want an honest answer?"

"Yes."

"I think I want the theater career enough to be your mistress to get it. And I'd know just how much you *really* care about me. Is that the way you want it?"

"Oh, Lord!"

They rode on in silence for a while and then she said, "I'm going to Philadelphia. If you don't come with me, I'm going to ask Dubinsky to help me get a part. I think he'll do that for me. *Are* you coming with me, Stuyvesant?"

After awhile she repeated the question.

"Are you?"

38

Even then he didn't answer. He was staring at the road ahead, and she watched him quietly. His eyes were half shut, but their odd, light color made them look fiery. Presently he glanced at her quickly and quickly away again.

"Yes, Goddamn it, I'm coming. You knew I would!"

Chapter Four

LAILEY was late. He said, "Good evening, Dodge," to the butler who opened the front door, without looking at him. Dodge had been the keystone of the Lailey household for fifteen years, and in all that time Lailey had never once really seen him. He left his coat hanging in Dodge's hands and hurried up the three wide steps which separated the vestibule from the great square hall. A white bear rug lay sprawled on the black and white marble floor, and Lailey was just crossing this toward the staircase when a tall, thin woman, dressed all in black, came out from behind the portieres of the reception room. Her attempt at a smile stretched the skin tight across her high cheekbones.

"Good evening, Mr. Lailey. I was watching for you."

"Oh, hullo, Edie. I'm late." He increased his pace a trifle. It seemed to him that his dead wife's secretary looked more like a black bed slat every day.

"May I speak to you a minute?"

He came to a reluctant halt by some potted palms which stood beside a *cinquecento* bench. The bench had once been part of the furnishings of an Italian palace. It had a high back of worm-eaten wood, and no one in the house had ever risked the discomfort of sitting on it.

Edie came toward him, skirting fastidiously the white bear rug, which she never willingly stepped on. Her thin fingers were climbing up and down a silver chain. She always wore the chain and Lailey still remembered that, when he and his dead wife Cornelia were driving across the Ponte Vecchio one day, she had said, "Stuyvesant, tell the coachman to go over to that stall and buy one of those silver chains for Edie. We simply must not go home without getting the poor thing something."

"I was going to say, Mr. Lailey, that perhaps Miss Reynolds ought to have dinner upstairs on a tray."

"Why? Is she sick?" He turned his eyes away from her because she was wearing a brooch in the shape of two clasped hands which, for no logical reason, irritated him exceedingly.

"No, but you could see for yourself, Mr. Lailey, that she is not accustomed to an establishment like this." Edie always referred to the Lailey house as an establishment, and that annoyed him too. "Dodge told me that she has trouble with the silver at dinner."

"Give her some pointers, then. She's a nice youngster. They'll like her."

Edie Tappen's mouth thinned to a stubborn line. "She hasn't a single evening gown, and her other clothes . . . Why, really, Mr. Lailey . . ."

"Fix her up in something of my wife's, then." She had no reason for looking as though he had struck her. She had been making a saint out of Cornelia these past years—the distant cousinship, plus the blight of spinsterhood, no doubt.

"Miss Reynolds is much taller . . ."

"Listen, Edie, Claire is a nice youngster, and even if she weren't, I wouldn't have my wife's sister's child . . ." The complication of the sentence brought him to a halt. "Don't keep alive old scandal," he said severely, and started up the stairs. He glanced at the clock on the tawny marble wall of the stairwell. The clock was gilt; it had no face, and the hands and numerals seemed to be floating in the

41

air. He knew that Edie was standing by the potted palms looking up at him, her fingers still climbing furiously up and down the silver chain.

When, a short while later, Sam Hadley transferred his weight from the hansom cab in which he had been riding to the Lailey carriage block, the springs of that ancient vehicle sighed with relief. Hadley straightened himself to his full height and put his broad shoulders back. The muscles in these shoulders made his coat bulge. He stood for an instant looking up at the gray stone front of the Lailey house, and light from the Italian lantern over the door shone down on his face.

It was a face which, in his youth, had been more aggressive than confident, but with the passage of time these qualities had become transposed so that now, on the threshold of early middle age, confidence was by far his stronger characteristic. It was the sort of face called "open," but the openness resulted from the fact that Hadley had enough strength, both of mind and of body, to have had little need in his life to practice subterfuge. He looked at the Lailey house with interest and with some astonishment at its grandeur, and a smile came into his eyes, as though he found it amusing that a plain man like himself should be coming to such a place. Then he turned back to the cabby on the roof of the hansom, put his hand in his pocket and drew out a bill.

Little of the old fellow was visible over the horse blanket in which he had wrapped himself like a gray cocoon, and Sam grinned.

"Cold up there?"

"Ain't nothing to what it's going to be in a few weeks."

When Sam grinned a number of unsuspected characteristics leaped suddenly to the surface of his face, not so much replacing the hard confidence as adding to it warmth and humor and enjoyment. The cabby reacted to it the way most people did—he grinned back.

"Mister, when you signaled me I didn't notice how big you was. You're built like a fighter."

"Well, I'm not. Anyway, not in a ring." The old fellow amused him. Sam liked people of all sorts.

"You ain't from these parts, either. I can tell."

"Nope. I came from the Northwest, the iron-ore country up around Lake Superior."

"Kinda tough country, ain't it?"

"Was till a while ago, anyway. You wanted something, you fought for it. Only way there was of getting anything. I left there about twelve, thirteen years ago. Miss it, sometimes." He looked the cabby over, an un-self-conscious appraisal that was habitual to him. "You look pretty wiry yourself. Here you are."

The cabby reached out from his high seat to take the dollar bill Sam was offering him.

"Oh, I used to be pretty good at holding my own. Ain't you got any change, Mister?"

"No, keep it."

Sam went up the red-carpeted front steps with the light tread some big men have and keep to the end of their lives. He was wondering what on earth it was that prompted a man to have a house like this, unless it was his womenfolk—and if his memory were correct, Lailey was a widower. Lailey was likable enough, but Sam didn't have a great deal of respect for him. Couldn't understand a fellow who left his mills to somebody else to run. Sam tried to picture Lailey in the midst of the roar and red dust, red-hot slag and leaping flames of a steel mill. The Lailey front door opened for him and as he went in he caught the butler suppressing, behind his customary mask, a look of astonishment at Sam's bulk.

Sam yielded up his coat and watched with amusement the deft way in which the butler, as he handed it to a footman, took a surreptitious look at the label. He was quite obviously reassured by what he saw. He said with complacency, "I will announce you, sir."

"I'll announce myself."

"But . . ."

Sam turned his back on him. He crossed the white bear rug without seeing it. Dodge said, "The drawing room is upstairs to your left, sir," and Sam began the long ascent of the marble stairway.

He was thinking that *she* would like this. It was just the kind of setting that she did like. There came to him one of those pictures of her which were always flashing into his mind, keeping him constantly stirred up with restlessness and angry resentment. He could see her ascending this stair, one hand in its white glove resting lightly on the rail, chin up, excitement in her eyes. She would walk as though a broad marble stair were her birthright, ignoring him because, when she got into places like this, she was ashamed of him. Some of their bitterest quarrels had been after parties where she had spent the evening showing herself off while he burned with resentment.

When he thought about her, his face grew dark and the easy confidence left it. He, who dealt with people so well, had not known how to deal with her, and so she had gone away, leaving him baffled and angry and oppressed by this disturbing sense of having failed. Such emotions as these were not natural to him—he was a man of action, not of moods—but he could neither conquer them nor rid himself of them. She had left him, but he had never, even in the restless dejection which his empty house sometimes gave him, thought of her as gone for good.

The square upper hall was lit, not by gas, but by clusters of candles in tall ormolu candelabra. They leaped and sparkled, bringing out fiery lights of gold and bronze in the dark, embossed Spanish leather which covered the wall behind. She liked candlelight. Sam stood still for a moment, staring at them, seeing with sudden, intolerable clarity their small drawing room in Cleveland, smelling the wax mixed with the odor of flowers and her perfume.

There were voices coming from the room on his left. He put these thoughts away from him and turned toward them. His gregariousness, his normal capacity for enjoyment, came to the fore. He went unhurried through the wide archway, relaxed, un-self-conscious, smiling, his hands thrust deep in his pockets.

The room was huge. Lailey and two others were at the far end of it, near the fireplace, and a young girl stood by herself a little way off, looking at a picture. They all felt his presence and turned around. Lailey started forward and Sam went to meet him, hand held out. When Sam felt pleasure and good fellowship, he put everything else aside for it. He glowed with it. He called to Lailey, "Hi, fella," in a big, hearty voice. He had taken possession of the room.

Beside him, Lailey looked more conspicuously what he was, the higher finish, the more complex nature, the greater detail standing out against the plain background of the big man. He took Sam by the arm and led him toward the others, and Sam looked down on him, amusement tightening the corners of his eyes, because, when people led him by the arm, he felt like a bear on a leash. Then he found himself being introduced to a small, black-haired woman whose name was Mrs. Maurice Herrick. She was sitting on a love-seat, her knees crossed, her foot, just showing under the flounces of her dress, jerking up and down. She gave Sam her hand indifferently, as though what he did with it was his problem, and she looked, not at him, but at Lailey.

Sam thought there was something strained and anxious in her eyes. When she finally brought them back to him and really looked at him, their expression changed suddenly to interest. Sam grinned at her, and her interest turned into coquetry. It was the kind of coquetry that Sam had seen in the eyes of saloon girls in the mining country and it astonished him each time he found it, as he frequently did, in the eyes of society women. He answered it with a cool, appraising look which traveled all over her small figure, amusement still pinching the corners of his eyes. She flushed and gave Lailey a swift covert look, hoping, Sam thought, that Lailey had noticed. He decided to leave her strictly alone. The undercurrent between those two was as perceptible as a draught.

Then he was shaking the well cared-for hand of Maurice, the woman's husband, and looking at a handsome shallow face with yellowish eyes which slid away from his. The fellow had a continental air about him and his clothes fitted him like a guardsman's uniform, but when he spoke his accent was purest New York. He said, "How do you do?" and, bending slightly from the waist, he touched the points of his waxed moustache delicately with the tips of two fingers. Sam's outgoingness dimmed perceptibly. The fellow was plainly a weakling, and Sam was dismissing him from consideration when he suddenly realized that Herrick was the broker he had been invited to meet. He looked at Herrick again, suppressing his astonishment. There must be some reason why Lailey would have a fellow like this for a broker. Smart, probably. That type often was.

Lailey called Herrick "Maurie," and he called Lailey "Stu," and their attitude toward each other still had a flavor of the campus. They had a good deal to say to each other which made them laugh, and Maurice said some things at which Sam laughed, too. His laugh was loud, but when he laughed with someone he didn't like, his eyes were not touched by it. His laugh ended before the others because nothing that a fellow like Maurice was likely to say could strike him as really funny.

Lailey took hold of his arm again and steered him over toward the young girl standing by herself. She looked as though she felt she didn't belong with the others but didn't mind. She had been wandering around the room looking at things, and now she had a small jade elephant on the palm of her hand. She put it down, smiling at it, and turned to greet them, her eyes wide. Sam thought they were the bluest eyes he had ever seen. The glow of friendliness came back to him.

Lailey was explaining that this was his niece, Claire Reynolds, who had come to live with him and cheer up his quiet old home. At that, both Sam and Claire laughed, because "quiet old home" was the last way they would have described the magnificence around them. And when he had stopped laughing, he smiled at her because this girl Claire and himself didn't belong in such surroundings and they both knew it about themselves and about each other. He didn't question how, but he knew this was understood between them. He put his hands in his pockets and rocked up on the balls of his feet and back again. He felt fine.

Mrs. Herrick called Lailey and he left them. Sam made a sort of barricade out of himself to cut Claire off from the others and, his hands still in his pockets, stood looking down at her. She felt the boldness first and then the kindliness. They both made her self-conscious, and she had to nerve herself to look straight at him. She did it, but she gave herself away by brushing nervously at the curls which lay against her cheek. This delighted him. She was young, she hadn't yet shed the appealing quality of childhood, but she had gained a good deal of the allure of maturity. Leaning over her a little more than he needed to, he said, "How old are you?"

Her eyes had flecks of light in them which made them alive and exciting, but they were not like *her* blue eyes because they had dark, smoky shadows in them. She lowered them quickly, and he said, "I certainly have a lot of nerve, haven't I? Don't answer me."

The eyes flashed at him again and they were dancing. "Seventeen," she said. "How old are *you?*"

"Say," he said, "Say, look here! By God, that's fair enough. Do you think I'd be fool enough to tell you?" They went off into a gale of laughter.

Sam saw that she had on a very ornate dress of cream-color satin and lace, which didn't suit her very well and was too short for her in front. She touched the lace with a slim brown hand and he thought she was going to explain something about it, but just then Lailey put a hand on his shoulder and told him to come and hear the "good one" Maurie had picked up on the Street. Sam gave Claire a parting look which made her blush, and the exhilaration of that carried him through the long and not very amusing "good one."

A footman came with glasses of sherry on a tray and Sam took one, amused at the look of the frail glass in his big hand. He didn't like the stuff. Rye was his drink. Maurice told the juicier parts of the story all over again and, at the end, laughed inordinately and ran his hands over the outsides of his pockets the way a man does who longs to put his hands in them but has too much concern for the fit of his clothes. Sam wondered if the fellow were aware of

47

Sitting there at the foot of the table, with the high back of the carved chair rising above her head, he thought she looked like a princess in a fairy tale. He was sorry when she and Mrs. Herrick left them to go back to the drawing room.

Claire and the little Herrick woman had been having difficulty in each other's company. When the men appeared Mrs. Herrick, in her relief, almost ran to Lailey.

"Stu, come up to the gallery with me and we'll pick out a place to hang the Fragonard." Then, over her shoulder to Hadley, "He's bought a Fragonard. You knew he was a collector, didn't you?"

Lailey said, "Let's *all* go," and she frowned.

The picture galley, which was also a ballroom, was at the top of the house. The walls were covered with crimson brocade and the floor with Turkish rugs. There was a musicians' balcony with a great loop of green damask hanging down from its carved railing. A double row of velvet-covered benches ran down the middle of the room, placed back to back with potted palms between each pair. The place was as big as an armory and three great mirrors at the far end, under the balcony, made it look even larger. All the rest of the walls were hung with pictures, so close together that Sam wondered how space could be found for one more. He looked slowly all around the room and up to the arch of glass skylight above their heads, the panes now black with night, and whistled softly. He squeezed Claire's arm against his side and said, "This place is big enough for a railroad station."

They strolled together slowly down one side, looking at the pictures. It was chilly and she shivered, so he kept her close to him. Vera had drawn Lailey to the other side of the room and they stood together by a window. Maurice was aimlessly wandering toward the far end. Sam looked down at Claire.

"Do you mind people asking you questions like I did?"

She felt, when they were alone together, as though he were enveloping her. It gave her an odd sensation both of security and excitement. Suddenly shy, she gave him a swift look through her lashes. "I don't mind if *you* do."

"I like you."

"I like you, too. You look so like Tad—my father, Tad—only without the beard—not *look* like him, I mean, but—well . . . He was big, too, and when he talked to you, he sort of brought all of himself to bear . . ."

"What did Tad do?"

"He was a newspaper man—a journalist. That's what he was in the East when mother ran away with him. Then he went to California to find gold—but he gave up prospecting when I was born. He said all the good claims went years before, anyway—and he started his own newspaper."

"But you knew your uncle before? It wasn't like coming to live with strangers."

"No—yes. Mother was Uncle Stuyvesant's wife's sister. When she ran away to marry Tad, the family disowned her. She died when I was born. But Uncle Stuyvesant has been wonderful. This is Aunt Cornelia's dress I'm wearing, until they can get me some of my own. We didn't have much money, of course."

Over by the window, Vera was saying to Lailey, *"Who is your new love?* You might at least tell me that, because I know you've got one. *Who is she?"*

"Look here, Vera—you said yourself that everything was over. You ended it."

"That isn't true and you know it. I said, *unless* . . ."

"You said . . ."

"Never mind *what* I said! You *knew* I was angry. You *knew* I didn't mean anything. We've had a hundred fights before. *Who is she?"*

"It doesn't matter to you who she is. Christ, do you think I belong to you?"

"That's right, swear at me. I don't care *what* you do. Do you think I do? I suppose you think I'm jealous. I suppose you think I *care* what you do with a woman like that!"

that far away, to see Vera's expression in the mirror, shadowed as it was by the overhang of the musicians' balcony. Sam relaxed a tension which seemed to have had no cause. Maurice raised the rapier slowly, held it upright in front of his face and slowly lowered it to the floor. It was the traditional fencer's salute to his opponent.

His next movements were so fast that Sam could not follow them. They were executed with grace and with a beautiful precision, and they left Maurice with one arm raised, elbow and knee bent and the rapier menacing his reflection in the glass.

"En garde!"

It was a shout that rang in the cavern of the musicians' gallery and echoed hollowly in the arch of the skylight. Maurice began to fence with the image in the glass. His motions were lightning-fast and his body had no weight. The sword flickered. The blade was alive. The point was everywhere. There was no sound but the light thud of his feet, the hiss of his breath, the wicked whisper of the sword. It was hushed and evil and somehow desperate.

An invisible sword seemed to be at his throat. He was fighting for his life. The sweep of his rapier narrowed, its motion grew more rapid and intense. Light flashing from the blade made a continual brilliance in the air. Then the rapier crashed to the ground and the vibrating blade sang. Maurice's hands were at his breast, his body bent sidewise.

"Touché!"

The effect of a mortal wound was real. For an instant Sam was paralyzed by the violence of it and by confusion. Then he pushed Claire's hand off his sleeve and started to run. Lailey was running too. Then Maurice took his hands from his heart, stooped for the rapier and turned to face them. Sam stopped where he was, still obsessed by the reality of the fight but not knowing whether it was Maurice against himself or the reflection in the glass or against some image in his mind.

When Maurice picked up the rapier and turned around, Lailey was close to him. Maurice's back was toward the glass and his eyes were full of light. The sword was pointed at Lailey. It stopped him.

Then, with one swift motion, Maurice leaped forward and the point of the sword was at Lailey's breast. Sam heard the echo of Maurice's shout and the air vibrated with Vera's high, thin scream. The scream tightened his nerves like caustic. Lailey jumped back and the sword followed him.

"It would be so easy to kill you . . ."

Lailey tried to turn away but the sword held him.

"Like this . . ."

There was a tiny rasping sound as the point of the sword touched a stud in Lailey's shirt.

"Or like this—or this . . ."

"Christ, Maurie, stop it!"

The point of the sword touched Lailey again and again. It made a cross before his eyes, it lingered flickering at his throat. It would not let him go. The room was full of the sound of heavy breathing and of the quick, sharp scrape of Maurice's feet on the polished floor. Sam was aware that Claire was clinging to his arm and that Vera's thin scream followed each flash of the sword. Then it was over. The point of the sword was resting on the floor and Maurice was shaking with laughter. He looked disheveled and a little drunk.

Chapter Five

WILLOUGHBY and Lailey went to Philadelphia on Saturday. At the theater they found that, because it was opening night, the curtain was delayed and the overture was only half over when they took their seats. Lailey saw Willoughby pull off her glove and poke fretfully at her hair, then feel her cheek with the back of her hand, as though she thought she had a fever.

He said, "Are you all right? We don't have to stay and see this thing if you don't want to—if seeing it is going to make you feel badly in any way, I mean."

"No. I *want* to see it. I feel altogether differently now I know you're going to help me somehow. Stuyvesant, you're a dear—you're an *angel*." There was something warm and intimate about the way she said it, and he laughed with pleasure because it made him feel that he knew something about her which nobody guessed but himself.

She seemed to understand this and she joined his laugh, and then she said soberly, "I think one of the nicest things about us, Stuyvesant, is the way we laugh together. I've never laughed just like that with anyone before."

People were talking loudly to make themselves heard over the noise of the overture and programs were rustling. The conductor's back had a stoic look. Many of the women were turning around in their seats to look at the audience and Willoughby did the same. Then she remembered the peephole in the painted curtain. It was round, just larger than an eyeball, and was disguised on the audience side by the design of the border. As she looked at it an eye appeared, blinked once and was gone. She felt startled and disturbed. Then the lights began to dim, and as it grew darker in the house, the noise of talking died slowly down. Now people were looking only at the stage. The music stopped and there was a moment of intense quiet. Willoughby put out her hand and felt for Stuyvesant's. The quiet deepened and the suspense mounted and then, before she was aware that anything had begun to happen, she heard the sound of the moving curtain.

Lailey thought the first act was good. Délice looked thinner but she seemed confident. Her voice was not as fine as he remembered and she had developed an odd trick of walking around the pools of light on the stage. She never came very close to the footlights either, and these new mannerisms gave her acting a quality that suggested furtiveness.

When the curtain came down he leaned toward Willoughby.

"You all right, dear?"

"Yes, of course."

"It's a good play—much better than I thought from the bits I heard. I don't think Délice is forceful enough for this Hester, though."

"She's ruining it! She's absolutely ruining it—the play and Hester too!"

She spoke with such vehemence that he was startled. She seemed really angry, and her face was red. After that she relapsed into brooding silence until he tried to draw her out of it by asking, "I don't quite get the significance of the name, The Rungs of the Ladder. Does it mean anything special?"

"You'll see in the last act. It's from Shakespeare. All Hester's friends are rungs in her ladder.

'. . . when he once attains the utmost round
He then unto the ladder turns his back,
Looks to the clouds, scorning the base degree
By which he did ascend.'

You'll hear John quote it. Stuyvesant, the applause was very thin."

"It's only the first act," he said. "The second is strong. I saw most of it, you know."

When the lights went down again, he felt for Willoughby's hand. She let it stay in his but she kept moving her fingers and he knew she was still stirred up about what was happening to the play and to Hester. He was interested, and impressed too, that she should care so much. Then his attention shifted to what was happening on the stage. Délice, or Hester, had not yet made her entrance. The other members of the cast seemed to be working hard, and he thought it was because they were worried by the quality of the response to the first act. Then it came to him that they were jettisoning every meaningless gesture, every wandering glance and, probably, every straying thought. The result was they were gradually building up an intensity of emotion which he had not imagined lay hidden in the play. And, as far as he could tell, the audience was reacting much more favorably.

Then Délice came on the stage. There were moments after that when he thought everything was all right and sometimes he was carried away by the diminutive, graceful actress. On the whole, it seemed to him, this act was going better than the last, but he knew that it was not going well enough or he would have been too absorbed to have these thoughts. The story, though, continued to hold his interest. The monologue began. Rita stood farther back from the footlights than she had during rehearsal, and that lessened its effectiveness. But the real trouble was, she seemed to be afraid of the audience. She was obviously trying hard—too hard. She should have spoken the lines as though she were speaking to the world, and she had the voice for it, but now her voice sounded flat and loud. Willow's fingers clutched his. People around them began to stir. There were scattered coughs. And then he heard whisperings—most ominous sound, except the crackle of fire, that the theater knows.

"What happened?" he asked.

"I don't know. She lost them. She'll never get them back. It scares me."

From there on the play sagged hopelessly. Rita moved through her scenes as though she were in a daze, and Lailey wondered once or twice if she had taken a drug. The rest of the cast worked desperately, supporting, covering up, but it was no use. The only spark of life which remained was the story, which was too good and too well set out to be quite destroyed. At the end of the third act Lailey suggested that they leave. Willoughby nodded agreement and set about collecting her things.

When they were once more shut in the odorous interior of a cab, he asked, "What on earth made it go to pieces, Willow? It got off to a good enough start."

She didn't answer him. She was sitting upright, with her wrist through the strap which hung from the padded side of the hansom. She was staring straight ahead of her, and he noticed for the first time how strong a profile she had. She carried her head well—and in a way that made him suspect she came of good stock. He speculated awhile about this mysterious background of hers, and then he said, "Willow, what are you thinking about?"

"What? Oh, I was thinking about the play. Stuyvesant, it's a failure—you know that, don't you? She killed it."

"As bad as that, do you think?"

"Yes, I do. Think of it! A play like that—a part like that. This Hester is magnificent—arrogant, selfish and magnificent—and the play sweeps you away. And what has she done with it? She *cowers* through it! She flinches away from the audience when she ought to dominate them. If I were the author of that play, I think I'd shoot her. If I were Délice, I'm sure I'd shoot myself rather than let the audience see I couldn't rise to it. She ought to be *ashamed*. She ought to be so ashamed she'd never set her foot on a stage again."

"Those are very hard words, Willow. She may be sick—she knows she's growing old . . ."

"All right, they're hard. That's what theater life is like. *I* could take it better than that. Oh God, when I think of what I could do with that part! I could play it right now, without any rehearsal at all, and I tell you I'd keep the audience in their seats. I'd hold them!"

After that there was silence and an atmosphere of tenseness in the cab. Stuyvesant's breathing was quick and shallow. Once he moved restlessly. Then he reached out for her hand and held it on his knee, his fingers tightening around it again and again. She moved closer to him and the silk of her dress rustled softly. After awhile he said, "Are you pretty sure the play is a failure?"

"I'm wholly sure. I *know* it is."

There was silence again. And then she whispered.

"Stuyvesant, what are you thinking? *What are you thinking?*"

He did not answer, but he held her hand more tightly.

"You're thinking I can play that part. I can. I can!"

"Just let me think about it."

They arrived at the hotel and he helped her down. She turned and put her arm through his.

"Stuyvesant!"

He glanced up at the cabby, who was wrapped like a cocoon in a horseblanket.

"Wait. I'll take the lady in and then I want you to drive me back."

He felt something like a shiver go through her body and he pressed her arm tightly to his side.

"Don't get your hopes up. It's just a wild idea. A very wild idea."

Inside the lobby door she faced him.

"I'll have them send a supper for us up to my sitting room." Then she left him.

The play was still in progress when Lailey returned to the theater, but the ticket-taker had left his post and the glass doors which separated the lobby from the house stood open. Lailey could see the distant stage, like a vignette in the darkness, and he could hear the sound and emotional tone of the words, though he could not distinguish the words themselves. Presently he saw Dubinsky, walking slowly, so deep in thought that he was oblivious to his surroundings, and the sight of him gave Lailey a stronger conviction than he had yet felt of the failure of the play, for Dubinsky appeared to sag with the lassitude of accepted defeat. Lailey watched him skirt the lobby on the opposite side and go through a narrow door. The door swung to behind him, showing the word "office" lettered on its face in shabby gold. Lailey, who was beginning to regard the emotions of all theater people as counterfeit, thought he saw in Dubinsky the physical aspects of true discouragement. He crossed the lobby rapidly and knocked, careful to temper his customary assurance as he might in the presence of bereavement.

Dubinsky's voice, sounding more brisk than he had expected, called out, "Come in," and Lailey entered. He found himself in a dispirited-looking room with one dusty window which darkly suggested an alley beyond. Dubinsky sat behind a table-desk, his arms flung out before him, blinking at Lailey in the light of a green-shaded student lamp. The skin around his eyes looked white. He seemed to have withdrawn so far within himself that his features were drained of expression, leaving behind only pronounced racial characteristics.

Lailey said, "Good evening. May I see you for a minute or two?" He was careful to keep any trace of his awareness of social disparities out of his voice. Not considering a reply necessary, he shut the door and advanced farther into the room. Dubinsky's face became animated with a look of marked uncordiality. Lailey said, "I was sitting behind you during the rehearsal on Thursday evening, if you remember. My name's Lailey."

"Oh, yes. So you were. What can I do for you, Mr. Lailey?"

Dubinsky sounded as though he were in the last stages of weariness. This and the quiet of the theater seemed to Lailey very different from the tension and excitement which he had supposed made up the atmosphere of an opening night. Then he realized that the weariness, the quiet he was sensing were the reaction. The striving was all over, the uncertainty was gone, and nothing but the weariness remained. A point had been reached and passed, and now the play, for better or for worse, was what it was, and no one could any longer change the outcome.

Although Dubinsky had extended no invitation to sit down, Lailey looked about him for a seat. Most of the chairs were piled with dusty stacks of playbills, loosely tied with hemp, and Lailey deposited himself with some caution on a low sofa upholstered in a nameless shade of plush. His seat brought him below the circle of the green lamp shade, and Dubinsky's face, seen thus through the light, with an odd green shine on the part of the lids which normally is in shadow, had a Mardi Gras appearance. Lailey said to the weary devil-mask, "I saw the play tonight. I was wondering what you thought its chances were for a successful run."

"Are you from one of the papers?"

"No, excuse me, I should have explained. I'm *Stuyvesant* Lailey." He hesitated, but the name seemed to evoke no recognition and he went on. "I'm in the steel business. Tell me, do you think Miss Délice will be able to continue the run? What I'm getting at is that, in the event Miss Délice is not able to continue after tonight, I might, under certain conditions, be inclined to talk to you about a financial interest in the production."

"Why should you be interested under circumstances like that?" Lailey's words seemed not to arouse Dubinsky's curiosity. He picked up a pencil and began to tap with it on the shabby blotter, and when he spoke again, Lailey had the impression that he was not continuing the discussion so much as crystallizing his own thoughts by giving them expression.

"As a matter of fact, I have about made up my mind not to take *The Rungs of the Ladder* into New York at all. I'll wait for the morning papers before I decide, but I know pretty well what they'll say. A little will depend on how Rita Délice herself feels about it and I want her to get a night's sleep before I talk to her, but I expect, almost surely, to call the cast together and announce the closing before noon tomorrow."

Lailey sat with his knees crossed, regarding his patent-leather toe in silence, watching the highlight travel across its surface whenever he moved. It seemed to be absorbing his whole attention. Actually, his mind was occupied with the fact that neither himself nor his words had been taken seriously, and he smiled slightly. The conventions of financial deals, like the conventions of good society, were, after all, familiar only to a fairly select group, and the pushcart could not be very far back in this man's ancestry. Moreover, if the name Stuyvesant Lailey meant nothing . . . Outside the theater a clock began booming eleven. The notes sounded clear in the night air. Almost immediately, as though there were some connection, there came a distant burst of applause. Dubinsky listened intently, his head cocked to one side.

"Show over?" Lailey asked.

"Couldn't be—yet. Not for a few minutes. That must be the table scene. That will please Rita."

Lailey put the patent-leather-shod foot on the floor and shifted his weight on the sofa.

"I said I might be willing to consider taking a financial interest in the production under certain conditions. I would like to suggest to you that, if Miss Délice cannot continue the run, Miss Cleveland be put in her place."

Dubinsky's attention came back from the applause and he stared at Lailey with the first real interest he had shown. It was annoyingly apparent to Lailey, however, that the interest was not in his proposition, but in himself as a kind of human curiosity. Dubinsky's interest transformed itself into amusement, which he was almost able to conceal, and he put the pencil down on the desk decisively, as though by that gesture he closed the interview.

"I'm sorry to say that is scarcely practicable."

"Why not?" There was a trace of belligerency in Lailey's manner

63

the same as a guarantee of quality. I have a reputation to maintain, Mr. Lailey. The failure of this play puts me in financial difficulties, I admit, but it won't ruin me—not by a long way, and if I close it now, the name of Isaac Dubinsky won't suffer. People will come the next time. But where do you think I'd be—dear God, where do you think the name of Isaac Dubinsky would be if it got around that my new star couldn't act—that she was just some good-looking girl that a rich man wanted to treat to the limelight—that Isaac Dubinsky let himself be paid to do a thing like that? I wouldn't dream of such a thing, Mr. Lailey. I wouldn't touch it! There's no use discussing it any more. Go find some other producer!"

Dubinsky pushed his way out from behind the desk angrily, crossed the room, took a match from a tin holder on the wall and scratched it as though the miniature violence of the action relieved him. He put the match up through the bottom of the fluted glass shade of a wall bracket and turned the key. The flare of light brought the cluttered, ugly room into sharp relief. Lailey stood up. He was a little pale and plainly angry. At that moment there was another distant burst of applause, and Lailey added to his growing stock of impressions about the theater the item that applause at the final curtain has a quality all its own. Dubinsky was listening intently, and he seemed, without actually doing so, to hold up his hand to silence Lailey. The applause was not prolonged and Lailey watched the expression drain out of Dubinsky's face again, leaving only the racial mask. The white look had come back around his eyes and he blinked stolidly.

The end of *The Rungs of the Ladder*. No doubt the final curtain had for Dubinsky a significance beyond money, since it was in all likelihood the end of Délice also. The end of a long association—the end, just conceivably, of romance, though the word did not associate itself easily with the stocky producer. This bit of insight on Lailey's part calmed his anger and made him feel tolerant.

The applause was followed by a strange sibilant sound that had a muffled roar behind it. Lailey could liken it to nothing he had ever heard, but it seemed to him that the onrush of flood waters must

66

sound like that. And then he identified it—the audience coming out. Odd that he had never heard it when he himself had been part of an audience, and he thought he was beginning to understand why every sound from the audience was listened for by theater people with such intensity.

Dubinsky was saying, on a shallow breath that made his words almost inaudible, "There were no curtain calls at all!" His anger seemed to have evaporated in the face of this appalling fact.

The first of the audience were passing the door. They were laughing and chattering as though they felt released, and Lailey thought he could never again see a play without an uncomfortable awareness of the emotional tensions behind the scenes, but he did not linger with the thought, for Dubinsky seemed at this moment vulnerable to fresh attack. Lailey launched the attack without delay.

"If you will excuse a businessman for saying so, I think your attitude is a trifle sentimental. The point here is that you have a good play. I admit the situation might be different if this weren't true, but if the judgment of a layman is worth anything, I think the play is so good that it might easily carry some acting in the lead part which wasn't as technically perfect as Miss Délice could give you."

Dubinsky did not, on the surface, appear in the least interested in this argument but Lailey, groping for the undercurrents of thought and feeling which, more than words, determine the course of such meetings as this, realized that for the first time Dubinsky had accorded his remarks some value. He pressed this slim advantage quickly.

"I'm not for a moment suggesting you take on Willow Cleveland without a trial." Lailey acknowledged to himself that, in his abysmal ignorance, he had been doing exactly that. "All I'm proposing is that you 'read' her, or whatever you call it, in the part some time tomorrow. You say you are going to convene the cast anyway. Why, good heavens, man, here's an actress who, though she may not be experienced, certainly has exceptional good looks. She's right here on the spot. She's already familiar with the play—which I should think would be a tremendous advantage. There won't be any financial risk to you if the play isn't a success. I'm *not* asking you to risk your reputation because, if you don't like the way she reads the part, that will be the end of it."

Dubinsky was standing with his hands behind his back. He was listening to Lailey's words, but no more than that. Outside the door the audience was still streaming noisily by, and the little office was beginning to seem intolerably stuffy. The harsh light showed the dust on the photographs hanging crookedly on the wall, the scratched japanning of an ancient safe and the bare threads appearing through the pattern of the inadequate rug. This, then, was the setting of the romantic life Willow longed for so ardently. Lailey sat down on the couch again. The light picked out a gleam from one of the diamond studs on his shirt front and it flashed rhythmically, like a tiny beacon, with every breath he drew. Dubinsky's indifference angered him.

Lailey hitched himself forward onto the sharp edge of the couch.

"Look here! Don't you think you owe Miss Cleveland a trial? You certainly owe her that much after the way she was dismissed. That was the most completely high-handed—the most completely unfair . . ."

"Fair? *Fair?* Good God—*fair!*" Suddenly Dubinsky was shouting. "What do you expect? This is the theater. There's no question of what's fair. Of course it isn't fair—but Rita's a valuable property. Rita can't be upset, or the show suffers. Fair! Do you think what's happening to Rita tonight is fair? Holy Moses, nobody's fair in the theater."

Dubinsky walked rapidly back to his desk chair and threw himself into it. He pulled a rumpled handkerchief out of his pocket and wiped his forehead and then, because the moisture started out once more, he wiped it again. Lailey could hear his breath coming fast and harsh. There was a look of deep unhappiness in Dubinsky's eyes and Lailey himself was shocked at the unfairness of a fate that could wind up an actress's long, triumphant career in so cavalier and cruel a fashion. Lailey thought he understood the sentiment

68

which would make Dubinsky prefer, if Rita's career were dying, to let the play die too. If so, then Lailey felt he saw at last the real obstacle in his path. He waited to give Dubinsky time, and when he spoke it was almost gently.

"The world goes on, Mr. Dubinsky. Miss Délice is not herself now, but if she were, she would not want a chance for success withheld from someone else."

They were both silent, and in the silence Lailey could hear Dubinsky's breathing slow down to normal. Dubinsky smiled, and it seemed to Lailey an odd smile, compounded of reminiscence and tolerance.

"Rita was never particularly anxious to help new people. She thought everyone should come up as hard a way as she had herself."

"I'd better be more specific about the suggestion I came to make. My lawyer will work out the details with you, but roughly, what I had in mind was to underwrite the play for two weeks after it opens with Miss Cleveland in the lead, so you won't lose anything if the show fails. You don't pay your cast while rehearsing, I believe, but there may be other expenses. I'll take my share of those—that's one of the things to be worked out. If you want all or part of the money in advance, all right."

Lailey stopped to wait for a reply, but Dubinsky said nothing. When it seemed plain that he was not going to answer, Lailey said, "What time tomorrow shall I bring Willow to the theater?"

Dubinsky passed his hands over his face and the top of his head and dropped them heavily to the desk.

"Ten o'clock." He rose with an air of putting everything but the present moment behind him. "Promptly at ten o'clock. I'm not promising a thing. I expect she'll be impossible. You'd better be here, too, so you can see for yourself." He started for the door and Lailey rose hastily.

"It's most kind of you. Let me thank you . . ."

"No more time now. Don't get her hopes up. I'm a fool to go *this* far!" Dubinsky jerked open the narrow door and went out, letting it bang shut behind him.

Chapter Six

LAILEY went with Willoughby as far as her dressing-room door. She had been very silent all the way to the theater, but now she did not seem to want him to leave her. Shivering a little, she stripped off her gloves with quick, nervous motions. He took her hands in his and found that they were cold.

"Did you get chilled, Willow?"

She shook her head.

"Frightened?"

Her fingers tightened on his.

"Don't be, darling. You'll be fine. You'll be wonderful. Dubinsky will be more than satisfied, you'll see."

She shut her eyes and he noticed that the lids were faintly blue. She looked almost ill.

"Are you all right?" His voice betrayed his anxiety.

"I'll be all right when I get out there on the stage."

At the other end of the corridor they heard the call boy's bored singsong. *Places, please. Places, please. Act One curtain. Places, please.*

Lailey kissed her cheek quickly, released his hands from her clinging fingers and opened the dressing-room door. "You'll be all right. I'll be out in the house with Dubinsky, cheering for you." She seemed a little dazed and he shoved her gently inside the room.

When Lailey entered the house, Burt, the stage manager, was directing some last-minute shifts in the furnishings of the set and Dubinsky was sitting in the middle of a row in the center of the theater, waiting, with one arm thrown out along the backs of the seats beside him. Lailey's intention had been to join the producer so that he might hear Dubinsky's comments on Willow's performance as the play progressed. When Dubinsky saw him, however, he made only a slight gesture in acknowledgment of his presence, a gesture which made it perfectly plain that he would not welcome interruptions, and Lailey, after a moment's hesitation, turned down a seat for himself in the row behind and several places removed. He was astonished to discover that he was nervous also. Show business! he thought disgustedly. Show business giving Stuyvesant Lailey nerves!

The moving operations on the stage were completed and the stage manager squinted into the house, shielding his eyes from the glare of the footlights with his hand.

"Want the curtain brought down, Ike?"

"No. Bring Miss Cleveland on."

The stage manager faced the wings. "All right, folks. Take it easy. Miss Cleveland on stage, please. House lights."

The house was plunged in darkness. Willoughby stepped onto the stage and Lailey's heart began to beat a little faster. She was, he noticed, beautifully and simply dressed. She walked with dignity, not timidly, not with too much assurance. Exactly right, he thought, and let out the breath he had been holding.

She came straight down to the footlights, not squinting or shielding her eyes as the stage manager had, but taking the full glare in her face as though they were not there at all. When she spoke her voice was calm and distinct.

"Yes, sir?"

Dubinsky rose and sidled out of the row of seats. He had been,

Lailey suddenly realized, watching Willow as critically as he himself. Dubinsky walked down the aisle to the orchestra rail, which he leaned on, looking up at Willow, and Lailey wished that he could see his face. Dubinsky spoke in low tones, for Willow alone, and Lailey had to strain to hear the words. His voice sounded friendly and calm, as though he meant it to be confidence-inspiring.

"Do you have your sides, Miss Cleveland?"

She held out a large, dog-eared pamphlet bound in chocolate-colored paper which she carried folded over.

"Good. We'll do the first act. Take it easy."

These words eliminated a fear of Lailey's that Dubinsky might not be going to give Willow anything but a perfunctory trial. Evidently he was in earnest and not intending to put any impossible hurdles in her path.

The producer was saying, "Just walk through it and read your lines. Never mind the acting for the time being. But above all, don't try to imitate Miss Délice. See if you can get her out of your head and make a fresh start, just as though you'd never heard the lines before in your life. Understand?"

"Yes, sir."

"That will be the hardest thing you have to do this first try. It won't be easy, but you have to do it. Never mind if you don't put anything into the part at all, but don't put Rita into it! The reason I say that is that no artist ever got anywhere by trying to imitate another. If you haven't got it in yourself, then you haven't got it, and trying to get it by imitation is never good enough. Just be yourself. If we go on, the result will be a different interpretation of the part altogether and we will work this out between us in time. But for now, just be natural, be yourself and don't worry."

Dubinsky turned his back abruptly and plodded up the aisle. Willoughby hesitated a moment and walked to her place in the wings. Lailey, expecting some sort of comment from Dubinsky as he edged into the row in front, leaned forward, but Dubinsky passed him without so much as turning his head, and Lailey realized again that he was there merely on sufferance. Dubinsky's words to Willow had calmed Lailey's own trepidation somewhat. Apparently the fellow expected to build a new character based on what he could use in Willow's own personality. Interesting! A lot more to all this than you'd think, apparently, from just seeing a play from the front.

He abandoned his thoughts, for the scene was under way. The cast, it seemed to him, was working easily together, building up to Willow's entrance. Was it all in a day's work to them—this leading lady or that? Were there no secret jealousies, no heart-burnings? If so, there were no outward signs of them, though perhaps the actors seemed a trifle more keyed up than at the other rehearsal. But why was Dubinsky beginning here rather than with Willow's entrance? To make it easier for her, perhaps, so that she could come in, carried along, as it were, by the action of the play. Again Lailey realized that Dubinsky was doing everything he could to give Willow a fair chance, and he recalled the producer's outburst about fairness at their last meeting. Curious fellow! A lot to him, conceivably, in his own way and in his own line of work.

As the time for Willow's entrance neared, the cast seemed to Lailey to grow a trifle tenser. So they did find Willow—the unknown quantity—a strain. He sat forward on the plush seat until he became ashamed of this display of eagerness, whereupon he sat back and tried to cross his long legs in the narrow space. So far the play had seemed interminable and dull but he knew that, in reality, it was not. He longed for a cigar with something like desperation, and then he forgot the cigar and sat on the edge of his seat again, for there she was, altering, by her mere presence, everything. How beautiful! He folded his arms along the back of the seat in front of him and opened his senses to her.

She was not frightened now, he realized with pride, or, at least, she did not let it show. She was moving easily, with her fine carriage, to her appointed place. There was about her all the radiance he knew, but there was also a dignity he had never seen before. He would have called it confidence except for the memory of her cold fingers. She was obeying Dubinsky's instructions to the letter, he saw with approval, not trying to act, being herself, but with what amplitude! She held herself within the limits laid down for her, but she filled his requirements and more than filled them, managing in some subtle way to convey the impression that she was holding herself in check only because that had been asked of her. Clever. He glanced quickly at Dubinsky, but the little producer had not so much as changed his position and the view of the back of his round head told Lailey nothing.

He returned his attention to the stage. No trace, not even a memory of Délice there now. Willow was, at the moment, making a long cross with her superb dignity, and Lailey remembered that Délice had all but made a dance out of it, fluttering and swaying as though each chair or table were a destiny to which she yielded with reluctance.

Lailey glanced at Dubinsky again. The fellow was too quiet! Did that bode ill? In the ordinary course of things he would have stopped the rehearsal a dozen times, Lailey supposed. What did the silence mean? And again Lailey turned to the stage, trying to see the action through Dubinsky's eyes, searching for flaws. This time he saw a thousand, and fear gripped him. Dubinsky's silence could mean only one thing. He would let the act run to the end, thank Willow with that odd kindness of his, thank her for coming and tell her that was all. This scene in Lailey's mind came between him and the stage. He saw her listening to Dubinsky, saw her turn and walk toward the wings while the rest of the cast, in their places, watched her walk away. Heartbreak, and—his fault! Cruel to have raised this hope in her. Perhaps she would never forgive him, and it was most deeply certain that he would never forgive himself.

So vivid was all this in Lailey's mind that it had superseded reality and it was with a sense of shock that he was recalled to the present. Something had happened on the stage that Lailey had not seen. His mind held an impression that Willow had hesitated and that Dubinsky had shifted restlessly in his seat, but what had caused this, or what had really occurred, he did not know. The scene was running smoothly again, with perhaps a little more tenseness in the air. The escape from his daydream was a relief to Lailey. He passed his hand over his face to rouse himself fully and gave his attention to the stage.

One of the other characters was speaking now and Willow was standing still. She used this short interval to open the script she carried and look inside and for the first time Lailey realized that she had been speaking her lines, not reading them. So, in one brief night, she had learned this part! No wonder she looked ill. But the amazing thing was that she should take the pains for this slim chance. He himself would certainly not have done it. Even granting a considerable knowledge of the play, the fact that she had done so hinted a conscientiousness he had not suspected. Or perhaps not conscientiousness so much as a determination which left no stone unturned. The discovery disconcerted him somewhat, as had the like discovery of breadth and ability in Dubinsky, and for a moment he felt himself unpleasantly an outsider, until he remembered that all this would not be taking place but for the authority of his money. She was, after all, no more than proving herself worthy to receive his gift.

Possessed of this appeasing thought, he waited for the end of the act. All was running smoothly now, to all outward appearances. The rest of the cast seemed to be behaving well, giving Willow all the support they could, working hard, "giving it to her," Lailey thought, amused at his own garnering of this piece of theater jargon. But was it really all going as well as he thought? He found, shortly, that the only thing of which he felt really convinced was his own inability to judge. Dubinsky's ominous silence began to oppress him once more and Lailey found, to his annoyance, that he was sweating a little.

The end of the act arrived, the stage manager stepped out of the wings, announced "curtain" and made a semaphore gesture which, since no curtain appeared, Lailey supposed was meant to symbolize its descent. He rose and edged along the row until he was almost directly back of Dubinsky. He sat down again and leaned over the seat in front of him.

"Well, what did you think of her?"

Dubinsky did not answer. He stood up, glanced swiftly at Lailey, as though he found his presence unacceptable, worked his way out of the row and went swaying down the aisle. Instantly Lailey's attention transferred itself to Willow, and he had no time to feel resentment. Now, in an instant, suspense would be over. Was she finding this brief pause as intolerable as he? She gave no sign of it. She was standing where the action of the play had left her and by some trick of personality she had merged herself with the half-dozen others on the stage, so that she seemed no more conspicuous than they, and Lailey thought that you would never know that the next minute might bring her everything she dreamed of or the end of all her hopes.

"Miss Cleveland!"

Here—now—this instant.

"Yes, sir?"

She left the group and became, for Lailey, the only person on the stage. She walked quickly, without hurrying, toward the footlights. "Yes, sir?" she said again, and again Lailey noted that her inflection was exactly right, not eager, not frightened, but polite and almost impersonal.

Dubinsky clasped his hands behind his back. "We'll take the act again. Not from the beginning, but from just before your entrance. Now, this time, see if you can put a little more into it. Lift it. Don't try to act. Just go on being yourself, but wherever you can, lift it. And try to think about what you would be feeling if these things were happening to you which are happening to this girl—Hester—in the play. You're not being this girl—you're not being someone else—but these things are happening to *you* and they make you *feel*. Understand what I mean?"

"I think so."

"Good!" Dubinsky turned toward the wings and yelled "Burt!" in a tone which, for the first time, Lailey thought, sounded like the Dubinsky of the previous rehearsal. The other actors were leaving the stage, but Willow hesitated and her lips moved as though she were about to speak to Dubinsky, but she did not do so. Watching her follow the others toward the wings, Lailey knew, as though he had read her thoughts, that she had just mastered an impulse, almost too strong for her, to ask Dubinsky if she had done well, and again Lailey applauded silently.

Burt arrived on stage with a suddenness that suggested he had been watching from the wings. With a name, the stage manager had acquired a personality in Lailey's eyes. Even so, he looked to Lailey the way he supposed all stage managers everywhere must look, namely, tired, thin and baggy at the knees. When he opened his mouth, Lailey discovered another attribute, for the fellow was hoarse from much shouting.

"You want Act One again, Ike?"

"Not the whole of it. Give them a cue a few lines before Miss Cleveland's entrance."

"All right. Now, folks, on stage—all but Cleveland. *Prompt desk!* Got it?"

This last appeared to be addressed to a youth in an exceedingly dirty shirt without a tie, who rose up from a front seat where he had been slumped low. It was the same youth who had risen from the same spot at the previous rehearsal. The lad held a sort of lapboard with the script fastened to it, which he tipped to catch the shine from the footlights and, taking a pencil from behind his ear, he searched a page. Presently he found what he wanted, glanced at the actors and read in a sort of nasal whine, *"I hate her because she gives me her charm like a gift to the poor and because,* and so forth and so forth, and so forth." He sat down and slid forward until all but the crown of his head was invisible.

There was rapid movement on the stage: Burt walked off; the actors resumed the exact places they were in when these lines were last spoken. That every move an actor made was planned and prescribed was a new idea to Lailey, who would have supposed, if he had thought about it at all, that they moved on the inspiration of the moment. He watched again the change which came over the actors as they became the characters in the play, and he tried to see

77

the mechanism of the transformation, but it was too swift, too subtle. One of the women raised her hands and spoke. *I hate her because she gives me her charm like a gift to the poor, because she deprecates herself to me with such grace, while she despises me, laughs at me.* The words were as full of passion as though they were the outpourings of real hate, and Lailey marveled again at these theater folk who seemed able to turn on emotion as effortlessly as he turned on a bathroom tap.

He shifted his eyes to the wings, and when Willow entered he saw at once the change in her. She seemed, in this short interval, to have become more alive, with a vitality that made her former appearance seem shadowy. Her very presence buoyed him. Magnificent. Oh, magnificent! The excitement stayed with him as he watched her move into her part, beginning to portray Hester, a beautiful and selfish woman, demanding her own way from everyone around her and demanding, at the same time, their adulation. She was putting something into the part, something which he recognized with a faint feeling of uneasiness as belonging to herself, and he felt as though he had made a not altogether pleasant discovery about her. Délice had covered this Hester's meanness with transparent winningness and pleadings. Willow put the whole thing on a broader scale and made her, not mean but insatiably egotistical, not winning but condescending, not pleading but wielding a determined charm.

Lailey's enthusiasm grew. "She's got it! By God, she's got it!" He was breathing fast with the excitement of her success, and his hands clasped tightly the arms of his stall. She would be great—and with a breadth of greatness the facile, waspish, miniature Délice could never reach! She stood out from the others on the stage with a boldness that reduced them to a tapestry of moving shadows. With the essence of herself she filled the stage, the house, his heart. Suddenly this overwhelming enthusiasm was too strong to be contained. He leaned over the back of the seat in front of him and spoke to Dubinsky, who was sitting motionlessly three places to the right, and as he spoke Lailey pounded the plush with his fist.

"She's wonderful! By God, she's wonderful! We've made a discovery that will have all New York talking a week from now."

Dubinsky stared at Lailey and hitched himself around in his seat to bring a shoulder as a shield between them. He made no other reply.

"For Lord's sake, man, can't you see it? She's marvelous!"

Dubinsky mumbled something, and Lailey got up and sat down again directly behind him.

"I didn't catch what you said."

"She's made of wood."

"You don't like her?"

"Listen to her! Where does she come from—what part of the country?"

"I don't know. Out West somewhere. Why?"

"It would take ten years to get it out of her accent. Now, do you want me to watch the rehearsal or do you want to talk?"

Lailey leaned back and for a few minutes he was too angry to focus his attention on anything. Presently the anger melted into a listless discouragement, and he ceased to take any interest in the stage or Dubinsky or anything at all but his gloomy conviction that his enterprise was about to fail because this fat little autocrat was too stupid to see what was so plainly before his eyes. Lailey was discovering, moreover, that he had been counting on the success of this venture more than he had, up to this moment, realized. There had been images in the night of himself at Delmonico's with this glittering new star, and other, more intimate images. How much luster these had derived from her stardom he appreciated now when, in imagination, he saw himself with plain Miss Willow Cleveland of uncertain future and antecedents unknown.

He thought, she'll want me to help her try again with some other producer. There's nothing to that. Nothing at all to that. He brooded with his head down, not watching the stage at all, and while he brooded the act came to an end.

The end startled him. He sat up straight, the suddenness of it making the blood in his fingertips tingle. The actors were walking

79

off the stage, but Dubinsky had not moved and Lailey wondered with animosity whether he had fallen asleep. Presently the theater became very still and Lailey listened to the odd, muffled sounds which underlay the stillness, rustling as of silk, whisperings and sounds like the distant tramp of armies, listened without knowing it to the secret ghostly life inside the walls of all old theaters everywhere. So remote from the world this crowded stillness seemed, he was startled to discover Burt leaning motionlessly against the proscenium arch. Burt looked exhausted and he drooped so that his thin figure seemed to hang from his own back collar button. He was evidently waiting for Dubinsky to rouse, and something about him informed Lailey that such waiting was not unusual. The idea that two men should attend thus the reverie, or doze, or whatever it was, of this little czar suddenly angered Lailey, and to Dubinsky's back he said loudly, "Well?"

Dubinsky squirmed as though the word had hurt him, and his voice was both peevish and pleading. "Keep quiet, can't you, and let me think?"

Lailey made a noise in his throat and threw himself back sidewise in his seat, shoving his legs out as far as he could. He felt intolerably cramped and stiff, and since there seemed to be no use in prolonging this business, he had an urgent desire to have done with it. Dubinsky rose, without looking at either Lailey or the patient Burt, and went up the aisle. Lailey turned to stare after him. Was the fellow preparing to leave without a word? Apparently not, for with hands clasped behind his back and bowed head, he was pacing slowly down the open space behind the seats. He resembled, to Lailey's irritated mind, a fat monk meditating in a cloister. Nevertheless, Dubinsky's meditation did seem to imply at least a ray of hope.

Burt had abandoned his vigil and was coming agilely down a sort of temporary bridge, which had been rigged up over the orchestra pit at one side. He dropped loose-jointedly into an aisle seat near Lailey and the queer silence took possession of the theater once more. A moment later it was shattered by Dubinsky shouting

80

with what seemed to Lailey unnecessary violence and full-blown irascibility.

"Burt. Where the hell are you? Oh, all right. All right. Get Miss Cleveland on, will you?"

"You want Act One again, Ike?"

"No, the monologue. Let's hear how she'll murder *that!*"

Dubinsky was coming down the aisle, swaying from side to side. Lailey's nerves were still jumpy from the unexpected shout. The fellow looked like a duck. Burt rose, taking his time, and going to the orchestra rail called, "Miss Cleveland," in a low tone. The thought that Willow must have been waiting, just off stage, all this time startled Lailey.

She came on docilely, her radiance all turned off. Dubinsky had come to a halt halfway down the aisle, his feet wide apart, his hands still behind his back and on his face a look of ferocious suffering. It dawned on Lailey that if the producer had at one time, or conceivably still had, a deep affection for Rita Délice, he would quite possibly hate to hear Willow in the monologue. Whatever the cause, he seemed inclined to take it out on Willow, for his tone was peremptory.

"Well, what are you waiting for? Begin!"

Odd that the little fellow, who had certainly proved himself, in Lailey's view, capable of generosity, should now be letting his feelings master him—and it did not occur to Lailey until much later that there might have been a purpose in Dubinsky's attitude. Willow, for the first time, seemed flustered.

"From here, sir, or the way I do—the way it is in the play, from upstage?"

"Holy Moses, I don't care! Begin."

Willow walked upstage and as she turned swiftly to face them again, Lailey saw that she, too, had caught that trick of empathy, for when she began to speak, her voice was low and vibrant with feeling that Lailey could have sworn was real. Dubinsky stopped her immediately.

"Speak up. For the love of Moses, speak up! How do you think

81

an audience could hear you? *I* can't hear you and I know the damned speech by heart."

Willow raised her voice. Dubinsky waved his arms and shouted.

"No, *no*. NO! The beginning. Begin at the beginning."

Willow began again, not so easily, and Lailey thought, "That's hard—with no cue—nothing to set you off." Obviously she was finding it hard.

"No—*no!* Stop it!" Dubinsky's manner said plainly that he was speaking to a person stupid enough to try the patience of a saint. "Good God. There's an audience out here, a whole lot of people that have paid a whole lot of money and they can't *hear* you!"

Willow began again, too loud, and Lailey could hear the strain in her voice. Dubinsky raised his arms to heaven and dropped them again, letting the palms slap against his legs. He ran a little way down the aisle and Willow faltered and stopped. At that, Dubinsky turned his back on her and walked slowly up the aisle again. He seemed deep in distant thought, and as he walked, he put his hand on the back of each seat he passed. He gave the impression of dissociating himself from all present. Willow hesitated and began anew. Dubinsky was behind Lailey now, presumably still playing his private game with the seat backs. Knowing he was there made Lailey's neck prickle and his anger rose. Willow experimented with her voice, now loud, now low, until she found a volume which seemed right to her. She appeared to gain a little confidence and began, Lailey thought—using the phrase which was so oddly expressive—to "lift it." Dubinsky broke into her new confidence with another shout for his stage manager.

"Right here, Ike." Burt's gangling form rose from a seat down front.

"That table. It crowds the big Act One scene. It ought to go farther stage right. Have it moved, will you?"

"Now?"

"Now! I wasn't talking to *you*, Miss Cleveland. Go on! Go on! I didn't tell you to stop."

Burt took the bridge in long strides and disappeared into the

82

wings, whence his voice could be heard calling, "Hi, Joe, lend a hand here, will you?" Something like panic lit Willoughby's eyes, but she kept doggedly on. Dubinsky grasped the orchestra rail just below her and, stooping, appeared to be trying to see into the high places of the stage house. Lailey was, by this time, so angry that he could scarcely contain himself. An ordeal for her, truly!

Dubinsky was shouting again and it sounded to Lailey like "Bridge! Bridge!" What in time did the fellow mean by that? Some sort of structure above the stage? Apparently, for, some twenty feet in the air, a head appeared around the proscenium arch and inquired aggrievedly, "You want me, Mr. Dubinsky?"

"Yes. What you got up there, Mac? Turn off those damn foots. I can't see what you got up there."

The head disappeared, the footlights went out and the absence of the hissing they made was more audible than the hissing had been. At another time Lailey might have been amused at these recurring Jack-in-the-box appearances of the backstage personnel, but now he was too much concerned about Willow. The sudden change in the light, altering everything she saw, might well have been a disconcerting shock, but if so, she gave no sign. She had moved out onto the curved apron of the stage and she was speaking her lines into the void. Dubinsky was still shouting.

"Well, what you got up there, Mac?"

The head appeared again. "Up where? Them floods are off."

"Why are they off? This is a rehearsal, isn't it? And where's the spot? Put those floods back on."

There was a moment filled only by Willow's voice, and then a white spotlight hit her with the impact of a blow. She never wavered and, watching her, Lailey felt a thrill.

Dubinsky was darting about now in the space between the front row and the orchestra rail, right below Willow, looking up, not at her, but into the mysterious realms over her head. He took off his coat, tossed it on a seat and pushed up his cuffs.

"That looks like ambers up there. Why you got ambers, for the love of God? Ambers! This is a night scene, isn't it? Night. Night. Burt!"

The table was being dragged with the noise of thunder across the stage. Willow's chin was up, and there was a flush high on her cheeks. Some beauty had departed but something else had come into her face which, though Lailey could not know this, was her father's image—a reflection of John Fenno's fighting grimness. Her voice was raised above the tumult as though she were determined to dominate. Lailey slid to the edge of his seat, folded his arms along the back of the stall in front of him, his fingers holding hard. Her chances were nothing—less than that—but, by God, she was going down fighting! A magnificent thing to watch. His heart responded to it, pounding in his throat. He wanted to shout, to cheer, to proclaim the gallantry of this defeat.

He scarcely heard the noise around him now. Dubinsky was shouting, "Burt! What the hell you got ambers for? Ambers!" The man on the bridge was shouting also, and pounding with his fist on a ragged notebook.

"I got it right here in the cue book. Act Two—ambers! I got it right here since the first light rehearsal. Ambers, it says . . ."

Lailey saw Dubinsky glance swiftly at Willow. Was he, Lailey wondered, watching her secretly? Had he been doing so all the time? And the illuminating idea came to him that, conceivably, this din and commotion were intentional, a test, perhaps, of her fortitude. If so she was, in his estimation, proving her mettle. He watched the ungainly antics of the little producer with considerably more interest. Burt, it seemed, was now the target of his wrath.

"You got that table way over in the wings. For the Lord's sake, put it back. Put it *back!*"

"Right in the cue book . . . Right back where it came from?"

"And the top picks up too much light."

"What you want us to do about that?"

"How the hell should I know? Paint it black or pretend it's a desk and put a blotter on it."

"Props. *Props!* You got that? Blotter. Act Two, blotter."

"This center stuff is too hot anyway. Cool them down. Cool them down."

Good Lord, why didn't they all go crazy?

"Just look once, Mr. Dubinsky. Right in the cue book, ambers!"

"Burt! Burt!"

"All right, Ike. We'll fix it. Mac, make a note to take bridge 8 and 9 over here. Kill the ambers and put in some blues."

But Dubinsky had suddenly calmed down. He sounded, in fact, almost affable. "Never mind the ambers. Never mind 'em. The table's all right there. Mark it, though, before you lose it." The individual called Joe extracted a grubby piece of chalk and, going down on his knees, marked with care all around the four legs of the table. While this was going on, Dubinsky again gave Willow a swift appraising look. Lailey was sweating. And then Willow stopped.

"What's the matter now?" Dubinsky inquired almost politely, as if she had just caught his interest.

"That's the end of the speech, sir."

"All right. All right. Do it again." Dubinsky threw himself into a seat and, resting his chin on his hands, gave her his whole attention.

Willow walked upstage, made her swift turn, animating herself with emotion and began once more to speak. Dubinsky stopped her instantly.

"The word is *true*, not *troo*. And it's *hair*, not *ha-rr*."

"Thank you, Mr. Dubinsky." No shade of irritation, no hint of impatience or fatigue. She began again and Lailey put his head in his hands and suffered for her.

Dubinsky stopped her every few lines, sometimes with biting criticism or bursts of anger, sometimes with bored weariness. She stood it all. She grew a little white, but her control seemed never to desert her, and she never ceased to work hard for the things Dubinsky demanded of her. It was inhuman and Lailey's jaw was set with anger, but he did not interfere and his admiration for Willow was boundless.

Once Burt came out on the stage and said, "Excuse me, Ike, but the whole cast is still here. Want me to tell 'em to go?"

And Dubinsky replied, "Certainly not. When I want the cast dismissed, I'll say so!"

When he turned toward Burt, Lailey saw that Dubinsky's brow was beaded with perspiration. Burt shrugged as though to say that it was no affair of his, hesitated a moment and came down the bridge over the orchestra pit to take a seat next to Dubinsky. Lailey's heart lifted a little, for surely there was no point in holding the whole cast together for so long a time unless Dubinsky felt that Willow showed some promise.

Willow's ordeal went on. She was obviously worn out but doing her best not to show it. Lailey knew she was accepting all this as a trial of strength and that she had made up her mind not to ask for quarter. She was very pale and even her hands looked thin with fatigue. If he had come on her suddenly, he would scarcely have recognized her, for all the animation and the light had left her face. She was not even beautiful, but he watched her with something approaching awe, for it seemed to him that all her qualities had been fused into the single quality of unshakable determination.

He rose and went quietly down toward the front to sit two rows behind Dubinsky. It was the only thing he could think of to do, and he hoped that Willow would see him and take heart. When this was over, nothing would be too good for her! Dubinsky had just delivered himself of a fresh tirade, and as Lailey took his seat, a little to the side where he could watch Dubinsky's face, he heard Burt say in an undertone, "For Chri' sake, Ike! The girl's human," and Lailey was filled with a warm liking for Burt.

The monologue came to a conclusion at last, and at the end Lailey saw that Willow was trembling. He himself felt exhausted— how must she, then, be feeling! After a moment's silence Dubinsky said, "Thank you." He said nothing more. Willow stood uncertainly and then turned toward the wings. To Lailey's overwrought nerves the sounds of her heels on the boards were like great stones falling in the stillness around him.

86

"Miss Cleveland—just a minute."

Willow straightened as though she had received an arrow in her back. She came back to stand inquiringly at the edge of the stage.

"Yes, sir?"

"Are you tired?"

"No!"

There was defiance in the word and Lailey saw Dubinsky's swift, amused smile. There was a spark in her eye, too, and she was not trembling any longer. She leaned down a little toward them.

"Would you like me to do the speech again?"

Dubinsky laughed. "No, dear, no. You've done enough. Call the cast, Burt. Call the cast."

Lailey remembered now with surprise that the theater was full of people. In spite of Burt's reminder, there had seemed only the four of them in a great emptiness. Willow turned her back to them and, walking upstage, leaned over a table. To Lailey her back was eloquent. Burt left via the wings and presently Lailey heard far off the faint shout of the call boy. "On stage please. Everybody on stage. On stage." This time he resisted the impulse to question Dubinsky. He shut his eyes and discovered the beginning of a headache.

Burt came back and the cast trooped on noisily, all of them staring at Willow with, it seemed to Lailey's overwrought mind, a rather horrid curiosity. Burt was on his feet clapping his big hands.

"All right, folks. Quiet please. Mr. Dubinsky has an announcement to make."

They gathered at the edge of the stage. Willow attempted to hide herself behind them but, prompted by their theatrical instinct, they left a sort of aisle open toward her. Someone called out, "Do we get our fares paid back to New York?" and Burt shouted, "Now quiet, folks, please. Quiet." Dubinsky got up and rested his hands on the back of the seat in front of him.

"I have to tell you that we are moving to New York as soon as Burt can make the arrangements. Don't any of you leave the theater without seeing him. There will possibly be two weeks of rehearsals there. Miss Délice is ill. I saw her this morning and her doctor advises a prolonged rest in the south of France. She will leave in a few weeks. She asked me to say good-bye to all of you. While we are in New York, Miss Cleveland will work on the part of Hester. It is possible that, after a few days of rehearsals, I shall decide to disband the cast. On the other hand, there is a possibility that the play will open with Miss Cleveland in the lead. I'm sorry I can't be more definite at this time. That's all. Thank you."

Chapter Seven

THE cast of *The Rungs of the Ladder*, including Willoughby, went to New York the next day on an early train. Lailey took a later train after telegraphing his lawyer to see Dubinsky at once. When he arrived he went straight to his office, where he found a request to meet Dubinsky at the theater that same afternoon at six o'clock. The request, which was rather like a summons, at first angered him. Then certain aspects of the situation struck him, and he began to laugh. He thought it funny, to say the least, that he was being ordered about by a man who was, well, what he was. A producer who was being paid by him to put on a show to star a woman who—and this part made him laugh too, but without much enjoyment—a woman who refused to be his mistress.

When he appeared at Dubinsky's office, Dubinsky rose and the two men shook hands for the first time. Lailey said, "I wired my lawyer this morning. Did he see you?"

"Yes, briefly."

"Satisfactory?"

"Yes. We worked out a preliminary agreement to be signed now, saying, in effect, that if Miss Cleveland proves satisfactory to me in the rehearsals of her new part, a more formal agreement will then be signed between us at the time she receives her contract from me. The terms of the formal agreement are stated, and they're those you proposed in your wire to your attorney, amplified a little. If you approve the preliminary agreement, we'll sign it whenever you like."

"Is there anything else on your mind?"

Dubinsky did not answer at once, and Lailey looked around at the office. It was small but its furnishings showed taste—a different place altogether from the dusty, shabby room in which they had last met, and then Lailey remembered that this was Dubinsky's own theater and so the taste was also, presumably, his own.

"Before you begin," Lailey said, "I'd like to say that what I saw yesterday at the theater was one of the most remarkable things I ever saw in my life."

"In what sense?"

"I couldn't have done it—not many men could have, I'm sure of that."

"You mean . . . ?"

"I mean, stuck to it—kept going even after she thought she'd failed. I know she thought she'd failed—and she went right on. I tell you, it did something to me to see her standing up there . . ."

"I'm sorry I had to be so hard on her. At that stage it was almost more a question of finding out whether she had the character qualifications to be an actress than of testing her acting ability. She has determination, there's no question about that, and it's an important quality. But I asked you to stop by, because there's something else I want to talk about."

Dubinsky made a steeple out of his fingers and studied it carefully before he continued. Lailey had the distinct impression that he was embarrassed, but when he spoke there was no evidence of it.

"I'm afraid that what I have to say is going to sound very personal, but it's absolutely essential that we discuss it now, before we get any farther along with these rehearsals. You must believe that it's

90

pertinent, not impertinent. I assume, of course, that your interest in Miss Cleveland is considerable or you would not have offered to put up this money. I am going to ask for your assurance that, during the next two weeks, she will not be subjected to any outside distractions whatsoever."

Lailey looked at him sharply and his face flushed, but he made no attempt to interrupt and Dubinsky continued.

"Miss Cleveland is going to find the theater a very arduous life, indeed. It's that, even for an experienced actress. In Miss Cleveland's case it will be doubly, triply so. I'd guess the two weeks ahead of her will almost surely be the hardest she's ever experienced. I venture to say that, before it's half over, you yourself will be both shocked and angry at the demands which will be made on her. And it won't be only the hard work. It will be the nervous strain and the constant fear that she will fail."

"You could relieve her of *that*, at least."

"No, unfortunately, I can't, until I'm sure myself whether she can carry the part. But I can't overstate the difficulties ahead of her or the necessity for her to give her work every ounce of herself. The point I am making is, she must not only have no outside distractions, but no outside thoughts or wishes or inclinations. She must give herself to this work in every sense of the word, if she is to succeed, and even then I can give no guarantee that she will succeed."

"Have you said anything like this to her?"

"Yes."

"And she's willing to go on with it on those terms?"

Dubinsky smiled. "I think so. The lure of the stage is very strong, especially for a woman of her type. But as I was saying, she must be able to give herself wholly to the work. I must be satisfied in my own mind that her interest and her energy won't be divided, that she won't have demands on her time other than those I shall make, and that she will be allowed to work with the singleness of purpose I describe."

Lailey said nothing to this, and Dubinsky went on. "It may

sound odd, but I'm less worried about it in connection with Miss Cleveland than I am in respect to you. She wants this part very much. She'll work for it—if she's allowed to. If she's left alone. What I want to know from you is, are you prepared to make that sacrifice for her? Are you prepared to leave her completely alone, as far as emotional distractions and pressures are concerned, until the play is into its run? If you think about it a little, I'm sure you'll see why it's absolutely necessary that I have that kind of assurance, and that it's necessary to seem to pry—no, actually to pry—into your affairs to get it."

Some of the native self-confidence had left Lailey's face. He looked troubled and older. His hands were folded tightly around the arms of his chair. He was not looking at anything but his own thoughts. After a while Lailey said, "I hate to think of her having to go through all this."

"I'm glad you're thinking of her. I'm very glad. It's almost the key to the whole thing. If you hadn't been willing to do that . . ." Dubinsky finished the sentence with his hands held palms up. "But you thought of her instinctively. That's a very good sign. You're quite right in saying that, in some ways, she's a remarkable person. She deserves your consideration."

Lailey said, "This whole thing has been something of an experience."

"I can understand that. You never had any contact with theater life before."

"What I saw yesterday was for me a profound experience." Lailey was looking straight at Dubinsky, and his eyes had none of their customary coldness. "I will confess that it did something to me. You've been frank with me, and by being frank you've assumed that I'll treat you in the same way. Good. I will. I like the way this whole thing is being done. So I'd like to put the cards on the table and tell you exactly how things stand. I met Miss Cleveland, more or less accidentally, not so very long ago, at Saratoga. I liked her at once. Then I found she was an actress. I went to Philadelphia to see her. I suppose I had in mind exactly what any man in such a situation would have, considering her looks and the actress part of it. After she lost her part I asked her to be my mistress. She refused, and the reason she gave was that she wanted to establish herself in the theater and become somebody in her own right. She didn't think of acting as just a pastime. She made that decision before we went back to Philadelphia, and for her sake I'd like you to know that—though I don't believe you need any more evidence than you had yesterday of her sincerity. I intended to make her my mistress, yes. That's why I agreed to put money in the show—but now, Goddamn it, I don't know. She's got quality. I think I admire her more than anyone I've ever seen. I don't think she could be anybody's mistress in the generally accepted sense. I'm beginning to think I don't want her that way. Right now, I don't know *what* I want. Yes, I'll leave her alone until the show's on. Jesus, that's the least I could do for her."

Dubinsky smiled, slapped the arms of his chair and stood up. He said, "Very well, I'm glad you see it that way. We'll sign the agreement your lawyer proposed, whenever you're ready. I only hope everything works out well."

Lailey rose more slowly. "Miss Cleveland is concerned about her contract. Mightn't it be just as well if that were signed at the same time? It would give her confidence . . ."

"I'm sorry, but I'll have to wait until I've had more opportunity to see her working in the part. For my own sake I hope she succeeds, but I can't give the final answer now."

"But you've already . . ."

"I can't sign the contract now."

"Don't keep her in suspense longer than you have to."

"I'll try not."

"Am I right in understanding that you're proposing I don't see Willow at all these next weeks? I'd like to take her to supper and come to watch rehearsals occasionally."

"Oh, *that's* all right."

They shook hands and then, suddenly, both were embarrassed. Lailey left the office quickly.

By the time the first of the two weeks of rehearsal had come to an end, Willoughby had lost weight. The loss was most apparent in her face, but as some of its roundness disappeared, the underlying strength became more noticeable. She developed a habit of moving her hands restlessly. Her eyes were brighter, but there were faint shadows under them.

Lailey noticed these signs of strain and they troubled him. He himself had grown a trifle gaunt in the cheeks, and the lines around his mouth were deeper. He spent all the time he could at the theater, for he discovered that it was a comfort and a support to her to have him there, though she never admitted this to him. Rehearsals became a torture. To have to sit silently in the dark house and watch her subjected to grueling work, arbitrary demands and a discipline more exacting than the average man encounters in a lifetime was almost beyond his endurance.

Sometimes, during a brief break in the rehearsal, when Dubinsky's attention was elsewhere, she would turn and smile toward the place in the dark house where she thought he might be sitting. Then he would stand up and wave to her, but he was never quite sure whether, with the shine of the footlights in her eyes, she saw him. These smiles of hers, and their unconscious fortitude, moved him greatly. Long before the first week was over he admitted to himself that he was deeply in love.

His office saw little of him except in the mornings. On one of these brief visits to the financial district he met Sam Hadley at the paper-littered corner of Broad and Wall Streets. Hadley's stock had just appeared on the Exchange. There was only one other steel stock listed, Colorado Coal & Iron, and the regular operators, both bulls and bears, who were more accustomed to railroad shares and the politics behind them, left the new stock alone. It remained at a fairly steady seventeen and a quarter, which was, in Lailey's view, about right.

Hadley looked even bigger on a crowded street than he did in a room with a few people. The two men raised their arms in greeting, and Sam gave Lailey the same warm smile but they did not stop to talk because Sam had someone with him. Lailey thought he recognized Sam's companion as Michael Brodi, consultant to Hadley's company, a man who was beginning to have a national reputation because of his writings on economic and financial matters. With the thought that it might be a good thing to lure Brodi into his own employ some time, Lailey went on his way.

The Brodis were Sam's only real friends. In spite of the warmth of his nature and in spite of his hail-fellow attitude toward all he liked, he kept everyone else in the category of acquaintances. This had been more than ever true since his wife had left him, but that same event had seemed to draw him even closer to the Brodis. He had fallen into the habit of discussing all his personal problems with them and especially with Lettie, partly because she was his sister-in-law and so not an outsider, and partly because she was as different from his wife as a sister can well be.

Lettie was tall and, even without the long welt of a scar which slanted downward across one cheek, most people would have called her plain. Because of this scar, not many looked directly at Lettie and so her eyes could, and did, observe others with freedom. They were fine eyes, gray and calm, with depths of understanding in them, and they saw a great deal. She had a way of assuming that others saw with as much clarity as she, which sometimes made the things she said not a little mystifying.

She had a talent for quietness and she liked, if she could not be with Michael or Sam or her daughter Dulcie, to be alone, for it was then that she renewed her strength. She liked to sit in the late afternoon by an open fire if possible and, as she put it, to "gather up the ends." She did this in her little drawing room, which was on the second floor of the rented brownstone house. An aging red setter named Shamrock shared these quiet interludes with her, stretched out on the hearthrug.

It was here that Sam found them one afternoon. He called from the stairs, in the cordial way which Lettie liked so much, and she called back, "Why, Sam!"

"You make a nice picture," he said, coming into the room. She rose to light the painted china lamp. Twilight and Sam didn't seem to go together. Shadows receded where he came and, holding the glass chimney raised above the wick, she thought how easily and frankly he showed it, when he felt pleasure, wanting it to be known.

He waited, standing, until she had finished with the lamp and then sat down facing the fire in a chintz-covered chair which was too small for him. With one extended foot he stroked Shamrock's loose red hide. Lettie picked up her darning basket but instead of sewing, she sat with the basket on her lap and looked thoughtfully at Sam, who was staring at the glowing coals. This, she thought, was no life for a man like Sam—without a wife, without a home. He hadn't seemed to care much just at first, but now, and especially since he had met this girl, he had grown restless. She seemed, in some mysterious way, to have waked him up. Presently she said, "You've been seeing Claire Reynolds, haven't you?"

"How did you know?"

"Because you looked like this the last time."

"Like what?"

"As though you felt things more."

"Felt things?" He laughed. Then he grew serious again. "Maybe I do. It's a hell of a life I'm leading these days, Lettie."

"I know. Tell me about Claire."

"I took her for a drive—her and a black scarecrow of a woman. Chaperon!"

He laughed again, not so much with enjoyment of the picture of himself being chaperoned as with an effort to make her enjoy it. She turned her sewing basket slowly around and around in her big hands, frowning at it, her mind trying to cope with Sam's problems. Then she said, "She's very young, Sam. Don't hurt her."

"Don't worry, Lettie. I remind her of her father!"

He was making a joke of it, but she could see it piqued him. Sam with piqued vanity!

"If you don't watch out, you're going to cause a heartbreak, Sam.

I could see, when we went to call, that she's turned to you. She's given you something."

She watched him while he thought about this. How open he was! Letting the people he was fond of see right into him—not trying to hide anything. He was pleased with what she had said, pleased with the idea that Claire should turn to him. Then she could see him beginning to worry about it. He wouldn't want to hurt her. He had it in him to be gentle, perhaps, though there had been little enough in his life so far to bring it out. But while she was trying to reconcile this with the tough, ruthless streak in him which had made it possible for him to fight his way up from nowhere, his expression had changed again. Amusement was crinkling the corners of his eyes. He was laughing at her.

"You've let your imagination run away with you. You always were romantic."

"I know, Sam. You can tease me all you like, but this time I'm serious. Anyone as young as Claire—when they're young they're so *vulnerable*."

He thought about this for a while, leaning forward in his chair, hands hanging between his knees. The clock in the hall made a whirring sound, premonitory to striking five. Lettie heard the front door bang open and Dulcie's flying steps go down the passage to the kitchen. Shamrock's feet twitched as though he were racing joyously after her in his mind. When she glanced at Sam again she saw that his thoughts had veered once more. He looked, she thought, beset, and she sighed because she knew what was the one thing in the world which could bring that look to his face.

And as though driven by his thoughts, he rose and began to walk around the little room. His hands were thrust in his pockets. He jingled loose silver and, wandering, looked at the objects around him without seeing them. She watched him with the concern of real affection, thinking that for the past year he had been forced, in a sense, to mark time, he who, of all people, couldn't stand inaction. He needed something to fight, something positive, with a clear-cut issue. And she had a moment of profound uncertainty as to whether she and Michael had done right in persuading him to this inaction.

Sam's wanderings had taken him toward the window. As he neared it there was a tiny, swift movement on one of the chintz curtains with which Lettie had relieved the drabness of this small room. He knew what it was—Dulcie's chameleon. He could see the tiny gilt chain, swinging slightly, and the pin which tethered it, but not the creature itself. He smiled at it and then the absent look came over his face again. After a moment he said over his shoulder, "A man can't live alone forever, Lettie."

It sounded as though he were talking more to himself than to her, and Lettie said nothing. She set the mending basket on the floor beside her and folded her hands. Her brow looked troubled.

He came back and stood with his hands on the back of the chair and stared at the fire. She thought, what a *waste*. He's handsomer than he ever was—not so bold, but stronger, more compassionate. And the way he can make you feel that he likes life and enjoys himself. Oh, why couldn't they have worked it out together?

She was still deep in these thoughts when he said with a sudden decisiveness which startled her, "I'm not going to put up with it any longer. I'm going to get her back."

"Oh, Sam—no. Let her go. It wouldn't work. Let her go."

"What do you mean, let her go?"

"I mean, let her be free—let her have her own life. If she wants a divorce, give it to her."

"A *divorce*? There's never been any question of that—there's never been any question of her leaving home for good—you know that yourself. Why, some of her clothes are still in her bureau drawers—she's left letters she hasn't answered in her desk. You and Mike both know she never said anything about not coming back. She's been away long enough—that's all."

"I know—but Sam . . ."

"I'd have put a stop to it before, only I agreed with you that, unless she'd gotten it out of her system . . . What we didn't any of us know was that she'd get a part in a play. Well, she's had her chance at that, too. It's time she came home."

"I'm afraid it's worse than you think."

"What do you mean?"

"You know, I thought—I don't know whether you really agreed with me—but I thought if you *didn't* let her take that part she'd always go on thinking she might have been a great star if it hadn't been for you. We all thought she ought to be given time to get sick of it. But now it's not as simple as that. It might have been better . . ."

"Has something happened?"

"Yes. She *is* a star."

"What do you mean?"

"Sam, it's one of those miracles of the theater. I don't suppose you ever read the theater news in the papers. I do, so I found out. The leading lady in her play got sick and they've put Willoughby in her place. It's a wonderful thing to happen to anyone, Sam, if only . . ."

Sam stared at her a moment, taking in the implications of what she said. Then he turned away from her and walked thoughtfully to Michael's writing table. He picked up a glass paperweight which Lettie had given Michael a long time ago. Inside was a landscape and a little red church. He shook it, watched while a snowstorm rose to envelop the church and subsided. Then he put it down decisively and went back to Lettie.

"She's in New York, then?"

"Yes, but Sam, if you *must* see her, wait just a little while. Her play hasn't opened yet and she's working terribly hard and, naturally, she's anxious."

"You've seen her!"

"Yes."

She waited but he said nothing. She liked him least when he looked like that. Implacable was the word her mind found for it, and it was an expression which was often on his face when he talked about his wife.

Lettie said, "I wasn't going to tell you. I went to the theater yesterday and saw her in her dressing room. After all, she's my sister,

Sam. We never got along very well, God knows, but she's my sister."

"How was she?" Sam said it carefully, as though he had to take pains to pick these words out of a violent tumult of thought.

"Tired, I thought. She wouldn't have said so for the world, of course, but you could see it around her eyes. She was being the great star for my benefit and—oh, Sam, it made me want to cry. She has the same kind of courage Father had. It was *you* who finally defeated Father. Don't do it to Willoughby, too."

"I didn't defeat him, Lettie. He lost the mill in the financial crash and I bought it."

"Yes, and he hated you, he'd fired you."

"Never mind all that now."

"No, you're right. Sam, it's a funny thing—you know how Willoughby used to make me feel before I married Michael—so shy and self-conscious and miserable? I was afraid of her and I hated her— of course I didn't really hate her, but I used to think I did. I thought I'd outgrown all that, and I have, but there's a little of it still left— just a little. I put on my very best dress to go to see her. I've been awfully proud of that dress—I loved it—but the minute she looked at it I knew it wasn't really smart and it didn't fit very well and then —can you believe it?—I got all self-conscious, the way I used to be. As awkward as a schoolgirl."

Lettie's eyes were shining with amusement at the memory and Sam smiled at her, liking her.

"It was so funny, really, me behaving like that and she being the gracious, condescending star. She showed me the stage and I followed her, letting my skirts trail on the dirty floor because I wanted to have her think I didn't care about a little dirt on my best dress. *Hers* was so new style—it didn't even touch. Naturally, each of us behaving like that, we didn't say much that mattered, but she did ask me one thing. She asked me if we would all of us, you and Michael and I, keep it a secret that she's married."

"But Lettie . . ." He thought a minute. "I don't like that," he said gravely.

"It's all right, Sam, really. Actresses usually keep their marriages secret, but it's more than that. She told her producer she wasn't married and I think she would be afraid it would weaken his faith in her to tell him the truth at this critical time. It *is* a critical time. But maybe it's because she wants to be somebody in her own right, Sam. Had you thought of that? I somehow think that may be it, Sam."

"What did you say when she asked you that?"

"I said she was quite right and we *would* keep it secret."

"How could you . . ."

"It can't make any real difference to you—not for a few weeks. It's only the idea you don't like. Since she's working so hard—working *magnificently*, Sam, I'm sure of that—don't put any obstacles in her path."

"She's my wife and I won't have her acting as though she were ashamed of it!" The implacable look was back on his face again.

"Oh Sam, don't be petty. You've never been petty—that's one thing you've *never* been. You've always been generous and fair. That's why you and Michael and I could be friends, even after what happened to Father, because you didn't take the mill just for revenge—maybe a little, but not *just* for revenge. Anyway, it won't hurt us to keep it secret because we won't be likely to meet anybody here who knows her. She can't hope to keep it secret in the long run but if it will help her now . . ."

His face was like a thundercloud and she thought, irrelevantly, his anger is on as big a scale as the rest of him. He had picked up a poker and was attacking the fire. The coals split apart, crackling. She thought, poor Sam, poor thwarted man of action. The violence seemed to relieve him. He put the poker down.

"Is she happy, do you think?"

"It's not a question of happiness. No, she's not happy in the ordinary sense, but it's her life—that was perfectly plain. It's what she wants. It's *right* for her."

"How can you say it's her life? You don't make a new life in a year. Her life is back home, and by God, that's where she's going.

This business is the last straw. When it gets to the point she isn't telling she's married . . . I'm going to see her!"

"Not until her play opens, Sam, please. Don't upset her until she has that behind her. You simply *mustn't*, Sam."

"All right, but this situation isn't right or normal—for either of us. I know it isn't for me. When I get to the stage where I look at other women—a girl . . . Lettie, nothing like that ever happened to me before."

"Sam, does she—Claire, I mean—know you're married?"

"You've just been saying that no one should know."

"You oughtn't to be seeing Claire at all, under the circumstances."

He started to answer her but gave it up, and she thought, what wicked, unfair power women have in their tongues. Men are so helpless against it. But, though she added nothing more, she did nothing to soften the effect of her words.

Presently he said, "What made you say that, Lettie—that she's in love with me?"

"Because when I went with you to call, I could see it."

"I'd only met her the night before."

"I know, but I could see it in the way she lifted her face when you spoke to her, the way she leaned toward you when she shook hands, the way the shadows came into her eyes when she was looking at you. I tell you, Sam, if you don't watch out you'll do a cruel and heartless thing."

"You're dreaming."

"Sam, what do *you* think? Look back on it. You've seen her—how many times? Four? Five? What do *you* think?"

"I think you don't fall in love that quickly."

"Look at Michael and me!"

She said it with so much pride and complacency that Sam burst out laughing and Lettie, who was faintly hurt by his outburst, couldn't resist the contagion of it, and laughed too.

In the midst of it the old dog sat up, listening to sounds in the hall below. He rose and trotted out, coming back, presently, preceding Michael Brodi and walking as though his master's coming were something to his credit. Michael was short and thick-set and his face was deeply furrowed by the force of his own emotions. He belonged, however, to that special breed of men whose feelings are never so deeply stirred by their fellow men as they are by thoughts and ideas. He had once been a teacher in a small Ohio college, a labor leader and, more recently, a writer whose opinions carried weight. He was, secondarily in his own mind, a consultant to Hadley's company and one of its directors.

Michael threw down the newspaper he was carrying and said, "So *there* you are! I was wondering where the hell you were all afternoon." He said it angrily. The dog went back to the hearthrug and lay down, his loose-jointed body relaxing like a sack with some bones in it. Michael walked to the fire.

Lettie said, "Kiss me, Michael."

He kissed her and then he touched her shoulder lightly. She put her fingertips on the furrows of his forehead for an instant. When he straightened up and faced Sam again, the angry look came back.

Sam said, "All right, fella. Don't get hot about it."

"That's three times this week—and with the stock just listed. What do you expect me to do—run your whole damn company for you?"

"It's just routine."

"Routine, hell! Don't forget that, as the stock holdings stand now, it's theoretically possible to lose working control of the company. I didn't want you to take the risk in the first place, but since you have, you'd better stay on the job till we're in a safer position."

"Theoretically!"

"Yes, and so long as that's true . . ."

"Oh, for God's sake, stop worrying. And by the way, I've been thinking some about that Herrick fellow I met at Lailey's. Have you happened to pick up any gossip about him?"

"That fellow who's Lailey's broker? We've got a good man—don't tie up with *him*. He has a reputation for handling slick deals the big brokers won't touch. You've got to remember . . ."

if *my* wife acted like that . . . Then he remembered how his wife was acting and silenced his own thoughts.

Sam was too far away to hear, but Lailey was saying, "I simply must go back to Willow Cleveland, Vera. She doesn't know any of these people."

"Nonsense. She's the type . . . Oh, look! There's that big Hadley man. Come on." She almost dragged him. Seeing this, Sam thought, I'll be damned if I'll let her use me to make him jealous, but there was no escape.

Not far away, Maurice watched all this and took another drink. He was the best-dressed man in the room, if the definition included clothes which followed the fashions a little more closely and were a trifle more extreme than the average. With his free hand he touched the points of his waxed moustache, then stood thoughtfully fingering one of his sapphire cuff links. He had bought the cuff links with his own money and he often fingered them this way. A good many things about Maurice, his waxed moustache, these sapphires, his style of dress, were in reality small defenses against Vera's waspish authority of manner and the fact that all the money was hers. Maurice watched his wife a moment longer, then he shut his eyes and took another drink. He was not drinking sherry, like most of the other people. After the drink a slight film seemed to come over him, which blurred faintly everything about him.

Lailey had said something about coming across the room to meet someone—the guest of honor, but Sam couldn't be bothered now. He wanted to find Claire. He got away from Lailey and Mrs. Herrick and began to elbow his way through the crowd. Then he found her. She was standing in front of the fireplace, which had disappeared under a bank of flowers. No longer handicapped by the dead Cornelia's finery, she was dressed all in blue, the shade of her eyes. The gown was simple and soft, and made her figure look slim and boyish. More than ever, she looked as Lettie had described her, "delphinian." The light from two gasoliers above her shone down on her bright hair, making it gleam and shimmer.

She had just finished talking to an elderly couple when she saw

Sam and color rushed to her face. He said, "Hullo, there," and stood over her, looking down at her. She glanced up at him with one of the sudden flashes of her blue eyes which so disturbed his bloodstream, and when she saw the look on his face her eyelids flickered and fell.

She said, "Hullo, Sam," in a very small voice, and he laughed with colossal enjoyment because of the prim way she said it. Her shy awareness of him was tremendously provocative. He forgot about the things Lettie had said to him. He thought it would be fine to see what she would do if he really pressed her—if he could find some way of getting her alone just for once.

Over in the archway, Dodge was announcing the arrival of Mr. Isaac Dubinsky, but nobody heard him. Dodge had made a quick appraisal of this guest and, like the majority of people outside of the theater world who met Mr. Dubinsky for the first time, he saw no deeper than the rotund figure, the swarthy skin and the high, round forehead where the black hair grew thinly. Dodge received the name as though the quality of it impaired his personal dignity, and he spoke it into the space above the heads of the party as though he were glad to rid himself of it.

Dubinsky stood just inside the archway and looked around him. His face was expressionless but his deep eyes were quick, and he watched the people as though they were acting a scene in a play.

This detachment of his, this assumption of the role of observer, was more or less habitual when, on rare occasions, he went outside the circles of the theater. He had adopted it partly from choice and partly because it was the simplest way to meet exclusion with dignity. He stood now with his hands behind his back, allowing himself to receive impressions from the scene he watched. Everyone but himself had a glass of sherry in hand, and this seemed to bind them all together in the observance of a common ceremonial, but underneath the polite conventions he felt the striving and the disharmony as ego opposed itself to ego, shrill voice to shrill voice. You felt things like that, he knew, only when you stood aside and watched. The women in their strange bustles seemed to be animate beings only from the waist up, and the drapery of their skirts, pulled tightly backward, gave them all the look of slanting forward into a wind. The deep cutting of the sherry glasses made the wine sparkle and he let his eyes wander, taking pleasure in these recurring bits of brilliance which held the scene together as a repeated color note ties together the composition of a picture.

He made no move to become part of it. The gulf which separated himself from these people was too wide. He knew too well that, were he to attach himself to one or another of the groups, the people in it would coalesce invisibly against him and that he himself would supply the cohesive element, creating in them a unity they now lacked.

He did not mind—had not, he believed, ever minded—but his not minding had become more sure with the passage of time.

Willoughby was talking to the group around her and wondering where Stuyvesant had gone. He should be here to introduce people, but it didn't really matter. She knew she was being a huge success and she loved it. She wasn't paying much attention to what was said to her, though, because she was stealing quick looks around her. It was the most magnificent house she had ever seen, and each swift look went in a new direction. It was hard to see what the room was really like because of all the people and the flowers, but she could see that some of the furniture was gilt and covered with Aubusson tapestry and some inlaid with brass and tortoise shell. Buhl, she thought they called it. The last quick look was at the ceiling and that really made her gasp. Most of it was carved and gilded, but in the center was a large oval painting of godlike people and a chariot and prancing horses. What she liked most was the scale of the place, the quality of being larger than life, and she laughed with sheer exuberance because she had the feeling that she had finally found her proper setting.

Claire said, "Come and meet our guest of honor, Sam."

She began to work her way through the crowd and he followed her reluctantly. Then, over the heads of the people around him, he caught sight of an elaborate headdress of blond curls. On half a hundred occasions, in a crowd or in a passing carriage, he had thought for a tumultuous moment that he had seen Willoughby's blond head. He always knew instantly that he was mistaken, but afterward he felt shaken. He forgot Claire and began to elbow his way forward.

Willoughby was turned so that she did not see him. People were crowding around her and she was laughing. She seemed to be graciously disclaiming their homage, but at the same time accepting it. He had not expected that, when they met, his foremost emotion would be anger. He planted himself in front of her and waited grimly to see the shock of recognition in her face. It was a full minute before she turned and saw him.

The light in her eyes leaped like the flame of a candle in a draft. She might have had the same look if he had struck her. But before he had recovered from his shock, she was holding out her hand. Her eyes were sharp but she was smiling, the same smile which, a minute before, she had been giving to strangers—a celebrity asking everyone to believe that she was simple and sincere at heart. He wanted to strike her, and at the same time he couldn't help admiring her. She was looking right at him with her cold, arrogant eyes, sure of herself, and the intensity of his feelings choked him.

She was saying, "I'm Willow Cleveland. Won't you introduce us, Miss Reynolds?"

Claire said something in a voice too low to be heard. He looked at her but he did not try to understand. Except for the violence of his feelings toward Willoughby, his mind seemed to be paralyzed. Before Claire had finished speaking, Willoughby began talking rapidly and he turned his head back to her. He tried to pull himself together. It was like a dream in which he could not move.

She talked about the largeness of the party, the beauty of the room, the certainty that she could not remember all the names. He knew it was only a few sentences, but it seemed to have been going on a long time. He started to break in just as Claire touched his arm. She looked like a child, and he did not want to say the things he was going to say while she stood there with that look on her face.

Then he realized that Willoughby had been quietly trying to get her hand out of his grasp. He hadn't known he was still holding it. He squeezed it hard and saw her eyes react to the pain. People around them seemed to be waiting for a chance to talk to her again. He turned his back on her and pushed his way through them.

Claire did not follow him. She said, "You knew him before, didn't you, Miss Cleveland?"

"No, of course not. Don't be a stupid child."

She was holding the fingers of the hand Sam had squeezed. They hurt her and made her cross. Then she stooped and brushed at the lace-trimmed flounces of her dress. It was blue like Claire's and, though it was nowhere near so simple, that they should be wearing the same color filled her with annoyance. She straightened up, beckoned a footman who was passing with a tray full of sherry glasses, took one, drained it and put it back on the tray. Then she faced the people who were waiting. She wasn't even tired any more. She felt sure Sam would keep her secret and, though she could probably expect trouble from him now that he had seen her, she didn't have to think about it just yet. She was already smiling and shaking hands. Claire had gone back to her post in front of the flower-banked fireplace.

Another footman was standing in front of Dubinsky with a tray full of glasses. He took one, smiled to himself and raised his glass in a silent toast to emptiness. In a mood of not unpleasant melancholy he sipped the sherry. No sour grapes in *his* wine. The foolish simile pleased him and he began a careful survey of the room, missing nothing. One of the many clusters of people seemed to him rather especially compact and, from something eager in the lines of the backs which were presented to him, he concluded that these people were probably crowded around Willow. She would enjoy that homage—she seemed to need it. If he guessed right there was something in her—ambition, craving, call it what you like—that would always outrun her current achievements, so that homage would never really satisfy her. A hopeful thing from her producer's point of view, since it was likely to keep her always striving, even though the ambition was for nothing more worthy than ever greater homage.

He shifted his gaze and found he was looking down one of those channels which open up of themselves through a room filled with people, like rivers of space in a page of type, straight to the fireplace where Claire stood alone in front of the bank of flowers. She stood in a pool of light which shone down on her from two gas jets high above her head on the chimney breast. His eyes on her, Dubinsky lowered his glass slowly. His face wore again the mask of the race for whom beauty and sadness are so closely allied. He had forgotten the people around him. He was moved as he sometimes was when his stage was visited by one of those rare moments in which all the elements of the theater combine to produce perfect beauty. Then he would watch, transported and not very far from tears, wrung both by the beauty and by the knowledge that it would not linger.

He moved a little nearer. *"Guardaci ben! ben son, ben son Beatrice."* Like Beatrice in the flowery meadow of light. *". . . una nuvola di fiori, che dalle mani angeliche . . ."* He moved a little nearer. *". . . saliva e ricadeva in giu dentro e di fori."* Di Fori! Ah, so within a cloud of flowers. She in light and he in shadow, veritable shadow. Beatrice had stood on the other side of a river—Lethe, was it? Uncrossable. The room suddenly felt hot, and the noise of talk was like a roaring in his ears. He took out his handkerchief and patted his forehead where little beads of perspiration glistened. No doubt she had a tinny voice and a nervous laugh. He found he had no great desire to speak to her.

She, however, seemed to feel his steady gaze. She looked up and saw him, smiled with spontaneous warmth and came toward him, holding out her hand.

"I'm Claire Reynolds."

Her voice was not tinny but, to his sensitive ear, unexpectedly rich and mature. He lost himself for an instant in the blue eyes and, realizing that he must do something, he threw away some of his reserve and smiled too. Nevertheless, he wished she had not moved.

She was saying, "I'm Uncle Stuyvesant's niece," and, laughing,

"That sounds silly, doesn't it? If he's my uncle, of course I'm his niece."

"There isn't any other way to say it." The river was there between them. Thought of the river reminded him of something. "My name's Dubinsky. Isaac Dubinsky."

He waited for the name to bring a shadow to her face or, worse still, a forced brightness. He waited with an expression so often resorted to that the lines of it were always in his face. He saw no evidence in her of either.

"Mr. Dubinsky. Oh, then I know who you are. Uncle Stuyvesant says that a producer-manager is the closest thing there is to an absolute monarch. I've been longing to meet you."

"Then your uncle hasn't learned much about the theater. He should have told you that I'm everybody's slave. They all take it out on me. The actors, the stage manager—everybody. Actresses are the worst."

The banality of what he was saying appalled him, and he was relieved to see that she was not giving him all of her attention. He thought she was looking for someone. He said, "Perhaps you'd like to come to the theater sometime and let me show you my kingdom."

That brought her back to him.

"Oh, I'd love to. May I really?"

"Of course. Of course."

There didn't seem to be anything more to say or any need to say anything, for her eyes were wandering around the room again. Watching her, he began to imagine himself showing her his theater, talking to her about it and a little, too, about himself. People were moving toward the door. Dubinsky said with sudden eagerness, "May I take you down to dinner?" and realized the instant he had said it that there would most certainly be other plans for her.

"I'm supposed to go down with someone—a Mr. Hadley. A friend of Uncle Stuyvesant's."

"Oh, yes—of course."

"But you won't forget about the theater, will you? You really won't forget?"

He smiled. She did not seem to expect an answer and he gave her none. Still smiling, he watched her move away. More people were beginning to drift through the archway and the rest of them were waiting to go through, formed into a v-shaped mass, like the sands of an hourglass about to trickle out. The little court clustered around Willow had broken up. The sands were running out fast now. He looked around for Claire and found her standing beside a big fellow with an angry face waiting, Dubinsky supposed, to bring up the rear of this procession. He thought that was how they did it in houses like this. Then he realized that he could not merely stand still, watching. He himself must find a partner.

Everyone else appeared to have done so already but he knew there must be some unmatched person somewhere, wondering probably where her partner could be. Presently he found her—an ill-tempered woman, by all the signs, apparently full of indignation at finding herself alone. He crossed the room and bowed to her, offering his crooked arm.

"My name's Dubinsky. May I take you down, Madam?"

She flashed him an angry glance and looked swiftly around the room. He knew she was still hoping for a better prospect. She took his arm in an abrupt, ungracious manner, not troubling to transfer her fan to her other hand. He felt her arm trembling. He glanced at her profile and saw that her lips were compressed into a thin line. She was not, he felt sure, as young as she thought she looked. Halfway down the stairs she turned on him.

"Who is this Cleveland person—do you have the faintest idea?"

"She's an actress."

"Oh, I know that. But who *is* she?"

"In the sense you mean, I haven't the slightest idea, ma'm."

"Well, good heavens, I think Stuyvesant Lailey has lost his mind. She seems to be the guest of honor but the invitations didn't say a thing about meeting her. I wouldn't have come!" The spokes of the fan made a crunching noise.

A thin figure dressed in black stood against the frame of the dining-room door. She had a paper in her hand. She looked like the skeleton at the feast. Dubinsky's partner disengaged herself from his arm with obvious relief and spoke to her.

"Where have you put me, Edie? If I don't like it, I'll make you change me!"

"At the first table, Mrs. Herrick. Your name, sir?"

"Dubinsky."

She referred to the paper in her hand. "The first table also, sir."

Mrs. Herrick turned her back on him and began to circle the nearest of the two tables, reading the place cards. Dubinsky did likewise but in the opposite direction. He found his—an affair of padded white satin standing on a miniature easel. The satin was painted with rosebuds and a dove, holding a streamer in its beak. On the streamer was lettered in gold, "Mr. Isaac Dubinsky." He smiled and glanced at his neighbor's card. The smile deepened. Mrs. Herrick was just completing her circling of the table. He eradicated the smile and, gesturing toward the card, bowed gravely. She glanced at it and gave him a look of pure venom.

Mrs. Herrick sat down and turned her back on him. The lady on the other side glanced around and moved a shoulder, like a barricade, between herself and him. He accepted his isolation. From farther down the table he heard Willow's laugh and thought that he really must do something about her voice. It was worse than usual tonight and more high-pitched. He tried to see her, but though he could see Lailey at the head of the table, Willow was hidden because she was on the same side as himself. He watched Lailey a while, wondering why no actor could ever reproduce that kind of unconscious confidence without overdoing it. Then he found that Claire, at the next table, was just visible through the intervening people.

She seemed distressed and he could see that she was very much aware of the big fellow—Hadley—on her right. Hadley did not seem to know that she was there. He looked angry and morose. His face was flushed, and he seemed barely able to keep his feelings in check.

Just then Willow laughed loudly and Hadley looked up, startled. The anger made his face dark. Dubinsky leaned as far forward as

118

he could to try to see Willow. When he straightened up again, he saw that Hadley was staring at his plate. After that, he watched Hadley all through the rest of the meal. Before tonight he could have sworn that there was no more in Willow's life than her determination to be an actress—and Lailey at her heels. How little, after all, you knew about the people who worked for you. And you fell into the habit of assuming that the theater was the whole of their lives, for no better reason than that it was the whole of your own. Hadley looked like a more forceful person than Lailey, and capable of being a disruptive factor. Dubinsky had the uneasy feeling that something was in the wind. Willow needed, above all, to be left alone.

Lailey, too, glanced from time to time at Hadley and back again at Willow. He had a strong feeling that these two had known each other before. It made his nerves tingle when he thought about it. Whenever he had asked her to tell him about herself she had put him off, but what was it she had said to him that night on the piazza of the United States Hotel? "I once let my happiness depend on someone else." A lover—a love affair that had gone wrong? He had not pressed her too urgently to talk about herself because he felt he would rather let her do it in her own time and in her own way, but this feeling that there had been something between these two was profoundly disturbing. When he had her attention, he said, "Did you ever know that fellow Hadley before? Somehow I got the idea . . ."

She put her hand on his sleeve. "Darling!" She laughed. He told himself that he had been a fool, and shortly after that the ladies rose to go to the drawing room.

To Dubinsky the dinner had seemed interminable, and when everyone rose, his relief was great. He stood by his chair, waiting for the ladies to leave, and he watched Claire all the way out of the room. When they were gone, the men from the other table came over to cluster around Lailey. The atmosphere of the gathering had changed completely. All the chairs had been pulled toward one end of the table and someone began to tell a story. He did not want to hear it. He found he was feeling very weary and he sat down where he was, glad of his isolation.

A glass was put in front of him and filled with Madeira. When he looked up again, he found that the fellow with the angry face had taken a chair farther down, on the other side of the table, evidently with a similar desire for solitude. He was turning his glass around and around by the stem and staring at nothing. Dubinsky smiled a little. He had never let his actors use that particular piece of business because it seemed to him stagy.

He wondered if it would serve any useful purpose to try to find out something about Hadley. He went slowly around the vacant end of the table, pulled out the chair next to Hadley, said, "Good evening," formally and sat down. He received a look of surprised dislike.

"My name's Dubinsky." It obviously meant nothing to Hadley. "Yours is Hadley, I believe?"

"Yes. Pleased to meet you."

Hadley hitched his chair away. His voice was as angry as his face.

"I was wondering if you were interested in the theater, Mr. Hadley."

"Not in the least."

He said it over his shoulder, his back half turned. Dubinsky raised his eyebrows. They sent a wave of ripples over his forehead.

"Miss Cleveland is pleasant to look at, don't you think?"

This time Hadley turned all the way around and stared at him. Dubinsky said, "I saw you watching her during dinner. Did you, by any chance, know her before this evening?"

"Yes, I knew her some time back."

"Was that long ago?"

There was a burst of laughter from the men at the other end of the table and Hadley either did not hear the question or pretended not to hear. Dubinsky thought it was probably the latter. He was behaving like a hurt bear that wants to be left alone to nurse its wounds. He turned his back on Dubinsky and began incising long lines in the damask tablecloth with the back of a fruit knife, giving the work his whole attention.

Dubinsky said gravely, "Could you tell me anything about her background, where she comes from, that sort of thing? It seems to be something of a mystery."

"What are all these questions about?"

"I have an interest in Miss Cleveland. I gather that you have too. That's true, isn't it?"

Hadley leaped to his feet and, putting both hands on the back of his chair, leaned down toward Dubinsky, and Dubinsky, meeting his look with equanimity, saw that this man was not, as he had supposed, angry and sullen by nature. There were lines around his eyes, ironed out now, but discernible, which meant humor and kindliness. Behind the anger, shielded by it, was real suffering and Dubinsky thought that he was looking at a man who had been driven to a point where he could stand no more.

"An *interest* in her? Yes, I've got an interest in her. She's my wife, Goddamn it!"

He walked away and, seizing a chair which stood near the group of men at the other end of the room, whirled it around with its back to Dubinsky and planted himself in it.

Chapter Nine

WHEN the men went upstairs to the drawing room, Sam followed them slowly, keeping by himself. He stood in the archway looking for Willoughby, but before he found her he saw Claire alone on a settee opposite him. She was leaning forward watching him, her face eager. She was trying to make him look at her, and her face lighted up when she thought he saw her. He knew that she was sitting alone because she wanted him to join her. He pretended he did not see her.

Willoughby was not hard to find. She had chosen the most conspicuous place in the room, a sofa with a low back which stood near the fireplace. She sat in the center of it, with her arms flung out along the back and her knees crossed. The toe of her satin slipper was swinging in little jerks, and he knew by this sign that the evening was exciting her. There was something eager about her also, but it had an avid quality which contrasted unpleasantly with the eagerness in Claire's face.

She had always loved to sit like this with her arms stretched out. He knew she did it because it showed off the lines of her figure and it always seemed to him that she was deliberately trying to look bold and provocative. They had quarreled about it often in the past. He wondered if tonight she were doing it deliberately to provoke him. It did provoke him, but it roused his old hunger for her too.

People, mostly men, were pulling up chairs to sit near her. They made a sort of barricade around her. She looked up and saw him on the other side of the barricade, and she smiled. Then she made a motion with her body. It was hardly more than a deep breath, but it was provocative and faintly lewd. It was meant for him and he understood it. He knew that she knew exactly how she looked to him and how her pose was affecting him. She was smiling. Maybe she thought it was an amusing thing to do. Maybe, because she was safe with all the people around her, she was defying him. He stopped where he was. She was still smiling and he knew that, in a moment, she would move her body that way again. He turned his back on her.

It was hard to see objects clearly. He had to concentrate on it. He could feel the blood in his temples. He did not know whether she was watching him or whether she was giving herself to the men around her. He wanted to know, but he would not turn around to find out. He jammed his hands in his pockets and went straight across the room to Claire.

She was smiling, too. He had not realized how clear and straightforward her eyes were, even with the dark shadows in them. He said, "May I sit down?"

"Of course."

"How does it happen that you're way over here all by yourself?"

"I thought if I sat where we talked that other time, perhaps you'd come and join me." She flushed, but she did not lower her eyes.

"You were right."

He liked the way the blood fanned out under her tanned skin. Her hands lay on her lap quietly, just as Lettie's sometimes lay, and he wondered if, like Lettie, she were at peace with herself.

"You have nice hands, Claire."

"Oh, I've been ashamed of them all evening—they're still so brown."

She held them out with the fingers spread, laughing at herself and inviting him to share in the laughter. He took hold of her wrist and pretended to inspect her hand solemnly. He was thinking that one reason he liked her was that he liked the sort of person he was when he was with her. Willoughby often made him hate himself. She had tonight. He felt almost grateful to Claire for being so unlike Willoughby. Without thinking very much about what he was doing, he raised Claire's hand and let the back of it brush his cheek. Then he kissed it. He let go of it quickly and folded his own hands tightly together between his spread knees. The kiss had suddenly meant more to both of them than he had intended it should.

When he again looked up, it was at Willoughby, not at Claire. She was still sitting in the same position, the toe of one satin slipper swinging back and forth, rippling the ruffles at the bottom of her skirt. He began to think about the meeting which was ahead of them. He would go to wherever it was she lived, and they would quarrel, and then they would be caught inescapably in their old relationship once more, with no chance for a new beginning and no hope that things would ever be any better or any different between them.

He was still staring at Willoughby when Claire said quietly, but with a little strain in her voice, "She told me you had never met before. That isn't true, is it?" He realized then that she had been following the direction of his gaze.

"No, that isn't true."

"I don't like her, Sam."

"In many ways she's not an admirable person."

"She's beautiful."

"Yes, she's beautiful."

"When was it that you knew her?"

"A long time ago—or it seems so." He was still so angry with Willoughby that it was hard to keep from blurting out everything about their marriage and his resentment.

She made no reply and after he had calmed down a little,

he made an effort to bring them back to a normal footing. "Each time I've seen you I've forgotten to ask you—did you like Mrs. Brodi?"

"Oh, yes. She seems to have the most wonderful way of going for important things and just brushing everything else aside."

Sam laughed. "That's it exactly. You've put your finger right on it. And because Lettie doesn't pay any attention to things most people think are important, they think she's vague. She summed you all up in one perfect word."

"Me?"

"Delphinian."

"Oh!" The lovely color rose to her cheeks once more.

"She ran away from home once."

"Mrs. Brodi?"

"Yes, to marry Mike. For all her vagueness she keeps Mike's papers in perfect order. Mike says by the time he's finished writing about something she knows more about it than he does himself. I'd like it if you were friends."

He knew he shouldn't be saying that, because he had told Lettie —almost—that he wasn't going to see Claire any more. She put her hand on his sleeve, pressing down with the strong fingers. "You're wonderfully kind, Sam. I do get lonely."

The marvelous eyes were earnest and a little misty. He picked up her hand again and held it. He looked deep into her eyes because he wanted to see if Lettie were right. He wanted to know if she loved him. She was not afraid of his gaze. She did not turn her eyes away or try to hide anything, and he saw it coming into her eyes slowly, very slowly. Watching her eyes begin to fill with love was a wonderful thing. He had not seen this in any eyes ever. And then he knew he must stop it at once. He was suddenly ashamed, deeply, humbly ashamed, so that he did not want to look at her. He had forgotten he was holding her hand. He dropped it and got to his feet.

"Claire, I'm going now, if you'll forgive me. I won't disturb the others to say good-bye. Forgive me, Claire."

As he went toward the door he felt her eyes on him. He did not want to think about what was in them now. He walked slowly, with his head down. Claire aroused a gentleness in him that had never found any outlet before. A man needed someone to develop that side of him, someone to expend gentleness on. He had not known the need existed in him, but Lettie was right, it was unfair to Claire to see too much of her and, he was beginning to think, because of the tug of her youth and defenselessness at his heartstrings, it might be unfair to himself as well. That made him think of Willoughby and the violence which had always been the essence of their relationship. He turned to look for her. She was there, still surrounded by her court, and as he looked he saw Dubinsky detach himself from the group and go toward the settee where he had left Claire. The sight of Willoughby brought all his anger back to him. He thought about going over where she was, with all the people around her, and saying something to her which would shock them all, but he knew he wouldn't do it. He had thought of a better plan. By the time he reached the archway he had forgotten Claire.

The crowd around Willoughby had begun to thin a little. She noticed this, without appearing to notice, and listened to an instinct which told her not to outstay her audience. Accordingly, she collected her fan and flowers, but she caught sight of Sam just as he was going through the archway. She prolonged her farewells until she felt sure he had left the house. When she was about to leave herself, she remembered, just in time, that she must find this niece of Stuyvesant's and say a polite good-bye.

"Miss Reynolds—where is she, Stuyvesant?"

"Over there with Dubinsky. Willow, won't you call her Claire? She's a nice youngster and I know she admires you tremendously."

Willoughby laughed. "What an odd-looking couple she and Isaac make!"

Claire rose to receive her. "I'm very glad to have met you, Miss Cleveland."

"Call me Willow."

Claire flushed but said nothing. Their hands touched briefly,

126

each feeling a tingling physical reluctance in her fingertips. Their eyes did not meet.

Lailey walked with Willoughby as far as the arch.

"I wish I could take you home, Willow."

"Well, obviously you can't, with all these people here."

"May I come later?"

"Not tonight, Stuyvesant. If it weren't for the show opening tomorrow—but I really do have to get a little rest."

"All right, then. Luncheon tomorrow?"

"No, dear, I'm sorry."

"Can't I see you at all until I come to take you to the theater?"

"I'm afraid not. You'll just have to understand, Stuyvesant."

"Haven't I always understood?"

"Yes, you have. You've been a dear. And this party was lovely. We'll see a lot of each other once the show is on."

They went through the arch together and at the head of the stairs, where they were out of sight of everyone, he stopped her. He leaned over her, one hand on the wall, one hand on the top of her arm just above the lace trimming of her dress.

"Willow, you know how I feel about you, don't you?"

She smiled and touched his cheek with the tips of her fingers. Then her eyes grew dark and serious.

"Yes, I know, Stuyvesant. And you don't know anything about me, really."

She had guessed his thoughts. Leaning over her, so close, his heart began to pound in heavy thumps and he knew how much he wanted her and, at the same time, how he had been fearing what she might be holding back from him. She laughed lightly, and put her hands on his shoulders. She leaned forward and kissed his cheek almost tenderly. He shut his eyes. Her perfume was all around him. He felt weak and shaken.

She said, "When all this is over, I'll tell you all about my dark, dreadful past. You can ask me anything you like."

"Is there anything to tell?"

"You're so absurd. So darling and absurd!"

She was laughing at him again. He drew a long, deep breath of relief and pulled her to him and kissed her.

She went slowly down the stairs. One hand slid smoothly over the cool marble banister rail; her feet touched the padded carpet silently. The susurration of her train sounded like wind rustling in dead leaves, and her thoughts were wholly occupied with the ill chance that had brought Sam here tonight.

The point was, would Sam really hold his tongue? Would he take his cue from her and, if the question of herself came up with Stuyvesant, behave as though she and he were strangers? She couldn't imagine it, and suddenly a chill of apprehension ran down her spine. She must find Sam and talk with him—that was clear to her now. Perhaps he had not yet left. She picked up her skirts and ran the rest of the way down the stairs.

Dodge said the gentleman had gone several minutes ago. He even opened the door and peered into the night, shut it and shook his head with sad dignity.

"No, Madam."

Willoughby went into the little gold and white cloak room, where she gave a sleepy maid a square of cardboard with a number on it and received in return her fur cape. How tired she felt! Perhaps it was just as well Sam had gone. There would be no danger tonight—perhaps no immediate danger at all—and she must avoid a scene, save every ounce of her strength for the opening.

She stood still, turning over in her mind all the implications of what she had done. It had been done instinctively, but she doubted if she would have acted any differently if there had been time to think. But that niece knew something was wrong! Even if Sam could be kept out of the way, she might go blabbing to her uncle, saying things that might make him suspicious.

She put on her gloves and smoothed the wrinkles out of the fingers with great care. Her face was troubled but she remembered not to frown. It was too late now, whatever happened, for Stuyvesant to withdraw his support from the play—that much, at least, was hers. But if the play failed? The possibility had never seemed real until this instant, and a sinking feeling that was like a wave of physical weakness swept through her.

Presently she sighed, touched with the tip of her gloved finger the place where the frown might be and, going to the dressing table, picked up a button hook and began working the pearl buttons of her gloves through the tight holes. She should have told Stuyvesant long ago about her marriage. It would have been easy then, whatever she thought at the time. Now, it was almost impossible. They were at the same time too close and not close enough. She threw the button hook down with a clatter. Unjust that this should come on her just as she needed all her strength. She must put her problems out of her mind somehow and concentrate on the main issue of the play. Succeed in that and there would be no problems. All this was too much to bear alone. It would be comforting to tell Isaac the whole story. He would understand—or at least, he would understand the longing to be free of every burden but her work.

For a moment she considered sending Dodge to find him. No, the relationship between herself and Isaac was still too new, needing her success to cement it into friendship. Wiser at this point not to let him know that there was anything in her life at all but just the single purpose. She went slowly out into the hall and through the double doors that Dodge and a footman held open for her.

The cold night air made her shiver and, descending the red-carpeted steps, her long train bunched over her arm, she drew her cloak more closely about her. From the doorway behind her Dodge was calling, "Mr. Lailey's carriage for Miss Cleveland." She stood in the spill of light and waited, aware that, late as it was, there were still curious people restrained from crowding forward onto the strip of red carpet by the outstretched arms of two policemen. She raised her face to the cool air, liking the sting of it on her cheeks. Now she must rest. Now she must make her mind a blank into which not even thoughts of the opening must enter.

Below her, at the curb, a carriage was drawing up. She descended the steps quickly, bowed her head and stepped into the dark box. The door slammed behind her and she leaned back and shut her eyes. In a short while Suzanne would undress her and leave her in the dark, where she would cry a little and then sleep. She let her head roll sidewise on the cushions behind her.

The door was jerked open violently and the carriage swayed on its springs. She sat up in fright. Someone was in the carriage with her, and the close interior was filled with thick, rapid breathing. How she knew, or at what point the knowledge came to her, that this was Sam, she could not have told. The carriage was stopping with a clatter of hooves and one of the men on the box was climbing down. The door opened and a street lamp showed her an anxious red face under a silk hat with a broad band and a cockade. She heard Sam say, "It's all right."

"Madam?"

"Yes, it's all right, thank you." The carriage started to move again.

"Well, Willoughby?"

She did not answer.

"I think we have something to say to each other."

"Yes, we do. But I won't talk about it tonight. I just want you to promise me . . ."

"Tonight, Goddamn it!"

He had found her wrist and his fingers closed over it hard. Suddenly the old fire, the resistance he had always aroused in her, came back to her. Fatigue vanished in a blaze of anger. She struggled to pull her wrist away and he held on, his fingers pressing the pearl buttons of her glove into her flesh until she cried out with pain.

They sat in fast-breathing silence. His grasp relaxed a little. She could feel his disgust with himself and she knew, as clearly as though he had spoken his thoughts aloud, that he was thinking that they were both caught in their old relationship again, exactly as it had always been, and that the sudden, instinctive violence between them had very nearly put an end to all hope for anything different. She pulled her hand away with a quick jerk.

"I didn't want it to be like this," Sam said.

"It's never been anything else."

"Willoughby, we're going to have a talk."

"Not now, Sam. Not tonight. I have to rest—the opening—and I'm so desperately tired. I have to save my strength."

"It's going to be now. I'm coming to your rooms—or whatever sort of place you live in."

"You can't. Not at this hour." She stopped. The same thought was filling both their minds.

His mirthless laugh rang out. "Hasn't anyone else ever . . . ?"

"Sam!"

"This fellow Lailey. That's one thing I'll want to know about."

"Sam, how can you! I won't have you speak to me this way."

"How can I? Jesus—what kind of a fool do you think I am? We're going to have it out!"

"No! I won't talk to you till after the show opens. I won't talk to you at all. Why should I answer a thing like that? I'm tired."

"I don't give a damn how tired you are. There's some things you are going to explain to me now."

"You're the most selfish person I ever met in my life."

"Selfish—Jesus!"

"Selfish! Do you realize how hard I've worked for this play? Have you any idea what it will mean to me to succeed in it? I suppose you think my having the lead just happened. I worked and worked and worked and fought for it, and now, when I need rest, you can't even wait until the morning. No, you don't think of me at all. You just think about yourself. You were always like that. Stop the carriage and get out."

"You weren't too tired to go to this damn dinner and show yourself off."

"If you don't get out, I will."

She leaned forward and reached for the catch which opened the door. He grabbed her arms and held them to her sides.

"Coachman," she called loudly. Another carriage was passing, and there was no response from the box.

"Shut up!" Sam said. The weight of his body was pushing her

into the corner of the carriage. She was helpless, and she let herself go limp. He released her.

"What's the matter with you, Willoughby? What's the matter with us?"

"There's nothing the matter with me. It's you, and you haven't changed a bit. You were always like that. Always making me do what *you* wanted. Other men let their wives have lives of their own. *You* never did. We always lived the way *you* wanted to live—we saw the people *you* wanted to see." Her voice was shrill, and there were tears of anger in it. "Why, it's even in the little things you do —it's even in the way you make love. Other men bend down when they take a woman in their arms. They're tender to her. They hold her as though they were protecting her. You—you just used to pull me to you. You don't bend at all. You don't care if you hurt me. You just stand up straight with your chest out and pull me to you."

"Stop it!"

"Did you ever think about anyone but yourself in your whole life? I ask you—did you?"

"Stop it, I tell you." He grabbed her by the shoulders.

"Take your hands off me!"

"Have there been other men? Are you comparing that Lailey fellow to me?"

"Take your hands off me!"

He released her suddenly. In the dark interior of the carriage she could hardly see him, but she knew that he had put his head in his hands. When he spoke, it was with a kind of agony in his tones.

"Willoughby, can't we talk quietly? I didn't want it to be like this. I wanted it to be different from the way it used to be. I got to thinking maybe you'd want it to be different, too. Let's not just slip back into the old way. Can't we talk about it quietly?"

"You started it," she said sullenly.

After that they sat in silence. The carriage jerked rhythmically. The sound of the horses' hooves synchronized, broke the beat, and synchronized again. The air in the close carriage was thick with hatred and unhappiness.

132

was going to make you give it up and come home. The Brodis stopped me. They pointed out you weren't using my name and it was just a small part. They thought you'd get sick of it—that you'd always think that, if it weren't for me, you might have been a great actress. So I listened to them. Then Lettie told me you had this lead part. She persuaded me again not to interfere. Hell, I even have tickets for your show. I wasn't even going to let you know I was there.

"Then, after a week or two, I was going to say, that's enough. You come home now. But what do I find? I find that silly name isn't just a stage name, and that nobody knows you're married. You're behaving as though you weren't married. Are you sleeping with this fellow?"

"No."

"Answer me truthfully."

"No, I'm not! For the last time, I'm not."

Willoughby rose and, walking across the room, stood with her back to Sam. She began rearranging with meticulous care the objects on the little table. Sam said no more, waiting, she knew, for her to turn around. She could hear him breathing heavily. In her imagination she saw herself turning back to face him, saying, "Sam, I want a divorce." Her hands were shaking and she put them, palms down, on the edge of the table. It would have to be said sometime. If only the opening were behind her! She heard Sam get up and begin to pace around the room, and some quality in the restless motion told her that his anger had subsided and that again misery and despair were uppermost. She turned around.

"Sam, what is it you want?"

He stopped pacing and stared at her, and the depth of unhappiness in his eyes startled her. She had expected an instantaneous reply. It did not come and she watched the unhappiness slowly fade into thoughtfulness. He was thinkng about Lettie's pleading with him to let her go, to let her have her own life. Willoughby saw his expression with a kind of shock, because she knew suddenly that he was considering the possibility of life without her. She her-

self had come to take it for granted that they would never live together again, but never had it occurred to her that Sam's feelings
toward her might change. For an instant she felt the profoundly
disturbing sense of being all alone—not loneliness, but the first
frightening realization of what life could be like if she had no one
to depend on but herself. She knew that she could still turn back.
She knew that she wouldn't.

Sam had picked up a little porcelain box and was turning it over
and over in his hands, looking at it as though he were absorbed by
the landscapes on its sides. She watched him, glad of the respite, but
when he put the box down firmly she knew that his moment of uncertainty was over also. When he turned toward her, there was no
longer any trace of introspection in his face.

"I want you to come back and be a wife to me."

"Sam!"

"How long will it take you to pack up and get out of this place?
Lettie can come and stay with you till you're ready."

"But Sam—the play!"

"Damn the play."

"You can't say that. That's absurd!"

"Plays have failed to open before now. This is going to be another
of them."

"Sam, you *couldn't* be that cruel."

"Cruel—Jesus Christ—is it being cruel to ask a woman to do her
duty? I never told you that you could go on the stage."

Suddenly she was angry. She leaned back against the table, her
hands clutching the edge, her head held high. "You can't make me.
There's no law to make me come back to you."

"Make you!" Sam started to laugh. "I could make so damn much
trouble for you that this producer fellow would be glad to get rid
of you. And what about the money I send you? Want to get along
without that?"

They stared at each other for a moment, hate in both their faces,
both breathing fast. A swift look of calculation came into Willoughby's eyes and vanished again. She took out her handerchief and

began to cry softly, exhaustedly, her whole body drooping. She went across the room to him, swaying a little as she walked, and put her head down on his shoulder. He did not move and, leaning against him, she felt him holding himself rigid. She began to sob brokenly and he, with an inarticulate, grief-stricken sound, put his arms around her. She let her body go limp against him.

Presently she raised her head and looked at him. There was an expression of baffled defeat in his face, and deep in his eyes a look of desperate physical longing. She pressed her body closer to his.

"Sam—please try to understand—try to see it from my point of view. I have this job to do—so soon now. I'm frightened." She shut her eyes for an instant. "I want to do a good job. I think you can understand that. You always wanted to do a good job of running the mill. If I were another man, you'd know how I feel. Let things stay as they are, Sam, just for now. Please. It's going to take all the strength I have. I don't want any more upsets. Please, please, Sam."

He started to push her away from him, but she clung to him and before he could say anything more, she hurried on.

"When the run is over, I'll come back to you, Sam. I promise—I promise. I'll do anything you like, if you'll just let me play this part. I'll come back to you, and you'll be proud of me because I'm good enough to do things on my own and yet I come back to you."

He took her chin in his hands and raised her face. They exchanged a long look and when she could support it no longer, she shut her eyes again. Her lids quivered a little. He raised his hand and, with an awkward gentleness, stroked her bare shoulder.

"No, Willoughby."

She did not move, but tears began to run silently down her cheeks. He held her a little closer.

"Sam!"

"What, dear?"

"Sam, if you will let me do that—stay here alone—you could come here when you wanted to. Then, after—I'd come home with you."

She felt his body begin to tremble and she pressed hard against him, her arms around his neck, holding him tightly, pressing every part of her body against him.

"Sam, Sam, I've missed you, Sam. You always thrilled me so. Sam!"

She was almost sure of her victory now, and she tried to reach his lips with hers. He was holding her so tightly that she could hardly breathe. Her eyes were shut again, and her open mouth was soft with passion. His hands gripped her shoulders and she drew in her breath with a sharp hiss of pain. Her eyes opened a little way, and there was light in them. She felt a sudden convulsive movement of his body as he bent his head to kiss her.

In the gray light of the morning Sam dressed slowly. Willoughby lay on her side sleeping, one arm flung out, and he stood motionless, gazing down at her. She slept quietly, with all the outward aspects of serenity. He studied her face with a kind of urgency, hoping that her features might give him some clue to her, and it seemed to him that he had never really looked at her before. It was the face of a stranger. She was a stranger, and he had the illusion that, when they took up their lives together, it would be like beginning life with a stranger. It was a secret face and, without the sparkle of her eyes and the brilliance of her smile, scarcely beautiful. She looked older, and this made him feel a little pity. There were faint blue smudges under her closed eyelids and tiny hollows in her cheeks. She lay so still, seemed so utterly spent. Last evening, he himself had been one more obstacle in her path, and if she had taken this means to master him, had she not at least the excuse of her desire to reach her goal?

He turned away from the bed and struggled into his coat. Through the thin curtains of the windows he saw the first pale glitter of the sun touching the tops of the opposite buildings. Another day— separated, it seemed, by a lifetime from the last. The coat of his dress suit smelt rankly of cigar smoke, and the air in the room seemed full of complicated, faintly nauseating odors. He went over to the window and pulled it up.

A fresh breeze, clear and cool, bellied the curtains out and made the skin of his face tingle. He took deep breaths of the freshness and found that he was thinking about Claire. They were not definite thoughts so much as refreshing images of her broad, smooth forehead and of the lights and smoky shadows in her eyes. She seemed as fresh as the morning air, her whole nature as alien to the emotions of the night as the cool breeze to the effluvia of the room. Suddenly he was sickened with himself. He pulled the window down and sat on the edge of the nearest chair, his hands hanging between his knees, his shoulders bent. Thinking of Claire in this room!

He reached out, pulled his shoes toward him and put them on slowly. Then he rose and went to stand by the bed once more. Willoughby had not moved, and in the fresher atmosphere of the room the warm scent of her body rose up to him. He and she would shortly be taking up their lives together again, but he had the odd feeling—ridiculous in view of what lay ahead—that he was saying good-bye to her. He thought about this, looking down on her, until a growing certainty, which was like a physical sensation, came to him, that she was awake and fully aware he was standing by her bed. The knowledge made his flesh creep. He turned and left the room swiftly.

The streets were empty and the early sunlight seemed to possess the city as at no other time of day. The air glittered with it, the tops of the buildings were washed in it, and wherever the sun touched, colors of brick and stone and mortar leaped into life, so that the city looked like a painting which is half brilliantly completed, half unfinished brush strokes of shadow. The glitter had a liveness about it that suggested new beginnings, and should have lifted the spirit. But Sam's spirit refused to respond.

The fire was out, the ashes cold. Did he love her no longer? There it was—the doubt. He had at last acknowledged it.

Chapter Ten

ON OPENING night, Lailey took Willoughby as far as her dressing room, where Suzanne met them, and after the door shut behind her he stood staring at the white star on it, his forehead furrowed with anxiety. On the drive to the theater she had swept him with her in all her changing emotions. When she clung to him, as she rarely did, she tore his heart, and when she let him see that she needed him, it made him feel weak with tenderness, but when she was defiant toward the world, it made him want to shout. And he marveled at the emotional virility which could let her undergo these changes of mood without leaving her completely shattered. He felt exhausted by them. He hated to leave her alone with only Suzanne. He did not want to turn away from her door.

Two hours of waiting stretched between him and curtain time. He thought about leaving the theater and going somewhere for a drink, but his knees did not feel very strong and the idea of drink produced a slight queasiness. The air in the corridor was oppressive, and though he took deep breaths of it they did not seem to fill his lungs. That Willow should suffer from nerves on opening night was understandable, but he had not expected to find these symptoms in himself. He wanted very much to sit down, but there was nowhere backstage where he could sit except the greenroom, a noisy place where the younger members of the cast spent their exuberant leisure. Tonight, perhaps, they would not be feeling so exuberant. He decided to chance it.

When he pushed open the door he found that three of them were there, oversensitive looking youngsters known to him vaguely as Russ, Archie and Cam. Russ was sprawled in the semi-reclining position imposed by the lines of a Morris chair and Archie lay face down on a thin cushion which covered a quasi-medieval bench, one of his hands trailing lifelessly to the floor. Cam, who was perched on the fender, was talking in an eager, overexcited way.

"You know how Pop is about that make-up box of his—fussy as an old woman—always tidying it. . . ."

Crossing between them, noting the exaggerated poses and the tension in the high-pitched voices, Lailey wondered if these theater people ever did anything without overdoing it. No one paid the slightest attention to his entrance, and yet—somehow they always made an audience of you.

"Well, Eddie spilled the whole bottle in it, see? He's got this idea mineral oil makes a good foundation for grease paint—disgusting! That precious make-up box was swimming. When Pop found it, Eddie says he was shaking so he could hardly mop it up. Eddie said he thought the old boy was crying. Isn't that a scream?"

"Oh, dry up!"

"Say, what's the matter with you, Russ?"

"I'm sick. Those Goddamn oysters I ate tonight were bad, if you want to know."

This set off a peal of too loud, too high laughter.

"Oysters on opening night are always bad, you fool. You ought to do what Pop does—eat after the show."

"Shut *up!*"

In the sulky silence Lailey concentrated on the sensations in his own stomach produced by this talk of mineral oil and oysters. Archie

himself off from the outside world. He was at once aware of the vastness of the place, and of the silence which was not silence at all but a complex of sounds, soft, hushed and almost ethereal. He had a sense of aliveness all about him. He moved quietly forward and saw that the curtain was raised and that, beyond the curving apron of the stage, the house was a cavern of blackness. He turned his eyes upward to the source of the dim light. In the vast darkness of the stagehouse overhead the light was like a suspended wedge, casting no illumination beyond itself, looking like something solid, and yet the motes in it making it seem to teem with fluid motion. A single strand of rope, its point of origin invisible, hung into the wedge of light, silvered by it. The curved-up end looked alive and it swayed slowly, moved by some mysterious stirring of the air far overhead.

Above the misty source of light the darkness was impenetrable, and from there he heard strange whisperings and sounds that were like quiet, long-drawn breaths. There was a rustling like wings, which died into silence as he listened to it, and then the unmistakable twittering of a bird. He felt the strangeness of the sound in all his nerves.

He lowered his eyes to the pool of light at his feet. It seemed to him like a different element from the air. A little self-consciously he stepped into it and imagined he had a physical sense of the change. He waded slowly through the light and out the other side toward the far wall. Here he found a sort of railing and sat down on it. Most of the mysterious magic he had felt was gone now, and he began a sort of stock-taking of his surroundings. To the railing on which he sat were tied a number of thick ropes. They were fastened with slip-knots, and the remaining lengths lay in neat coils under the rail. The ropes, disappearing in the blackness, looked like the teeth of a giant comb. The one nearest him and the railing on either side of it were painted red. A long ticket tied to the rope swayed in one of the sourceless drafts. He turned it over to look at it and found it said "Danger" in large letters. He tried to trace the course of the rope overhead and was astonished to discover that from this

146

angle he could see above him, hanging in the air, part of the set for *The Rungs of the Ladder*. A fireplace and its wall dangled in space, a bookcase seemed to be, incongruously, full of books.

Beyond the stage door someone was whistling a brisk air. The door banged open—irreverently, it seemed to Lailey—and a youth burst in. Lailey had seen him before. He invariably answered to the call of "Lights." Lailey thought his name was Mac. The dimensions of the stage shrank with his coming. The whistling stopped abruptly as Mac leaped with monkey-like agility up an iron ladder which was let into the brick wall near the door. A small light flared, showing part of an iron balcony attached to the bricks and hidden from the audience by the projection of the proscenium arch. A cat-walk above the long roll of the curtain melted into the darkness. Clamped to the balcony and cat-walk were odd-looking pieces of equipment that Lailey guessed to be spotlights and floodlights. They looked like heads with necks at grotesque, broken angles. Mac, clattering overhead, was touching up pinpoints of blue flame in each. Lailey heard him return to the balcony, and suddenly all the lights flared on. Before Lailey's eyes adjusted to the intense brilliance, they sank to blue pinpoints again.

With the same monkeylike agility Mac came down the iron rungs. He had an L-shaped taper in his hand. A chain of blue dots appeared, outlining the proscenium arch, each one inside a glass tube. The tubes, he supposed, were designed to keep the air currents stirred by the moving curtain from blowing out the lights.

Mac came toward him and Lailey said "Hullo." His own voice sounded strange. Mac looked into the gloom, holding the taper away from him.

"Oh, it's you. Evening, sir. Sitting it out?"

"Something like that."

"Won't be long now. Them lazy devils never let in the set until damn near curtain time, and I want to light my herse. Stagehands don't care about nothing."

"Do you always keep the scenery up there between times?"

"Yeah. Most theaters just leave it in place, but we're different in lots of ways. Fire protection. Dubinsky was in a fire on the road somewhere once. Lost a friend in it. Ever notice the scars on the palms of his hands? Burt tells me it was from then—a long time ago, I guess."

"What good does it do to keep the scenery up there? It isn't especially inflammable, is it?"

"Inflammable as hell. By the time the show's over the stage is full of gas, see? Pockets of it everywhere. The flats are rough-canvas and paint—and they catch dust. Dust doesn't burn—it explodes. I've never seen it, but they tell me the whole length of a flat bursts into flame at once—and then these pockets of gas. That's why theater fires burn so fast and don't ever get put out until they've killed some people and burned the place to the ground. Curtains are worse than flats—so, orders is, we take the curtain up and fly the set every night —though me, I never heard of a fire starting any other time except when the show's on."

Mac pulled worn gloves out of his pocket and took a firm hold of one of the ropes in the comb. A strange, gridlike contraption began to descend slowly. Lailey watched it come to rest about four feet above the center of the stage.

"What would happen if you pulled the one painted red?"

"Drop everything—flats and counter-weights. Kill you if one of the sand bags hit you. One reason why Burt don't allow no strangers on the stage. He'd put even you off, if he found you. Rope seems to have a kind of fascination. Burt says he saw a guy pull one once, stage full of people. No scenery up at the time, but the sand bags came down, wham! About thirty of 'em. Some miracle, didn't hit anybody. Burt says the guy that done it was so scared he got sick in the corner. Now I'm going to leave the herse down until them lazy devils let the set in, or they'll foul my pipes sure."

Mac hitched the played-out rope carefully—everything about the stage showed order and attention to detail—and went over to the herse. This seemed to be a framework of pipes and spaced gas jets with colored panels of some transparent substance that looked like mica. Pipes and wire cable rose upward and Mac, peering aloft, shook these, shaded his eyes, squinted and shook them again.

"That what you light the stage with?"

"Center of it. This thing's Dubinsky's pet. It's modeled after the one in the Paris Opera. We got the best lighting here any place in the city. Most managers think we're crazy. They just turn up the foots and some overheads and that satisfies 'em. Not the boss. He even took me abroad with him last summer just to study lights. Jes', I think we went backstage every theater, France and Italy. Saw everything from equipment we ain't dreamed of over here to those old-time wax things they call 'bougies.' France is the best—way ahead of us. Even the small houses coloring their lights with gauze —regular sunset, dawn effects—anything you please. Dangerous as hell, moving curtains of gauze in front of gas. Dubinsky won't let us, though I sure as hell bet he'd love to. We use gauze, too, but it has to be stretched in frames, and he makes sure somebody holds it all the time. Back in a minute."

Mac went to the iron ladder and performed his agile climb. A second later, lights on the herse flared, dimmed slowly and disappeared. He returned, saying, "*They're* all right. I don't quite trust 'em—all that pipe hanging loose."

"All your controls up there? You stay up there and work them during the show?"

"Sometimes. Depends on the show—how many cues—things like that. Never all the time. Gets too damn hot and the gas fumes get you. I got me a set of controls over there in the corner, too, but I do all I can from above. See the stage, don't miss any cues and, believe me, there's plenty of cues. Dubinsky runs me ragged changing light effects all the time. I never seen anything like it. Next show we're going to cut the foots and light only with bull's-eyes from the balcony rail. That will have 'em going."

"You like working for Dubinsky?"

"Well, it ain't easy, but it's interesting all right. He can't get along with any of the old-timers. Had about sixteen of 'em, they tell me. Too set in their ways for him. He's always trying something new. He wants this effect or that—no trouble's too much for him. He even has the lights colored special for red hair. And you learn pretty quick not to tell him you can't do it. Sometimes we'll stay up all night, just the two of us, working out the lights for some scene. I like it but most producers think he's crazy."

"I didn't know lights were important."

"Important! Why look, gas has brought in a whole new fashion in acting. Before, you couldn't see the actors' faces, so they had to get it across by big broad gestures and a lot of noise. Now you can see their expressions, so Dubinsky and the other good ones quiet their actors down and let 'em be natural. Much more effective—or so they say."

Lailey thought of something. "I could have sworn I heard birds up there awhile ago. I couldn't have, of course."

"Sure. There's a whole row of ventilators up there to take off the gas. They get in and they don't know how to get out again. Sometimes the gas gets them and we find them on the stage in the morning. Once one of them fell right on stage while the show was on— almost hit Miss Délice. She's scared to death of 'em but she never made a sign, though she gave Burt hell afterwards. We always meant to put netting over them ventilators, but you know how it is."

A sound of tramping and loud voices came from beyond the stage door and Mac turned to look at it, speaking over his shoulder.

"Here they come to let in their damn set. Ever notice how a bunch of stagehands can sound like a whole herd of elephants? Burt'll be along in a minute so you better get out of here, Mister. Now I got to see they don't foul any of my pipes."

Lailey rose, feeling cramped. A noisy group of men was coming on the stage. They were pulling off coats and slinging caps into corners. As Lailey passed them, he heard one of them say, "What you got that damn thing down for? Don't you know we gotta have a clear stage to let in the set? Every night. Every damn night."

"Like hell. You get here on time instead of playing pool over to Jake's place . . ."

The door swung to, shutting out further words.

Out in the corridor once more Lailey found that now the theater was full of brisk sounds, and the tension in the air had again mounted. The gas flames inside their wire cages had been turned up so high they hissed, and someone down the corridor was whistling a tune in which nervous strain was more apparent than the melody. Lailey felt his own blood stream quicken. He took out his watch—twenty-five minutes to go. He felt the need for some sort of action that would bring him in step with the tempo around him. He walked rapidly down the corridor, as though he himself had a purpose to accomplish and, because he found himself wondering how Dubinsky was passing this time of waiting, he headed toward the upstairs office.

Dubinsky was alone, his chair turned away from his desk so that he faced the door. He was reading quietly, and with seeming absorption, a very small book that looked faintly ludicrous in his plump hands. He laid down his book before he looked up, and Lailey had the impression that Dubinsky recognized his step. He wondered if Dubinsky knew the cadence of every step in this theater full of people. Dubinsky smiled almost sociably. He showed no sign of strain.

"Come in. Sit down, if you like. Finding the waiting hard?"

"Aren't you?"

Dubinsky lifted his shoulders in a gesture which said, as plainly as words, that his work was over and that there was nothing he could do now which could affect the outcome. He was still smiling. Lailey sat down on the edge of the chair by the desk.

"What do you think? How will she manage? Are her chances good?"

"They're not wholly bad—I don't anticipate a failure. She's not an actress, of course, but . . . There is, you know, a certain amount of similarity between Miss Cleveland and the Hester of the play. The audience will feel it, and I am counting on it to make up for some of the deficiencies in her acting."

Resentful of this comparison of Willow to the selfish, willful

Hester, Lailey flushed and glanced quickly at Dubinsky and found that Dubinsky was no more than holding out the truth to him, expecting him to have the strength to look at it, the breadth of mind to accept it. He looked down again, studying his clasped hands. A number of times recently Lailey had been made to realize, though not by anything Dubinsky actually said, that his own attitude toward the production of this play was not, even now, wholly serious. To everyone around the theater he was the rich man amusing himself. He was aware of this feeling now, and aware of the effect of his attitude on Dubinsky. He glanced swiftly at Dubinsky and saw an expression which seemed to imply that he knew the source of the trouble in Lailey's mind. Dubinsky eased Lailey over the rough moment by ignoring it.

"I have some theories of my own about casting, not shared by most of my colleagues in this country. The usual way, you know, is to pick an actor—or an actress—as versatile as possible, give him a long contract and let him play any kind of part that comes along. When an actor becomes good enough, he gets his own company together, calls himself an actor-manager and works up a repertory. That's called the 'star system' and it has its faults. In the first place, since the stress is put on acting, you are always aware that it *is* acting. It's as though the star were saying, 'See what a great and versatile actor I am!'

"Then, too, most of the stars surround themselves with a poor cast so they'll stand out by contrast, and the play suffers. The result of all this is that the theater has become a collection of great names, not a collection of great plays.

"I happen to think that's wrong, and I want to change it—shift the spotlight from the star to the play as a whole. One way to do it, I think, is to pick out an actor whose own character is as similar to the part you want him for as possible. Let acting ability come second. 'Type casting,' I call it. The result you should get from that is, first, a greater sense of reality and, second, a better balanced play. Miss Cleveland is only a passable actress, but I'm hoping that will be outweighed by the fact that she has it in her own nature to portray a convincing Hester. That bit of reality, that *nth* quality which would be lacking even in the performance of a truly competent actress, is what I'm counting on. *The Rungs of the Ladder* is likely to create considerable excitement in theater circles but . . ." Dubinsky smiled. "They aren't box office."

Lailey sat in troubled silence. Dubinsky reached for his watch, which lay face up on the desk, and pulled it closer to him. The motion jerked Lailey back to an awareness of the impending ordeal. He took his eyes off the watch and said, "I had no idea you were thinking of the play in terms like that."

They were silent for awhile and Dubinsky continued to smile slightly. Presently he picked up the watch and dropped it back into his pocket.

"We might as well be getting down."

The springs of his swivel chair twanged as he rose. Lailey jumped up in nervous haste and Dubinsky's smile deepened.

"Ten minutes to go. No need to hurry."

"Are you going to be out in the house to see the curtain go up?"

They were walking down the corridor, side by side. Dubinsky made a small outward gesture with one hand, and Lailey realized that he did not want to tell his plans. Dubinsky went with Lailey as far as the door which led into the lobby. There he stopped and put a hand on Lailey's back.

"Don't worry. She'll be all right."

Lailey went through the door alone and was at once engulfed in light and noise and movement. As he worked his way through the crowd, he had to respond to many greetings. The house was two-thirds full. He caught sight of Claire in his box, with Edie behind her like her shadow. Claire greeted him with a smile and some happy words about how excited she felt. He returned her smile mechanically and turned around in his seat to see how the house was filling up.

Claire said, "Look, there's Sam." She blushed and said quickly, "That's Mrs. Brodi with him."

"You like him, don't you?"

Claire nodded, and after that she was very quiet.

Lailey glanced at the program in his hands and wondered when he had picked it up. His palms felt damp. The orchestra was trooping in and some of them had already begun to tune their instruments. The uneasy feeling in his stomach had returned. The opening bars of the overture struck his nerves a blow. The lights began to fade. Suddenly he leaped to his feet and plunged through the curtains of the box.

In the corridor he ran. The theater was as quiet as though there were no one in it but himself. He leaped up the flight of steps to the stage and pulled open the door. He was at once confronted by Burt.

"Get the hell off. The curtain just went up."

"I want to see Miss Cleveland make her entrance. I'll go then." He had a swift impression of the brilliantly lit stage beyond the narrow opening of the wings, and of voices which sounded unnatural and loud.

"Nobody stays on my stage while the show's on." They were talking in fierce whispers.

A stagehand stepped out of the shadows and beckoned Burt urgently.

"I'll wait for Miss Cleveland," Lailey said decisively.

Burt gripped his arm. "If you're going to stay, sit over there where she can't see you. I gotta go. And don't speak to her. Don't speak to her. They're as brittle as glass just before they go on. You're liable to upset her so she'll forget her lines."

Burt pushed him down on a canvas stool between two barrels. It was too dark to see anything, but he knew the barrels were full of black, dust-coated water and that beside them was a rack of mops to be used in case of fire. Burt leaned over him.

"Don't let her see you."

Burt went away. It was dark. The voices from the set dominated everything, but they seemed remote, too. He didn't listen to the words. He felt very sick again. He tried to get his mind off himself.

Over his head a shaft of light cut through the darkness without affecting it. The shaft looked solid and square like a beam. Motes moved in it like larvae in a pond. He leaned back against the wall. The bricks felt chill and damp, and he leaned forward again. The big barrels fenced him in on either side.

Someone opened the stage door cautiously. He heard the rustling of silk, and he knew that she was there. He could hear her breathing. She moved slowly forward—he could just hear every carefully placed step. When she stood close to the edge of the wings, he could see her. She was watching the stage and listening. Her back was toward him and she was listening intently. She was standing straight and tall, and he thought her breath was coming quickly. She bowed her head, listening and waiting for her cue, the whole of her concentrated on the voices from the set. It was less dark and all the gas jets were hissing.

He heard the door open quietly again and looked around. Dubinsky was there. He was keeping his hand on the door to make it close soundlessly. Then he tiptoed forward. Lailey saw gleams of light move across the shiny surface of his shoes.

Dubinsky did not go to the wings. He stood back a little, where Willow could see him if she looked his way. His breathing was faintly audible to Lailey. He wondered if Willow knew Dubinsky was there. He felt sure she did.

Presently she moved a little, and he knew by the motion of her body that her cue was not far off.

Then she turned her head and looked at Dubinsky. She did not smile, but her look stirred Lailey. Something silent and deep was passing between them. Dubinsky's answering look was like her own —it was a mutual assurance. He had seen and he knew it, the very essence of the relationship between director and actor.

She was listening again, leaning a little forward, readying herself. She drew a long, faintly shuddering breath and let it all the way out again. Once more she turned to look at Dubinsky and, though the look was brief, this time there was fire in it. Lailey clenched his hands around the sides of his stool.

On stage some word was spoken. Willow drew a great breath and her whole body lifted, every part of her coming alive. She took one step and paused. He saw her tremble and then, head up, she stepped out into the brilliance of the stage.

Chapter Eleven

WHEN Willoughby came on the stage, Claire thought, 'She's so beautiful—could she have meant something important to Sam once? What about now?' Sam was thinking, 'When she's up there on the stage, everyone can see every line of her body.' Lailey, still standing in the wings, thought, 'If a woman has been an actress, other women whisper it for the rest of her life—would a man like that about his wife?' Dubinsky, walking with a more than usually pronounced stoop of his round shoulders toward the door which led from the stage, was thinking, 'She's too conscious of the audience.' Out in the dark house, Lettie thought, 'She seems a little larger than life—she's on a grander scale than the rest of us. Perhaps she always was.' Only Michael thought nothing at all about her. After the first glance he shut his mind to the whole thing and got on with planning his new article.

Up on the stage, Willoughby herself had a brief moment of panic. It seemed as though her throat were closing up and she wondered if she could get her first lines out clearly.

My dear friends—forgive me for not being here to greet you. Imogene dear. Seaton. John. Godfrey.

As she went to each of them in turn, extending Hester's charm, which was easy because it was like her own, everything seemed different and disturbing. It was different because the other actors were so concentrating on their own parts that they had no time to think of her. It was like a fire or a flood, each person wanting only to save himself.

It was so dear of you all to come to visit me. I want the people who love me to be with me. You do love Hester, don't you? All of you?

But it's a shock to you to find I asked you together? You wouldn't have come, would you, Seaton, if you had known these others would be here? Or you—or you? Only Imogene and John want to be together. It's going to be so amusing.

It seemed different because the audience was there. Her voice didn't seem to come back to her the way it did from the empty house in rehearsal. She wondered if she were speaking loudly enough.

Willoughby's next cue took her by surprise. She heard it in time —she was nowhere near missing it really, but the fact that she had so lost herself as not to know with precise clarity what was going on unsettled her further. She threw herself into her part with increased intensity.

You are all such clever people—you, Seaton, a statesman, John a writer, Imogene and her pictures, Godfrey's poems.

Too much intensity—the lines didn't warrant it.

Her cue came once more, and this time Willoughby went to the other extreme and anticipated it, not with her voice but with the motion of her body. This fault came near to flustering her. A pulse began to beat in her throat making it hard to breathe. She began to get angry at nothing and her voice rose a little higher.

Godfrey even looks like a poet! So chic to be a poet and look it! But think of poor me—poor Hester. No talents to give my friends or the world and so—I have to give them myself.

Hester, you never gave yourself to anybody.

Why, John, I give you all a piece of myself—to anybody who loves me I give a piece of myself.

158

Like a reward for merit, Hester. Are you sure the gift box isn't empty?

You're being cruel to me. He's being cruel to me, isn't he, Imogene? John, you're so amusing!

Everything seemed a little unreal.

Don't fool yourself, Hester. You are creative, like the rest of us. But you expend your talents on yourself.

She wondered if she had replied all right, because she couldn't hear the echo of her words in her mind. John was speaking.

Little by little you are making yourself a work of art, building your ego block by block, like a church to worship in. But remember, Hester, art must conceal art. Conceal yours carefully!

It was Willoughby's cue.

Oh, listen to him, everybody—listen to him. He's quaint, isn't he? John darling, you're quaint. You amuse all of us very much, but if we didn't know you loved me . . .

Now her voice seemed all right, and she could breathe down to the bottom of her lungs again. Now she could enjoy herself. The audience was here. This was what she'd been waiting for.

In the semi-darkness of her box, Claire sat forward on her chair. She was thinking, 'She's so real—it must be wonderful acting. It's so real that it's sort of horrifying. You hate her so that you're kind of afraid of her. She's so real. *Why, that's the way Miss Cleveland would be!* That's why Hester is so real. She *is* Hester, only Hester is intensified, the way all play characters are, so you see what she is more clearly. Was that why Mr. Dubinsky picked Miss Cleveland for the part—because she's really like Hester? If he did—if he knew how Hester would show up what Miss Cleveland really is herself— if he knew it would be like that, I think it's rather horrible. I think it is horrible—it's shocking, letting her expose herself like that.'

Claire felt a little faint. Close as she was to the footlights and a little above them, the smell of gas was already beginning to reach her. The stays she wore cut into her and she felt as though, if she drew a deep breath, she might be sick. She longed to push through the red velvet curtains of the box and escape. She leaned back and felt the gilded wooden chair cool against the bare skin above the low cut of her evening dress. Behind her, Miss Edie touched her on the arm and whispered.

"The chair will make marks on your shoulders, Miss Reynolds. Better not lean back."

Claire straightened herself, a little ashamed of feeling the way she had when there was really no reason. But it was like watching some indecency; it stirred up strange emotions and you couldn't help yourself. If Sam had known her in the past, he must be feeling things, too. She put her gloved hand on the brass rail of the box and tried to see into the darkness below her. Was this Hester revealing things about Willow Cleveland to him also? But suddenly she felt certain that Sam already knew about Willow. She remembered his words, "She is not an admirable person." He knew these things about her long ago, she thought. He knew them long ago, but there was something deep between them. There must have been. She held him, even though he knew. He must have loved her. Sam—oh, Sam!

She shut her eyes. Presently she knew that the velvet curtains had been moved aside and that her uncle had come into the box. She kept her eyes closed and her head turned a little away, but she felt his presence and she knew when he had settled himself in the chair beside her. He liked Miss Cleveland—he had said he liked her very much.

She whispered to him. "Uncle Stuyvesant." She slipped her hand into his exactly as though she were a child, and he held it and patted it as though she were a child, but she knew by the way he patted it that he didn't understand, and she felt lonely because she wasn't a child any more and couldn't get any comfort out of having her hand patted. She leaned forward and whispered in his ear.

"She isn't like that really, is she, Uncle Stuyvesant? It's just good acting, isn't it? She isn't like that?"

"Like what? Like Hester?" His whisper was loud and she thought, 'Some people don't whisper very well. It isn't in them. Sam wouldn't either.'

Lailey said, "You mean, is Willow like Hester? What a strange

160

idea! No, of course not. It's only that she's a wonderful actress—she's that, you know. Wonderful." But Claire felt the fingers of the hand which held hers stiffen a little, and she thought, 'I shouldn't have said anything. I mustn't say anything to Sam.'

Lailey was thinking, 'Of course it's only that she's a great actress. Dubinsky was wrong. There's not the least bit of likeness between Hester and herself—unless it is that they both have the kind of determination that is most unusual in a woman. Sometimes, after rehearsals, it *is* a little hard to forget Hester for a while, but then, Willow is so lovely that it drives it out of your head. It's all the proof you need that Willow is a born actress. If Willow seems to be Hester after she comes off the stage, it's all the proof you need. That's a good point. I must put it that way to Dubinsky sometime. It's the proof.'

Lettie shivered a little and leaned her shoulder against Michael's.

"She's stepped out into the open."

"What, dear?"

"Willoughby. She's stepped out into the open. We can see her now. She's clear. She never was before, *quite*."

"Be quiet, darling. You'll disturb people."

Lettie took her weight off Michael's shoulder and glanced at Sam. His profile, or what she could see of it, looked rather grim. 'He isn't over it,' she thought. 'I was right. Why, maybe he's seen her more clearly all along than the rest of us! But he still wants to beat it out of her. Funny, but I do believe that's always been one of her great attractions for him—he's never been able to beat it out of her. Her beauty, of course—but that's just made the other feeling all the stronger. Poor Sam. It's an impossible situation between them now, but he can't understand that. What's going to happen?'

"Michael, what's going to happen?"

"I don't know how the play ends any more than you do, dear."

"Oh, I don't mean the *play*."

At the back of the theater, in the open place behind the seats, Dubinsky was pacing, and listening to the lines from the stage.

After a while he stopped pacing and went to lean his arms on the plush-covered partition which separated this part of the house from the stalls, and because he was short and the partition high, this pose made him look like a Raphael cherub grown elderly. He was thinking, as he had thought on every opening night of his career, that you never really saw a play for what it was until the opening night. Until the audience was in the house you were never able, for some reason or other, to see it objectively. During rehearsals you tried, and usually you thought you were succeeding, but on opening night you knew you had only been guessing—and sometimes it turned out to be a good guess, sometimes not.

It was the audience being there that made the whole difference. You seemed to see the play through its eyes. Up to then you tended to believe that the production actually had in it the qualities you had been trying to put there, but on opening night you saw it as it actually was. Sometimes you found you had succeeded, and quite often you discovered that the play had values you never knew were there, and might have played up a little if you had. It was the great problem of the theater, how to get perspective on your production before you let the audience have it. If producers could learn that, there wouldn't be so many failures. Some were a little better at it than others, that was all. Here he was tonight, looking at *The Rungs of the Ladder* and finding it different, in a good many disturbing ways, from what he had thought.

Willow, for example. He began to pace again, listening with part of his mind to the words, not looking at the stage, but seeing the action in his mind with perfect clarity. Willow had been his weakest link—or so he had supposed—but here she was, dominating everything, even though she was a little off her stride, hadn't the "feel" of the audience yet, or quite found her voice.

She dominated the play, all right, so that the plot and the suspense which he had thought were too good to need any building up—were good enough to carry the play in spite of Willow—why, they were secondary! Why couldn't he have seen that before? And if he had seen it, wouldn't he have said that it was exactly as it should be and thanked his gods?

Of course he would, but the trouble was, the audience didn't like it. He wouldn't have foreseen that. He could feel their dislike, that intangible force or pressure that builds up when a lot of people are feeling the same emotions at the same time, and for which there is no adequately descriptive word. Why didn't they like her? Because Hester was a damned disagreeable character—but plenty of disagreeable characters had been great successes on the stage from Shakespeare's time until today.

Frowning, Dubinsky went back to lean on the partition, but her scene was nearly over and after a few more lines Willow left the stage. A great deal went with her—so much that the house seemed empty and the play seemed to have shrunk. She has power, he thought. She has that. He felt the audience relaxing, and he thought with relief that now they'd listen to the story. Now the play was in balance.

Only the four were left on the stage, and Dubinsky followed the dialogue without giving it much attention. That youngster was good as John. He had a technique you could count on.

Do you really think Hester has gathered us all around her because she loves us? Did you really believe her when she told you that? She wants us because each of us has some little thing she can take. Imogene, here, thinks she is Hester's best friend, but haven't you noticed how Hester is acquiring Imogene's gracious manner and her tricks of poise? And when she has acquired them, do you think she'll want the model near her any longer?

Just what was it that Willow had done to the audience in the devastating ten minutes on the stage? It made him long for Délice and her familiar competency.

And you, Seaton. Do you think it's you Hester wants? She never wanted any person in her life. She wanted the prestige of being seen with you—she's used that to mount higher. We're all just the rungs of the ladder. And when she's up, why then, she'll turn her back on the ladder. Watch out. She's nearly up!

163

She's so like Hester that she ought to be working out all right in the part. Why, that's it! She's too like. They hate her because she's real.

Hester is a thief. She'll take from you anything she can.

That's it! They all know Hesters—all the women here. Some Hester has probably tried to take a bit of security away from most of them—a husband, a lover. Rita wouldn't have been quite so real, they'd have thought of her as an actress. If they dislike Willow too much, it could ruin the play. Why can't you learn to weigh these things in rehearsal?

When Hester goes into a room, she wants to see every head turned her way. Once she wanted to make them look at her because of the men she was with—men of position like you, Seaton. And because of the diamonds she wore. That isn't good enough for her now. She wants them to stare because of what she herself is. Haven't you noticed she never wears her diamond collar any more?

Strange, when you came to think of it, that you never know your actors very well—even Rita, perhaps. Actors get to be so many people that their real selves have little more weight in the scales than the characters they play. If they were going to dislike her, that trick ending might just make all the difference. Nothing to do now but wait, with what equanimity you could muster, for the final curtain.

And you, Godfrey, you're young, you're nobody, you're poor. You fool, you think she loves you. She's asked you to take her to the ball tonight. Don't delude yourself—it's just that she's putting Seaton away with the diamond collar.

Dubinsky took out his watch. Two hours, more or less, till final curtain and the verdict—and after that there would be the verdict of the press to wait for. His feet hurt and he had the sensation in his stomach of empty queasiness which he associated with the suspense of waiting in a doctor's office. On opening nights with Rita the strain was never so bad as this—but also, Rita had never, even at the top of her career, swelled the walls to bursting as Willow did. He took out his pill box and popped a pill into his mouth. Shortly, he noticed with pleasure a shifting of pressures within him and, relaxing, he settled down to listen to what was left of Act One. It really was a good play, though the plot was a bit slow in unfolding, and that, also, gave Willow too much weight. "John" was working himself up beautifully.

I am the only one who will always be with her. Why? Because I see through her—because she can't fool me—because I'm the test of her art. So long as she can't fool me, she knows that she hasn't perfected herself. If she ever did fool me, I'd be discarded, as the rest of you will be—a rung in her ladder.

Dubinsky sighed and turned away. Willow would be on briefly now, and then the Act One curtain. She might come off stage close to hysterical—you never knew. Anyway, it would be a good idea to be waiting for her. He went slowly to the back regions of the theater and stood in the shadow near the steps to the stage. Presently the stage door opened and Burt came out. He had a wedge in his hand and he put it under the door to hold it open. That was a sign the act was nearly over. Why was it that actors coming off the set always ran like children let out of school? With the door open, Dubinsky could hear the voices on the stage plainly, and though the words themselves were indistinguishable, he listened critically to the tones. Willow was giving it the lift at the end that he wanted. Good. She had got over her inevitable moment of panic nicely—you never had to worry about her type. Ah!

The voices had stopped and there was a sound like the rushing of a great wind. Dubinsky leaned forward to listen, his head on one side. A far better hand than he had expected! Excellent, in fact. It just went to show you never knew. Still, there was nothing conclusive about it. This was going to be one of those plays where you couldn't tell until much later—until the final curtain, perhaps, whether you had a success or not. He took out his handkerchief and patted the beads of perspiration on his forehead.

Willow came running down the steps, her skirts rustling. She was breathing fast and she looked incandescent. The others were right on her heels. "John" saw him and gave him an angry look. Dubinsky smiled. They didn't like that rule of his that there were

165

to be no recalls until the final curtain. Rob an actor of his applause and you robbed him of the very thing for which he was an actor. Well, perhaps that was rather less than fair.

Sam stood up and, saying to Lettie, "Excuse me, please," he made his way out into the aisle. He felt Lettie's eyes following him and for an instant he was angry with her for intruding, even in her thoughts, into the business between himself and Willoughby. Then he was ashamed. The affair had made the first breach between the Brodis and himself, though he was not wholly sure why, but the fact that it had done so made him feel depressed and almost desolate.

As he went up the aisle it seemed to him that not only Lettie, but everyone in the theater, was staring at his retreating back, and then he remembered that no one but the Brodis knew about himself and Willoughby, and so it was all his imagination. The play was nightmarish. He could not dissociate Willoughby and Hester in his mind, and he had the feeling that, like a bad dream, the oppressive effect would linger, and that it would be a long time before he could get over seeing in Willoughby the exaggerated traits of Hester. They made her seem coarser. They gave her a crudity she did not have, or rather, they stripped away the veneer. The effect, he thought, might be much the same if he saw her drunk, that is to say, revealing, damaging—and the memory hard to destroy.

Half way up the aisle he remembered Claire. From her box she would have seen him rise. Perhaps she even thought that he was on his way to join her. He should at least have looked toward her, acknowledging her presence in some way, but he hadn't been aware of it, and now it was too late.

In the slowly moving crowd at the end of the aisle he suddenly found himself beside Lailey. He would have retreated, but Lailey, who seemed to be bursting with exuberance, gave him no chance.

"Hullo, Sam! Fine play isn't it? We've got a great actress in Miss Cleveland. I'm going backstage now."

A current of the crowd swept him away, and Sam followed at a more leisurely pace, glad not to have to prolong the conversation through the corridors to Willoughby's dressing room. He kept Lailey in sight, however, and saw him pause at a door, but just as he was about to knock on it, the door opened and a thin man came out. Sam knew, without thinking about it, that he must belong to the theater. He had the distempered look of too little sleep, chronically bad meals and worry, and he and Lailey seemed to be on cordial terms, on Lailey's side, at least. Sam heard Lailey call him "Burt" and repeat his remarks about the play in the hearty manner that men of his type invariably use when they want to seem democratic. Burt, who was obviously in a hurry, paused to reopen the door for Lailey. When he closed it again, Sam was standing in front of him.

"Excuse me," Sam said, and reached for the door knob.

"Can't go in there, Mister."

"I just saw you let someone in."

"That was Mr. Lailey."

"So what?"

"So it was Mr. Lailey."

"If he can go in there, so can I."

"Yeah? You got money in this show too? I gotta go back on stage and I haven't time to argue. You keep out of there."

Sam stood still, watching Burt's retreating back. Money in the show! She had not told him that. For a moment his mind groped, trying to track down all the implications of this discovery, until he realized the futility of attempting to think it through now and in this place. He went in without knocking.

The room gave him the impression of being full of people though, in point of fact, there was no one in it but Willoughby and Suzanne, Dubinsky and Lailey. Willoughby was seated at the dressing shelf, doing things to her make-up with feverish haste. The grease paint made her skin look coarse, and again he had the nightmarish sensation that this play had selected and magnified traits in her, distorting her, so to speak, so that though she was familiar to him, she was, at the same time, horrifyingly strange.

Her eyes met his in the looking glass, but she seemed scarcely to recognize him and he knew that she was not at the moment concerned with the undercurrents of their relationship. Suzanne, who was hovering over Willoughby in a way that seemed to him both possessive and proud, turned to stare at him. The stare was insolent, and she moved as though to shield Willoughby with her small person. She leaned over Willoughby and Sam heard her say, "Do not hurry so, Madame. It iss not necessary you hurry so." Her caressing tone, Sam knew, was largely for his benefit.

Lailey and Dubinsky were sitting in folding chairs at the far end of the room, watching Willow, as though this too were part of the performance. Dubinsky's expression was anxious, Lailey's full of triumph. When Lailey saw him, he raised a hand in greeting and then reached out and pulled another chair close to his own. Sitting in it gingerly because he did not trust folding chairs, Sam thought that Lailey was too pleased about his play to wonder what Sam Hadley was doing there.

Lailey put a hand familiarly on Sam's back. "A great actress we've got here. Great! Did you hear the hand they gave her? We've got a hit on our hands."

Excitement had affected Lailey. Sartorially, he was as perfect as ever, but he gave the impression, somehow, of disarray. In your mind's eye you saw him with a strand of hair out of place or a loose collar button. It was Dubinsky who answered him, in a low voice so that Willow could not hear, though she was concentrating wholly on herself.

"I keep telling him it's too early to judge." He continued to watch Willoughby while he spoke. "The audience doesn't like Hester. I can see now that there are a number of things which I should have done in the beginning."

Dubinsky was obviously only repeating something he had said before Sam appeared, but it seemed to penetrate Lailey's exuberance for the first time. Suddenly he was as anxious as, a moment before, he had been confident.

"Is that so? What things? What are you talking about?"

168

"I didn't give Hester enough shading. I should have made it easier for the audience to see that she's really a figure to be pitied—alone, unhappy, and underneath her confidence, perhaps, she's even a little frightened. She *is* these things, you know."

"What difference would that have made?" Sam asked, and Lailey picked up the sentence as though it were his own. "And anyway, you'd have had to rewrite the play."

"Oh, no. I might have the ending changed a bit, but in the main you'd get it across in little ways—inflections given to words already in the script, a droop of the shoulders, gestures. Sometimes a single gesture can throw more light on a character than all the playwright's words. The point is that Hester, as she stands, hasn't enough human weaknesses. If she had just a few, every woman in the audience would feel superior to her and, consequently, they'd like her better. Queer that you can't see these things in rehearsal, but you can't."

Lailey's confidence had come back to him. "I think you're wrong. The audience liked her, all right. But if you feel that way, for God's sake, why don't you tell her now to put in some of that stuff?"

Dubinsky smiled. "It's too late. Never tinker with a show on opening night. You're always tempted to try, and if you do, it's always a mistake."

He was only giving them part of his attention and Sam saw that, under cover of the talk, he was watching Willoughby closely. She was still hurrying, still fussing with her make-up, leaning forward close to the mirror, and Sam saw that she was tuned to a high pitch of excitement. He was not surprised when Dubinsky got up quietly and, taking his chair with him, went to sit beside the make-up shelf. When he talked to her, Willoughby stopped fussing to listen. Sam wished he could hear what the little man was saying, and he might have if Lailey had not put his arm along the back of Sam's chair and said, in a carefully lowered voice, that he thought all that stuff about wanting to change Hester was a lot of damn nonsense.

"Hell, they like her as she is."

Dubinsky was apparently telling Willow to take deep breaths. Anyway, she was doing it and he along with her. He looked rather ludicrous, Sam thought, swelling himself out like that. There was something possessive in the way Lailey talked about Willoughby, and Sam's anger began to smolder. Dubinsky was leaning toward her with one arm resting on the make-up shelf. Her pose was relaxed and easy now. Suddenly she smiled at Dubinsky and put her fingers on his sleeve. When she took them away again, there were white powder marks on the black cloth. Dubinsky looked down at them but he made no move to brush them off. He didn't, for some reason, seem like the same person whom Sam had found so annoying at the dinner party. In fact, Sam found to his astonishment that he almost liked him.

Lailey put a hand on Sam's back again and Sam moved away from it. The fellow had been saying something or other in that confident way of his.

"I didn't hear that."

"I was saying, I'm giving a little supper for Miss Cleveland after the show. Delmonico's. How about joining us?"

"I've got guests with me. Thanks."

"Bring them. Bring them."

Too Goddamn confident. So sure of himself that it hadn't occurred to him to wonder what Sam was doing back here in her dressing room. And what the hell was Lailey himself doing there?

"Sorry."

"Oh, listen—come on. I want to make it an occasion for her. It's a great thing she's done. We ought to make her realize we know it."

Willoughby had stood up and gone behind a screen and Suzanne, taking a dress off a rolling rack, had followed her. Bits of the dress came whisking into view around the edges of the screen. She might as well be changing her clothes in public. Lailey still had that unbuttoned look and something self-conscious had crept into his manner, so that Sam knew that he, too, was aware of Willoughby behind the screen. No doubt he planned to take her home after this dinner. Sam stood up.

"Thanks," he said. "I'll come. We'll all come." He said it angrily.

She came out from behind the screen. She stood straight and tall and full of confidence. She glanced his way and, seeing him, she smiled. He wondered if she had known, until then, that he was in the room. The door opened and the thin man put his head in.

"Ready?" he inquired.

She nodded and he shut the door again. A minute later they heard the voice of the call-boy.

"Places. Act Two, Scene One, places."

Lailey had leaped to his feet.

"Plenty of time," Dubinsky said. Willoughby was walking toward the door and Dubinsky held it open for her. Some whispered word passed between them, and she was gone. Dubinsky stood still for a moment. He seemed to have forgotten that there were others in the room, and his expression was grave and thoughtful. Then he carefully brushed away the marks of powder on his sleeve, turned his back on them and went out.

The second act didn't, in the language Dubinsky used to himself, "go over" very well. There was a young woman up on the stage playing the part of Hester, but there was no illusion of her being Hester. The mechanics of the theater showed through. The voices sounded loud and unnatural, like stage voices, and you noticed such things as backstage thumpings and the flimsiness of a painted door when it was slammed, things which never would be noticed if the spell had held.

Dubinsky, leaning on the partition at the back of the house, felt miserable and, as the act progressed, his discouragement turned into a sense of personal failure. He shut his eyes and found that he was remembering Délice. The memory was so vivid that the two women seemed to be speaking the lines of the play in synchronism, but with their individual differences of inflection and tone. When you acquired a competent technique like Rita's, you lost some freshness and vividness—but technique carried you over the rough spots. Thinking of her now increased his unhappiness and his feeling of being all alone.

Compelled by it, he left his post at the partition and went quietly down the passage to the box where Claire was sitting. When he parted the curtains, Lailey looked around and started to rise but Dubinsky put his hand on his shoulder and forced him back into his seat. In the luminescence from the footlights he saw Claire turn to see who had come in. She smiled at him. Edie rose to give him the chair behind Claire's and he lowered himself into it.

He felt very tired. Claire was still leaning forward and, quietly, he put his hand on the back of her chair. It gave him comfort to have it there. It was almost like touching her. He shut his eyes and let himself rest. The voices from the stage lost their meaning. He felt very close to her and at peace. He felt as though it were the first time he had rested for a long, long time—years, perhaps.

Then one of those disturbing moments came to him when he saw himself, for a moment of lonely clarity, as he was. He saw his short, round body, the black hair which was growing thin, the fat, scarred hand resting on the back of her chair. He saw how laughable he must look. Pitiable and laughable. He took his hand away.

After that he watched the stage critically. Willow was beginning to feel too confident, adding touches to Hester which had not been in the rehearsals. He decided he must have a talk with her. He leaned over and said to Lailey, "I'm going back now. Don't come this time. I want to see her alone. And keep that fellow Hadley out, will you?"

He reached the dressing room before she did. No one was there but Suzanne, who was moving around restlessly and talking to herself in French. Her words sounded monotonous, fluent, and they rose and fell on the swell of her breathing. He wondered if she were praying and he thought, not for the first time, how much real emotion from how many sources went into creating the false emotions of the stage.

Then, in the manner of a whirlwind, Willow came, her hair blowing, her skirts flying. The door banged behind her.

"*Isaac!*" She cried it out as though she had not expected to find him there. She seized his hands and he smiled, not at her but at himself because he felt himself responding to the rousing quality in her.

"Isaac, it's going *splendidly,* isn't it? I love it!" She kissed his cheek. She had to stoop to do it. He was pleased and annoyed, and he spoke gruffly.

"Change as quickly as you can, Willow. I want to talk to you."

She went at once behind the screen and Suzanne followed her. He sat down to wait for her on a French settee which had seen better days and bore scars of occasional appearances on the stage. Silky swishings and rustlings came from behind the screen. How vital she was—and she demanded the same quality from everyone. You couldn't call it magnetism—that meant to attract, and the effect she had was rather to fire, to galvanize. She must have had much conflict in her life.

She came out from behind the screen and he noticed with wonder that she had in this one night acquired the authority of bearing of the star.

"Sit down," he said, making room for her.

She sat sidewise, facing him. She was glowing. And she was carrying her chin up in that superb way she had which made you feel that she was offering you an exciting challenge.

"Yes, Isaac," she said.

He did not answer at once because he had noticed that her eyes had more depth in them than he had ever seen there before. He thought, she knows it's not going well and she's trying to hide it from me that she knows. How would she manage herself if the play failed?

He put his hand over hers. "Willow, I want to warn you. You're thinking about the audience too much. I want you to try to forget the audience is there. I know that's hard and you won't really be able to do it, but just don't think about them so much."

"I'll try, Isaac."

"And another thing." He held both her hands tightly to chain her attention.

The door opened and Burt said, "Ready?"

Dubinsky felt her start to rise. He said to Burt, "All right," and increased his pressure on her hands.

"Listen, Willow—this is important. Try to think it's a rehearsal and don't change any of it. Don't change it at all from the way it was in rehearsal. Don't try to add anything. Don't try to give it more force. It has force enough. Just do it exactly as you did in rehearsal. It's important. Will you try?"

"*Places, please. Places.*" The call-boy was right outside the door. Dubinsky could feel her eagerness to go but he still held her down, trying to make her focus on him.

She said, "All right, Isaac, I'll try." Her eyes still had the disturbing depth.

He let her go then. She went to the mirror for a last look. He was holding the door open for her. As she went through she gave him a swift smile that had an unexpected sweetness in it. Moved by it, he stood watching her as she walked toward the stairs, her shoulders back and her head up, and he thought what a superb woman she would be in later life when time had fined her down a little, added breadth and understanding to her courage. Then he sighed and went back to the house.

The third act started off better. In places the illusion mysteriously reappeared and lingered. Dubinsky, back at his watching post, thought that she had at least one quality which many a more experienced actress had not—she was intelligent. Tell her a thing and she grasped it. She was eminently capable of doing what she was told. The trouble was, that she needed to be convinced of the necessity for doing it. Your ideal actor would have brains and a kind of sixth sense that would tell him when not to initiate.

Willow was honestly trying not to initiate, and this touched him because it was evidence of a faith in him which he had not been wholly sure she had acquired. If she kept on like this, the play might have a run, and these were faults which could be eradicated, given time. Whatever improving you did to a show after opening night seldom affected box office. Nevertheless, the play really was going better and he felt a little lighter in heart.

As the act drew to an end he thought about going to her dressing room and admonishing her again. In the next act Hester would really begin to show herself in her true colors and if, at this point, the audience didn't like the play, and Willow took it personally, the result might be very bad indeed. He must balance that against the fact that all was apparently well enough at the moment, plus the risk of unsettling her further by more talk. In the end, Dubinsky spent the intermission alone in his office.

He waited until the house lights were down for the final act before he went back to his stand at the partition. He got there just as Willoughby made her entrance, and the minute he saw her he recognized disaster. The success of the last act, if you could call it that, had gone to her head. She wasn't Hester at all. She wasn't even remotely trying to be Hester, but at the same time, by being herself she was magnifying Hester a thousand times. She carried herself with an outrageous assurance which built itself on top of Hester's assurance into something insufferable. The arrogant, artificial charm, the triumphant, artificial smile, made a caricature, a monster out of Hester but—and this was the quality which made it all shocking to the senses—the monster had reality, it was convincing, it had life. And behind that was Willow's incredible force of personality.

The audience reacted at once and violently. Dubinsky felt and heard the wave of it go through the house. They hated her.

And he hated her. His face was red with it, and he began to pace up and down behind the partition, his short body rocking from side to side with the force of his feelings. A part of his mind heard and followed the lines; the rest was thick with anger and bitterness and despair. He had only seen a thing like this happen once before, the tremendous surge of antagonistic feeling of a whole audience against one person. It had awed him then and it awed him now.

Then his subconscious ear caught a change. He came back quickly and leaned on the partition. She must have felt the shock of the audience's reaction to her. He had not been watching when it happened to her, but she must have felt it like a blow. The triumph and assurance had gone and something else, equally strong, had taken its place.

He felt someone moving up to stand beside him and he glanced quickly around. Lailey was there.

Lailey said in a tense whisper, "What's happening?"

Dubinsky waited a moment to be sure, then he said, "It's the worst thing that could possibly happen, short of what she just did."

"I don't understand."

"She can't stand their dislike. She's trying to fight them."

He thought, she's trying to fight them the way she fought me that day she read the monologue in Philadelphia. If an actress were going to fail, she should go down acting, not fighting. But there was something magnificent about the way she fought, something which stirred his admiration as it had then. The audience didn't feel it. Their antagonism was less intense now and they sat there like lumps, waiting for her to move them. She couldn't fight them, of course, the way she had fought him. He hoped she would realize it.

She had begun to slow the tempo of the scene. He could see she was thinking. The new tempo was bothering the other actors and they were trying to adjust themselves to it. She was speaking her lines without giving them any attention, the way a well-rehearsed player can, and she was thinking earnestly. Dubinsky was surprised and interested. He wondered what it was, what she would do next.

Hester's words flowed on and then, gradually, Hester began to appear. Willow was sliding herself back into her part. When it was clear to him what was happening, Dubinsky grabbed Lailey's arm in excitement and jerked his head toward the stage, but he couldn't find words for his thoughts. He dropped Lailey's arm and, folding his own arms along the top of the partition, he leaned his weight on them and tried to hoist himself up as high as he could. She was using her intelligence, God bless her. He wished that she could know that he was there. Then he stopped thinking and listened to the play.

When he came to himself again Lailey was gone and the audience was quiet. It was the quiet of interest. She had recaptured them briefly, as she had him, but it was surely too late. He started to pace back and forth again, his hands clasped behind his back. Then he began to worry about the ending. It was not right for her, or for the play—another thing he should have foreseen. They wouldn't like it and that would be the last impression they would carry away from the theater.

He worried about it more and more, and then he sought the seclusion of the passage to the box. There was only one short scene between Hester and Imogene left now, and the voices from the stage came to him muffled by the velvet curtains of the box. He paced down the passage until the words became hard to distinguish, and then he turned and paced back again.

Imogene dear, you look so serious. Have you come to tell me something?

Yes, Hester, I have. I've come to say I can't stay for the rest of the visit.

But why? You wrote that it would be such Heaven to be under the same roof with John. I wanted you to enjoy that, since you didn't either of you have enough money to be married for a long time. I particularly wanted you to enjoy that. It was a gift I could give you—you'll never take any other kind. I feel sorry for you, Imogene.

Dubinsky paced restlessly. This last scene was a mistake—would have been a mistake even with Rita in the part. It made Hester—well, not quite a caricature, but overdrawn, certainly.

Why are you going, dear?

I could give you a conventional answer—John teases me sometimes—he says I always say the right thing—but this time I think I want to say what I feel.

You needed to shear away from a character every unimportant trait—the kind of contradictory qualities which, in real life, muddy our understanding of people. You needed to give the character what the writing boys called "dramatic clarity," but by shearing away, not by exaggerating. An important difference.

Hester, you frighten me. There's something universal about you

—you're what every woman is, secretly—even myself. You're ruthless and selfish. Most of us are restrained from doing the things we want to do by fear of the consequences, and we call it good breeding and being civilized. You're not civilized and you're not restrained. You do things that most women only imagine themselves doing in their most secret thoughts.

Dubinsky sighed. He could finish the rest of the lines from memory and the scene seemed flat and stale.

Why, dear, that was quite a speech. I always thought you were too much of a lady to say what you think. Being in love with John, you are catching his style. But I do feel sorry for you, dear. Stay till the end of the week—if you don't, you'll be throwing away three days of happiness, and the chances for happiness are so few.

What do you mean, Hester? You sound as though you meant more than you say. What do you mean?

Dubinsky parted the velvet curtains and felt a faint restlessness in the house. Here and there, he knew, women were pulling their cloaks over their shoulders and dropping programs to the floor. He saw Lailey lean toward Claire and heard him whisper, "When they start to clap, stand up and throw your bouquet on the stage. It may start other women doing the same."

Then, Imogene, I will tell you. I was going to be kind and not tell you until the end of the week. I was going to make John promise, so that you could have three more happy days. In spite of what you say, I am kind, Imogene!

Hester, what do you mean? Promise what? What are you talking about?

Why, dear, just that we were married this morning, John and I.

Dubinsky dropped the curtains and turned away. No need to hurry backstage. The recalls might be a lengthy business and Burt could be trusted to put a stop to them at the right point.

By the time he reached the back of the theater the lights were up and the long procession of ushers, each grasping a floral piece, ready to start down the aisle. He glanced back at the box and saw Lailey on his feet, inclining a little toward the stage, clapping noisily. He saw Claire rise and throw her bouquet on the stage and, in the middle of the house, another woman rose and threw hers. It fell into the orchestra pit and one of the musicians picked it up and tossed it on the stage.

Chapter Twelve

L AILEY was waiting to take Willoughby to Delmonico's, standing outside her door, hat and gloves in hand. He had only seen her for an instant after the last-act curtain and he was thinking about what he had seen, her eyes too bright, her hands too quick and the feverish glow on her cheeks showing through the grease paint. Her eyes haunted him still. There was anger in them—hate, he thought, might be a closer word—and suffering, misery. Trying to dispel the memory, he shut his own eyes and rubbed the lids with a thumb and finger.

When he opened them again, Dubinsky was coming toward him down the corridor. Lailey waited until the little man was abreast of him and then he said, "Just how bad do you think it is?"

Dubinsky looked at him gravely, and Lailey knew he had intruded on a moment in which Dubinsky would rather have been alone. His face was gray and drawn, and Lailey came far enough out of his own troubles to realize that Dubinsky was feeling the burden of his responsibility to be intolerable. While Lailey was searching for words to express this understanding, the now familiar mask of patient kindness slipped over Dubinsky's face again. When he spoke, there was gentleness in his tone.

"We'll be able to tell more after another night, but I'd say we might get an audience for the two-weeks run you've underwritten. I doubt if the play could last longer than that."

"Does *she* realize?"

Dubinsky took time to consider and Lailey could see he was so tired that it was hard for him to fix his mind. He was trying to do so with the patience of a man accustomed to letting himself be used. Finally he said, "I'm not sure. An experienced actress would, of course. I'd guess she knows, or she's beginning to know, and that she's trying to hide it."

"Isaac, I got her into this. I wish it had never happened."

Dubinsky stood silently staring down at the floor boards. After a moment he said, "She has courage, and she has yourself." Then he went on his way.

The door opened and Willoughby appeared. She wore a long wine-colored cloak with a small collar of fur under her chin. Her skin looked pale, almost bluish, and as thin as paper. She was still burning with the intolerable brilliance. She was smiling and her lips looked stiff, and he realized with a sick feeling that the smile meant nothing. She had withdrawn behind a barricade, herself on one side, himself and all the world on the other. He had never been so far away from her.

He tried to speak, could not, and cleared his throat. They walked down the corridor together. He put his hand around her arm above her elbow and found that she was holding herself with a tenseness that was almost rigidity. At his touch she turned toward him, still with the smile which she meant as a barrier. With that smile on her face there was no way he could tell her that he was deeply, terribly sorry. There was no way that he could reach her at all.

In the carriage she asked him to let the window down. She said that the gas fumes had bothered her, and that her mouth and nose still seemed to be full of them. She said she could *taste* the gas. She took a few deep breaths of the fresh air, and then she slipped her wrist through the hanging strap and leaned back against the cushions. He hoped that she had relaxed. He groped for her hand and

181

when he held it, he found that she had not. She did not respond to the pressure of his fingers and he leaned back beside her, watching the shadows and stray beams of light which played across her face, thinking how strong and proud her profile was and wondering how he could break through to her. He could feel her still hating the audience, still fighting it in her mind.

Then, without thinking about what he was going to say, he was talking to her, and the darkness helped him.

"Willow, it's all been my fault. I got you into this. I should have realized . . . I'm deeply, deeply sorry." He felt her stiffen but he went on. "If I had understood you, maybe you could talk to me now." He sat on the edge of the seat and leaned over her. She drew back in her corner as far as she could. He said, "Don't, Willow. Don't shut me out of your thoughts."

He could see she was trying to escape him. He said, "I hope you'll be willing to give up this terrible life now, darling. I wish to the Lord I'd never gotten you into it. I love you. You know that, don't you? I want to marry you. Will you marry me, Willow?"

The light of a street lamp fell across her face, and he saw that she was watching him with eyes which looked enormous. The hard brilliance was still there but it looked more brittle, and then he realized with a sick feeling that, with her intelligence, she would know he wouldn't be asking her to marry him now, in this way, if the play had been a success. He had only emphasized its failure. He said, "I was meaning all along to ask you tonight."

She moved a little and took her hand away from his. "Don't," she said. "Don't." He could see she knew it wasn't true.

"But I mean it, Willow, with all my heart. I want to marry you right away. Will you, dearest?"

"Let's not talk about it tonight."

"All right, if it's hard for you, dear. But it would be the right answer, the right thing to do—right in every way. Just tell me this much. You love me, don't you? You want to marry me?"

"I'd like nothing better, if . . ." She said it as though there were no more breath left in her.

182

"There's no 'if' about it, darling."

He took her in his arms and she put her hands on his chest to hold him off.

"There are so many things we have to talk about, and I can't tonight—I simply can't."

"Don't try, dear. Don't think about anything now. Kiss me."

She let him kiss her, but she didn't respond to him and her lips felt cold. She made a small choked sound and he knew that, all the time he had been kissing her, she had not stopped thinking about the play, and when she made that sound, she had come near to accepting things as they were. For an instant she clung to him, returning his kiss. Then she pushed him away from her and sat back in her corner. She sat very straight, and she was breathing fast. He knew that she hadn't been able to accept things and that again she was fighting something which was not there to fight. She began to open the front of her cloak as though the snug collar were choking her. She said with the same shallow breath, "We're nearly there. I'll have to . . ." She left the sentence unfinished. She seemed to have gone a long way back into her own thoughts. He watched her, feeling helpless and deeply troubled. She seemed so terribly alone.

At Delmonico's he waved the carriage starter aside and helped her down himself. She was smiling again, but he noticed that she stepped on the carriage block as though it were something which might break. He said, "Are you all right, darling?" and she turned the smile on him. Then he saw a group of people approaching and he said, "Here come some of our guests, I'm afraid. They must have walked over." He cursed himself silently for having subjected her to the additional ordeal of this party.

Their carriage drove away and she turned her back on the approaching people and stood on the curb facing the darkness of the park across the street. The fall wind was blowing, bending the tops of the trees, bringing them the sound of the fountain and revealing the bulk of Farragut's statue looming among the trees. She raised her face to the wind, letting her cloak fall open, and he watched her with deep concern, obsessed by the idea of her aloneness.

Then she put her hand on his arm and said, "All right," as though she knew her respite had to end. Her touch felt hard and he realized that she was not aware of him in any real sense. She was dealing with the present with only the surface of her mind. Looking at the slowly approaching group, she said, "I suppose it's some of *them*." He didn't understand but he felt her tenseness return. Something in her manner, something in the way she held herself, brought back with sudden clarity a picture of her on the stage facing the antagonism of the audience. So that was it—hate of their hatred. It was so strong in her that he wondered if it dominated even the failure of the play. He had no more time to think about it, for Sam Hadley and his friends were only a short distance away.

Lettie touched Michael's arm and said, "Remember, she's not supposed to know us." But it was Lettie who was red in the face while the introductions were being made. She hoped it would be taken for the half-shy, half-bold way in which housewives behave toward celebrities. Willoughby, her own sister, seemed as distant as she had on the stage, but Lettie felt so sorry for her that her throat ached. Michael, she could tell, didn't feel sorry for Willoughby, but then, he had never liked her, and Willoughby would hate having people feel sorry. Lettie said diffidently, "I think they're waiting for us." She and Willoughby led the procession up the walk.

For as long as Lettie could remember, whenever she was talking to her older sister, Willoughby always seemed to be looking at something beyond Lettie's shoulder and thinking about something else. It was like that now when Lettie said, "I wouldn't have worn this old cloak if I had known we were coming here. I really should get something especially for evenings, now I'm in New York."

"What? Oh—don't. I'll give you an old one of mine."

Lettie's flush deepened. She was glad Michael couldn't hear. She began to talk fast about nothing.

"Look, they're like candy—striped peppermint candy—the awnings, I mean. It's all so pretty—the light shining through the lace curtains and the flowers in the urns—so late in the year! And the little tree shaped like an umbrella and the iron balcony and fence."

She was chattering and all the time she wanted to cry out, "Oh, Willie dear, I'm so terribly, terribly sorry." And she wanted to say, "Oh, Willie, don't be so angry at things." Tears were close to her eyes.

Inside Delmonico's there were a great many people and they all looked at Willoughby. So that Willoughby, for a second at least, wouldn't have to look over their heads with that aloof smile, Lettie said, "Do you suppose they've *all* been to theaters?"

"Maybe, but it's late. Maybe they've been to Maddern and Mansfield's *In Spite of All*, at the Lyceum. That runs late, too. Or perhaps they're all part of Stuyvesant's party. They look at me like . . ."

"I know." Lettie could see it—the same expression on all those faces turned in the same direction, all waiting with uncharitable expectancy. Magnify that into a whole audience. Lettie shut her eyes. *"I couldn't* face them, Willie."

The cloakroom was deserted except for a maid in a black uniform standing in sullen silence by the cloak racks at the far side of the room. When she moved forward to take Willoughby's cloak, Lettie could see that her feet hurt her and wondered how long she had to stand there and whether they paid her anything but tips.

Willoughby's fur-lined cloak was slipped off her shoulders, and when Lettie saw the dress underneath, she forgot everything else and cried, "Oh, how lovely!" Then a wave of warm feeling went through her because, for an instant, Willoughby's hard, aloof self-possession vanished and she looked at Lettie softly, as though she were grateful. Almost, Lettie thought, as though she were grateful about something *else*.

The dress had been made from a Paris model by one of the best couturiers in New York. The underskirt was heavy satin in a soft pink, and a broad band of embroidered wild roses ran around the hem and climbed up the front. The roses themselves were velvet, darker than the satin. They were not stitched down—which made them look almost as though they were real. Each rose had a pearl, like a drop of dew, on one petal and there were many more pearl

185

dewdrops on the leaves and on the embroidered branches. The draped-up overskirt and the pointed bodice were velvet, matching the wild roses.

"I've never seen anything so beautiful in my whole life, Willie," Lettie said softly.

"Don't call me Willie. I've outgrown that silly name."

"I think you've outgrown us all."

At the other end of the room the door opened and two women came in, their trains rustling. They brought with them an air of excitement and gaiety; they moved in their own atmosphere of it. Their coming seemed to stir up the heavy air in the room. They went straight to the huge, gilt-framed mirror and began to fuss with their dresses. Their backs were toward Willoughby and Lettie, but Lettie could see their reflections in the glass. One of them was pretty, Lettie thought, admiring them, but her prettiness was spoiled a little because her quick, shallow brown eyes had none of the kind of stability which comes from understanding. Her voice was high and artificial, and when Lettie began to listen to her, she was in the middle of a sentence.

". . . not a bit," she was saying. "I don't think anyone did. Harry thinks it won't have any run at all. I'm not surprised. I thought she was simply hateful and so conceited . . ."

The other woman, looking into the depths of the mirror, said "Shush" in a low, warning hiss. The excited voice broke off and Lettie saw the brown eyes widen in horror as the speaker recognized Willoughby. They put their heads together and whispered nervously, then they turned away from the glass and rustled quickly out.

Willoughby was white and very still. When Lettie saw the stillness, the words she was about to say died. There were strange, intense pinpoints of light in Willoughby's eyes. Then Lettie saw a pulse come to life in Willoughby's throat and begin to beat against the white skin. Lettie took a step toward her. All the heartbreak she was feeling was showing in her face, and Willoughby moved away as though she wanted to keep a distance between them.

She moved as though she were not conscious of her own motion. Lettie thought Willoughby had forgotten she was there. Willoughby stopped beside a carved chair and put her gloved hand on the back. The way she did it was slow, precise and trancelike, controlled by a terrible tension. The tension held Lettie too, so that she could not reach out to Willoughby or speak to her. Willoughby turned away from the chair, and one of the wild roses on her skirt caught in the bracket between the back and the seat. She felt the tug and looked down. With that strange look in her eyes, Lettie thought she didn't even see the caught rose but suddenly Willoughby drew a sharp breath, stooped and, taking her skirt in both hands, she jerked fiercely. The rose was torn off, taking a jagged piece of satin with it, and Lettie cried out. Willoughby turned and walked out of the room without looking around.

The small reception room at Delmonico's was upstairs. It was a long, thin room with two very straight rows of very straight chairs along the wall. When necessary, it could be joined with another room by opening the double doors at the end, but now the doors were closed because there were only a little more than twenty people present. The most distinguished part of the room was the woodwork, which was carved and painted white, but it belonged to a period no longer fashionable. To nullify the old-fashioned effect of the white woodwork, the walls had been covered with rose-pink brocade. The chair seats were crimson and, because of the warm glow generated by all this, the room was generally believed to be flattering to women.

Dubinsky stood by a table which had a fringed felt cloth on it, turning over the pages of a handsome leather guest book without feeling any interest in what he was doing. A crystal chandelier hung over his head and its fringelike prisms shed drops of rose and orange and amethyst light on his round forehead. He had shut his mind to the noise of talking which filled the room, and from time to time he glanced at the door.

Lailey was watching the door also, standing near it, holding a lace-edged bouquet to give to Willow when she appeared. Lailey looked, Dubinsky thought, fined down, as though the night's experience had burned away some of the unessentials, leaving him more visibly what he was.

Dubinsky rather liked what he was. The experience of the last two weeks could not have been easy for him, and Dubinsky wondered if this might not be the first time Lailey had ever found himself in a situation where his background, his money, the fact of being Stuyvesant Lailey, were of so little use to him. All men live on as little knowledge of themselves as they can. These things—the money and the background—must have protected him, more than most men are protected, from the necessity for this grim sort of knowledge.

In the unrelenting light of the play's failure, Lailey could not have escaped some of that self-knowledge. He was standing up to it well, taking more blame than was rightfully his for the heartbreak Willow must be feeling, but Dubinsky wondered if he might not be doing it so well only because he had a lover's blindness. He was at least spared a clear vision of Willow as she really was, and prevented from realizing to what an extent she herself was responsible for the failure of the play. If disillusion must come, let it come later and, turning several pages of the book without seeing them, Dubinsky wondered if this wish for Lailey from himself, who had always believed in living by the cold light of things as they were, might betoken a weakening in his own fiber.

But Willow—was it heartbreak she was feeling? Over by the door there was a stir and Lailey started forward. She stood there, taking the bouquet from Lailey without looking at it. There were, he saw, a tear in her skirt and two bright, pink spots high on her cheeks. Dubinsky shut the book and came around the table. She had, it seemed to him, come close to the barrier of some final restraint. She was like a fire in the last incandescent instant before it bursts into flame. He went to stand near her.

She had taken her place beside Lailey, and Dubinsky stood in his customary attitude, with his hands behind his back. She was keeping some sort of precarious hold on herself while she said "How

188

do you do?" twenty separate times. She didn't shake hands with anyone. She kept her hands under her bouquet and if anyone came too close, she backed away. Everyone looked at the tear in her skirt —she never glanced at it. What she was feeling, Dubinsky thought, was not heartbreak. That would come later. She hadn't gotten over being angry as yet, or gone very far toward seeing things as they were. Dubinsky continued to stand, like a sentinel, but he felt relieved when supper was announced.

The supper table was oval and, since there were no place cards, Dubinsky chose a chair on the opposite side of the table from the one Lailey had pulled out for Willow, where he could continue to watch her. She was on Lailey's right and two men were disputing the chair on the other side of her. One, Dubinsky saw with considerable deepening of concern, was Hadley, and the other a fellow with a waxed moustache. Hadley took possession. He looked like a fellow who usually took what he wanted, and Dubinsky wondered what part this trait had played in his relations with Willow. Lailey, Dubinsky felt sure, was uneasy about the relationship of these two, without suspecting what it really was. And Willow . . . Placed thus between husband and lover, her position was intolerable. With this burden added to everything else, could she support it?

He tried to catch her eye to give her a steadying look, to warn her, if he could, of the dangers of her own frame of mind. Before he was able to make her see him, he felt his sleeve touched lightly and a voice which sounded agreeable to his always critical ear said, "I suppose they have a chef who does nothing *else*." He turned sidewise to find a pleasant-faced woman with a scar on her cheek. She was looking at him in an anxious, urgent way which had nothing to do with her words, and she was calling his attention to the centerpiece, a bluebird with spread wings perched on a flowering branch. The thing was made of thousands of little pieces of sugar candy. He had the distinct impression, though he couldn't have said what gave it to him, that she was trying to distract his attention from Willow, and that her reason for doing it was to give Willow such privacy as she could. Marveling a little, he allowed himself to be diverted to the centerpiece. They examined it together and then he found himself laughing with her, though he was not quite sure why they were laughing, and afterward he discovered he had the feeling of knowing her quite well. She told him her name was Mrs. Brodi, but something kept him from asking her about herself and Willow Cleveland.

A waiter was offering him a platter of small objects so disguised by pipings and flutings that it was impossible to guess their substance. He took some on his plate and glanced at the gilt-edged menu card with which each guest was provided for just such contingencies as this. The illegible scrawl in gold ink seemed to say, "Hors d'oeuvres Florentine." Dubinsky left the rococo objects untasted. The party was noisy now—all but Willow, who was staring at space, and Lailey, who was staring at Willow, and Hadley, who seemed to be doing his best to stare angrily at both of them. Then Mrs. Brodi was demanding his attention with some comments about the theater. He found that they were surprisingly intuitive for a layman.

Willow ceased to look through and beyond Dubinsky, and looked at him. He was sitting sidewise in his chair, one arm hooked over the back, listening to Lettie. He seemed really interested in what she was saying. Lettie, of all people! How strange! He looked more relaxed than she had ever seen him, and there was something in his face she had never seen there before. The difference it made in him was so surprising that, for a moment, it took her out of herself. He looked, not exactly younger, but for the first time she saw in him the dim outlines of the young man he had once been. His face had sensitiveness and animation. And interest—they were talking as equals who spoke each other's language.

He had never talked to *her* like that, never looked at her without a guard on his expression. Watching him, she had a disturbing sense of having failed, in some way she did not understand, to meet some standard of his which she could not define and had not known until now that he held. Why? Because she lacked, in her own character, something which he recognized at once in Lettie—plain, simple,

"You let me do the worrying. Let's get on with it."

Dubinsky turned a page, sighed but instead of starting to read he lowered the script to his knee. "Here I've been driving this poor author crazy making him rewrite for the last year and a half till he's got this show turned into the perfect vehicle for Délice. Now the script's finished, he's gone away for a couple of weeks' rest, thank God. If he'd seen Miss Cleveland last night, he'd be in here this morning yelling his head off."

"So you got a nice show for Délice, Ike—so why don't you call her back? Or are you going to drive the poor guy to suicide rewriting again? What I say is, you got to get somebody pretty quick. The sides are all manifolded." Burt glanced at the neat pile of sides in their new brown covers, on the corner of Dubinsky's desk.

Footsteps were sounding on the boards of the corridor and Dubinsky was looking past him out the door. The next instant Willow was hesitating in the doorway. Burt, getting to his feet, thought she looked as though she hadn't slept at all. She looked like hell. She seemed vaguely surprised to find him there. She smiled at him and that embarrassed him because always, before, she'd smiled *down* at him but now she smiled as though she'd like to make friends.

Then she saw the miniature stage on its tripod. A queer look came into her eyes and he knew that she guessed it had to do with the new production and that it was a shock to her to find he and Ike had been working on it without her knowing anything about it. He knew she was thinking that maybe she had no part in it, maybe she was all through. Actors led a hell of a life—even the successful ones. He'd never envied them. Backstage, you got the same excitement, the same satisfaction in rounding off a job—Burt never thought of anything he did as creative—and you didn't get your feelings all torn to pieces the way the Cleveland's were at this minute. Burt crammed his notebook into a trouser pocket, gave the trousers a hitch and said, "I'll be on my way, Ike." He didn't envy Ike's job, either.

Dubinsky hadn't risen. It wasn't discourteous, but a way of making things informal and as easy as they could be under the circumstances. He said, "Sit down," and motioned to the red leather chair. His expression was kindly, but she knew he wouldn't be kindly unless everything were over and he felt sorry for her. She didn't want his kindliness. She sat down, put her gloves on her knee and began smoothing them out with great care. Dubinsky waited for her.

Presently she said, "When I was a child I used to smash things sometimes." It wasn't what she had meant to say.

"It's a substitute for something you *can't* smash, isn't it?"

She looked up, startled. "Why, I suppose so . . ."

"It doesn't change anything, of course, but it makes you feel better, doesn't it? It relieves the pressure, clears your mind and afterwards you can think better. Isn't that the way you find it?"

He smiled at her astonishment and saw her expression change and become personal as she tried to make the things he had just been saying fit with the Dubinsky she knew. He had the fleeting thought that it was the first time she had ever been the least curious about him and, when he saw her give it up and return to her own problems, he was amused to discover that he felt vaguely disappointed.

She said, "When I smashed that glass, something inside me smashed too." Then he saw with pleasure that she hadn't liked the sententious sound of her own words. So she had taste—a thing he'd had some doubts about—the artist's kind of instinctive taste which is a matter, not of manners, but of values.

She made a gesture as though she wanted to wipe out the remark. "It was generous of you to say the things you did last night. I'd like to believe them, but I can't. The trouble was—I just wasn't good enough."

"I wasn't good enough either, Willow. I don't suppose it will help much, but I want you to blame me. So often the success or failure of a play—and the fortunes of the people in it—depend not on the actors, but on the judgment, the insight, the ability of the director. It's harder than you would think to see the errors you're making, while the play is in rehearsal. There are some things I should have had you do to the part of Hester that I can see clearly now."

"I guess I didn't even try to do some of the things you told me to do."

A brief smile crossed Dubinsky's face. "No, you didn't. But that's largely the result of inexperience. You have to learn to submit yourself entirely to the director, do your best to try to understand what he is working for and take all his suggestions. He may fail you in the end, but it's like the captain of a ship. He's only human, but his judgment and his orders have to be final. The system has its faults, but no other system would work at all. But as I said before, I would rather you blamed me than yourself."

She was leaning across the corner of the desk, her hand resting on the pile of sides for the new play. She hadn't noticed what they were. She said, "Isaac, I want you to do something for me. You *must* do it. I want you to let me rehearse the monologue for you, right now, and I want to put into it everything you've told me I should, and this time I want to *really* try. I want you to call a rehearsal today and start doing to the Hester part the things you think should be done. I want to bring Hester alive."

"But, Willow, there isn't any . . ."

"No, no. Don't say anything yet. You'll just say it's too late. Don't even nod your head like that. I won't be beaten. Maybe I am beaten, but I want to do it anyway. Isaac, I've been thinking about things all night. I still want to be a success in the theater more than I want anything in the world. I want it enough to try to be honest with myself, because I think that's the only way I can get it. It took me a long time to see it this way, but I know now I've been pretending to myself. I've been standing in my own way. You tried to make me see that once. I do see it now. Perhaps I *am* beaten, but before the play closes, if there's time, I want to do Hester *right*. Can't you see I can't quit and leave things as they are?"

She stopped and he sat very still, staring at the steeple he was making out of his fingers. He looked grave and his face was flushed.

He knew how much this had cost her, how bitter the night must have been to bring her to this point. After a while he said, "I don't think you ought to hope . . ."

"I'm not hoping anything."

He smiled a little then, and she saw that he knew she did still have hope. She hadn't known it herself until then.

She said, "Can't you grow up in a single night? I feel as though I have."

"You can get a grown-up understanding, Willow. You've had a great shock and a great disappointment. You've been thinking about it a great deal and trying to think objectively, which is courageous. You've seen things as they are, not as you want them to be. Let's say that you've had a sort of revelation of what it means to be grown up. It's what you do from now on that counts. Maturity isn't a permanent state but a life-long series of small choices between one way and another way."

"If you help me . . ."

"No one can help you. You chose to come here this morning and have this talk, and that was a mature choice. Last night, by saying what I did, I offered you an easy way out by making it possible for you to transfer all the blame to me. You didn't take it, and that was an exceedingly mature choice. Every day you'll be confronted with the necessity of making such choices, and maturity is something which must be perpetually reaffirmed."

She was looking down at the pile of sides under her hand, thinking about what he was saying. He stopped talking to her because he saw she had just discovered what it was her hand was resting on. She took her hand away, and the look on her face was the same as it had been when she first saw the model of the stage. He leaned back in his chair, giving her time, wondering why he didn't end her uncertainty and his own here and now, by denying her the part or giving it to her. He had never found a decision so hard to make. Was it weakness on his part or a justified uncertainty?

She was holding the fingers of one hand with the other, as though the contact with the sides had burned her. How little he really knew about her in any factual sense, where she came from, her background! Was she married, as that fellow claimed? Strange that things like these should weigh not at all in the decision he had to make, canceled out by her own determination to lead the life she wanted. Strange, too, that he felt so little compunction about her feelings when it was a question of the ultimate good of the play. But she was in earnest now—more so, he'd guess, than she had ever been, and if she wanted to rehearse, that, at least, he could do for her.

He said, "All right, we'll rehearse, if you like."

He could see she hadn't taken in his words. He said, "If you would like to, we'll do some work on Hester this morning. You're not too tired?"

"Oh, *no!*"

He thought that her eyes didn't look as tired as the rest of her face. His words had made her forget the sides and her eyes looked clear and fresh and very blue. He said, "I want to say a few things first. It's probably too late to save *The Rungs of the Ladder,* and you ought to understand that. It's only once in a great while that a play can be turned into a success while it's in its run. If you want to improve your work by rehearsing, I'm willing to help you as much as I can, but I don't want you to have any false hopes."

"I know. I understand that."

"Good. Then there's another thing. Your friend Mr. Lailey has underwritten the run of this play for two weeks. If the audiences drop off rapidly in the next few days, I should not feel inclined to hold him to that agreement. Let me add, however, that I don't think it likely. What we have on our hands in *The Rungs of the Ladder* is not a success and not quite a failure. We'll know more about that tonight. Now there's one thing I want to know. You've had a real taste of the theater and its difficulties and you say you still want to stay in theater work. If that's the way you really feel, I might be able to tell you some things which would be helpful."

Involuntarily, her eyes went to the pile of sides for the new play. She had not meant to betray her awareness of them again. She glanced at Dubinsky and his lack of expression told her that he had read her thoughts.

He said, "Do you want to stay in the theater even if you have to begin all over again with a small part?"

She didn't answer at once. She began to trace, with one finger, the curve of the arm of the chair, and her face grew flushed. Then she said, "Yes, if . . ." and stopped.

"If—what?"

"I'd be perfectly willing to begin at the bottom again if I thought that some day . . . Isaac, I don't want to be a second-rater. I don't want to do it unless there's a real chance that I can learn to be good —really good."

"Nobody can tell you that, Willow. It depends on yourself. You have it in you. If you don't let yourself be distracted or let the hard work discourage you, and if you remember some of the things you learned last night. If you 'grow up,' as you call it."

"But you think I have it in me?"

"I think you do. I can't say any more than that."

"Then—oh, Isaac!"

"But you've got a lot to learn. I don't mean merely the technique of acting. You're intelligent—you'll pick that up as you go along, and any good director can help you. I'm thinking about your attitude toward your work. We discussed it once before. You're a hard worker, and that's to your credit. You're trying to learn one of the most difficult of all crafts, and one in which you'll have a great deal of competition. In the long run you get into a part, into the portrayal of a character, exactly what you put into it. If you are an insensitive, unimaginative person, the portrayal is sure to be insensitive and unimaginative. If you are unintelligent, your portrayal is unintelligent, and so on.

"Now, I don't think that you are unimaginative, and intelligence is often a fair substitute for sensitivity. I don't think your trouble is any fundamental lack. If I did I'd advise you to give up acting. Your fault is what you say yourself, that you stand in your own light, so to speak. You have the qualities, but you want to be a

Lailey was not there, and Sam was not sure that what he felt at this discovery was relief or just the contrary. Dubinsky was sitting in the middle of the house, a lonely figure in a sea of empty seats. Dubinsky seemed to sense Sam's presence for he glanced around and then got up. As he came near to the place where Sam was standing, Sam spoke to him.

"I want to watch her."

Dubinsky stood with his hands clasped behind his back and he waited a moment before answering. Then he said, "All right, you can stay," and turned away but he stopped again and said, "I didn't tell her you were coming." Then he went back to his seat.

Sam found a place to sit where it was darkest, turned down the seat beside him, put his coat and hat on it and tried to make himself feel at ease. The curtain was raised and the set, in the cold white light of the arc lamp, looked to him shockingly tawdry. What he had taken to be paneling was revealed as paint, and crudely daubed at that. Books in the bookcase, which he had assumed to be real, were painted also. This dusty sham made the fascination of the theater all the more inexplicable to him. Two stagehands were moving furniture into place, making a great deal of unnecessary noise. A slight youth in dirty blue work-clothes was walking around, shading his eyes with his hand, peering upward. Another youth, with something that looked like a drawing board under his arm, came to the edge of the stage.

"You want the book held, Mr. Dubinsky?"

"Certainly I want the book held."

"All right, sir. Gimme a light, Mac."

Burt came on stage. "You want full lights, Ike?"

There was no reply. Waiting, Burt lowered one hip like a tired hack horse. The youth with the drawing board was propping it up against the back of the front row, like a slant-top desk. Mac, squatting at the edge of the stage, was feeding out a length of rubber pipe. "Catch," he said. A match flared and the thing turned out to be a gas fixture fastened to a clamp which fitted the top of the drawingboard. Burt's attention wandered to the stagehands and

216

success more than you want to use your ability for the pure joy of using it. I tell you frankly, Willow, you'll never be the kind of success you want to be unless you are more interested in the craft than in the success, unless you are more ambitious to be a good actress than a successful one, unless all your thinking centers on how good your work is and not on how good people think you are. I'm pretty sure that, with your appearance, you could get leading roles in a certain type of production where looks count more than craftsmanship, but I'm paying you the compliment of believing that's not the kind of success you want. Whether you could ever have the kind you do want, I honestly don't know. I say again, I think you have the qualities. What happened last night has shaken you up, made you think clearly, but whether you have it in you to subordinate your own ego, your own interest in yourself as a person, and whether you have it in you to love good craftsmanship enough to work for it the way you've been working for personal success, I simply don't know."

She was sitting very still, looking at her hands. There was a long silence and then Dubinsky said gently, "I'm afraid those were very harsh things to say. It's a compliment to you, really, that I think you have the fortitude to listen to them."

She looked at him then, and there was a flash of anger in her eyes. "You don't have to compliment me. I can take it without a sugar coat!"

He laughed. "I believe you can. The point is, what will you do with it?"

"You'll see."

"Do you still want to rehearse a while?"

"Yes!"

He laughed again and the laugh had real pleasure in it.

They rehearsed until past lunch time and when they had finished, the call-boy told Dubinsky that there was a gentleman in the greenroom who wanted to see him and that he had been waiting some time. On his way there Dubinsky found Burt and told him to

call a full rehearsal of *The Rungs of the Ladder* for that afternoon
—which wasn't going to be easy for Burt since the cast, not expecting such a thing, was probably scattered all over town. "And,"
Dubinsky said, "send out and get Miss Cleveland something to eat."

Dubinsky's visitor was Hadley. He was standing with his back to
the disorderly fireplace and Dubinsky, greeting him formally, wondered if he had chosen it because a fireplace at the back adds authority to man's attitude toward man. It gave Dubinsky a slight
feeling of pleasure to dislodge him.

"We can't talk here very well. Shall we go to my office?"

Having changed the balance of power by ensconcing himself in
his own swivel chair, Dubinsky inquired, "What can I do for you?"

Sam did not reply at once. He began pacing around the limited
space, as though the thing he had come to say could not easily be
said. The small, crowded office made him look more than ever like
a giant. As he walked, he rested his hand on a pile of books, touched
a chair back and moved restlessly on. He passed the miniature stage
on its tripod two or three times without noticing it, but when he did
he looked startled, and then faintly scornful, and Dubinsky, smiling
inwardly, knew that Hadley thought the thing was some sort of toy
or hobby. Presently Hadley came to stand directly in front of him.

"Look here, I told you something about myself night before last,
at Lailey's house."

"I believe you did."

"Have you mentioned it to anybody?"

"No. It seemed to me that you told me under the stress of emotion and that if you wanted it known, you would not have announced it in just that way."

"That shows considerable insight." Hadley sat down in the chair
beside the desk and crossed his knees. "Does *she* know that you
know?"

"No."

Dubinsky leaned forward to look at his watch, which was lying
face up on the desk. Hadley said quickly, "I won't take your time.
You've answered the question I came to ask, but there is something

I think you ought to know. Maybe she's already told you. She has agreed to give up the stage when the run of this play is over, and to come home."

"No, she hasn't told me that."

Hadley studied the look on Dubinsky's face a moment but it told him nothing. The fellow kept his thoughts to himself. Sam said, "There's hardly been time. It was only agreed on night before last. Perhaps I should have let her tell you herself."

"Perhaps so."

"We'll leave when the run is over. I live in Cleveland."

Dubinsky still said nothing and Sam gave up trying to read his face.

"In the meantime, for the run of the play, I've agreed to say nothing about the fact that she is my wife. She wanted it that way and I agreed. I shouldn't have said anything to you about it at Lailey's but, damn it, my feelings got away from me. Since then, I've talked to her about it myself. I thought I'd better come to see you and ask you not to mention it."

"I wouldn't think of it."

Part of Dubinsky's mind was obviously somewhere else. He looked preoccupied, as well as troubled, and Sam thought he knew why. He said, "I gather the play is not a success."

"No, not a success, though she can have the satisfaction—if it is any satisfaction—of knowing it's on the border line. It's almost a success, or hasn't failed by very much, however you want to put it."

"Do you anticipate any run at all, or will it close at once?"

"It may have a run of two weeks. Possibly more, though that's unlikely. I'm glad you came in and told me this because productions overlap and we'll be starting on the work for a new play right away. If she's really going home after this run, I'll make my plans without her. As a matter of fact, I was very hesitant about renewing her contract anyway."

"Then her leaving won't inconvenience you too much."

"It's nothing to which I can take any exception, if she stays to the end of the run."

Sam smiled suddenly and Dubinsky watched the change it made in him with interest.

"I don't like to play the part of a tyrannical husband, I assure you."

Dubinsky rocked silently for a minute. He was thinking back over the things Willow had said to him that morning. Nothing in them to indicate that what this fellow said was true. He studied Sam thoughtfully. What he had just said had the ring of truth—the man himself had about him an air of indisputable honesty. If there were subterfuge, Willow would be the one . . .

"I gather," he said, "you're not asking my co-operation in persuading her to give up the stage?"

"No. She's consented to that."

"I may as well tell you—though I believe the question isn't likely to arise—that if she seems, in the end, to be the best choice for a part in our new production, it will be offered to her without reference to what you've just told me."

"Why so? Surely . . ."

"In the first place, she herself has not yet told me she is giving up the theater and in the second place . . ." Dubinsky smiled. "I have my own interests to look after." The smile faded. "There's more to it than that. If she is not offered a part, it isn't because I'm willing to back you up. I recognize her right to freedom of choice. Call it a matter of principle, if you like."

Dubinsky watched with interest while Hadley thought this over. When, a moment later, Hadley raised his head and looked at Dubinsky, his eyes were smiling. Dubinsky found himself regarding the big man with liking. A good opponent—with qualities in him you relied on without further thought, even if he were an opponent.

As though to confirm this, Sam said, "I think I see your position. Fair enough."

Dubinsky, feeling now more inwardly at ease with this man than a few minutes ago he would have dreamed possible, said expansively, "I feel I owe her something. She has really worked extraor-

dinarily hard and well, and the failure of the play isn't altogether her fault. I've already talked to her about that. I really feel I owe her something. It's hard for a layman to understand the problems and difficulties that an actor has to meet. It comes as a complete surprise to me that she has agreed to go home, but if she has, I have an idea that it would help her in the future if you knew a little more about these problems. Please don't think that I have it in mind to influence your course of action in any way. The thought occurs to me, however, that if you were to see her working, if you were to come here and watch a rehearsal, you might have a clearer idea of what she is up against. It should make for a better mutual understanding. What do you think of the idea?"

"It would be interesting to watch a rehearsal. Beyond that, I can't say. It wouldn't, of course, influence the decision, but I'll come to one, if you like. I'll be glad to."

"There'll be one today. No, better give her a chance to get used to the changes I'm going to make. Come tomorrow morning at ten, if you like."

"I'll try to make it."

Sam went slowly down the stairs. He should, he knew, be feeling satisfaction at the way things were working out. If no new contract were to be given her, she would probably come home without being forced to. But the thought brought him none of the satisfaction it should. She would be heartbroken, and he discovered now that he didn't want it that way. He would prefer that she had succeeded. Was it just that he preferred to win in a fight rather than to have her beaten into submission by circumstances? But—he would rather have had her succeed! Preoccupied by these thoughts, in the maze of corridors he took the wrong turning.

He realized this at once, because it brought him close to the dressing room which had the white star painted on it. He stood by it and listened. There were sounds inside and it gave him a strange feeling to know that she was there. He had not thought of seeing her, but now he knew that he could not go away unless he did. It was a feeling stronger than his judgment. He was wondering what

reason he might give himself or her for intruding on her, when he saw Lailey hurrying down the corridor. Lailey was walking swiftly but with bent head so that he did not see Sam until they met, almost in front of Willoughby's door.

The encounter was plainly a shock to Lailey. Finding this interloper, this comparative stranger, hanging around Willow's door, and in the morning when he should have been at work, instantly aroused his antagonism.

He said, "Hadley! What the hell are you doing here?" and tried to place himself between Sam and Willoughby's door.

The proprietorship of Lailey's manner was even more of a shock to Sam who, in his mind, had just repossessed his wife.

"What am *I* doing? For Christ's sake, what are *you* doing? That's a question I want to ask you—what are you up to? What is this game?"

"Game! See here, Hadley . . ."

"You get the hell out and leave her alone, will you?"

They were shouting, and inside the dressing room there was an electric stillness. The stage door opened and Burt came out and leaned his lanky form on the rail of the landing above their heads.

"*You're* the one who's going to leave her alone. I asked you to my house to meet her, and what do you do—you come butting in where you're not wanted. Every time I turn around, for the love of God, there you are."

"By God, you . . . If you only knew it, *you're* the one who's butting in . . ."

"How can you say such a thing?"

"You know damn well . . ."

"Ask her, then, ask her. Let's have a showdown. She's in there now—knock on her door and ask her which one is butting in."

"*Both of you leave her alone!*"

Dubinsky had come up behind them. He was blazing with anger, as he often was in rehearsal. Sam, who had never seen the metamorphosis of the little producer from quietness to explosive emotion, was silenced by it, but not Lailey.

"Listen, Isaac, this big gorilla is making a pest of himself, annoying Willow. I'm trying to stop it."

"I don't care what you're trying to do. I won't have rows in my theater. Burt, what's the matter with you? Why didn't you stop it?"

Burt shifted his weight, glanced at Hadley's bulk and was silent.

"Holy Moses, I could hear you way upstairs! I won't have disturbances of this sort in my theater. If you want to shout, go out in the alley. This is not a public place. I'll ask you both to leave."

"You'd better keep out of this. It's a private matter between this fellow Lailey and myself. It's got to be settled now."

Burt came quietly down the steps.

Lailey said, "Yes, keep out of this, Isaac. It hasn't anything to do with you."

"This is my theater. I give orders in it. You will both leave at once, and hereafter . . ."

The door of the dressing room was thrown open and Willoughby stood there, in a wrinkled wrapper with slippers on her bare feet and her hair down around her shoulders. Back of her, Suzanne's face looked like a polished yellow mask.

"Stop it!" Willoughby said. "Stop it! Stop it! Stop it! I've only a little while to rest before rehearsal and you . . . Oh, leave me alone! What I'm trying to do is more important to me than both of you put together."

Lailey went to her and tried to take her hands.

"Darling, please!"

Sam said, "*Leave her alone!*" All the unnatural restraints that Sam, the man of action, had been putting on himself began to give way. As though a dam had broken, every penned-up and blocked emotion rushed suddenly into this outlet.

Lailey was facing him again, the light eyes bright with anger, and Burt moved closer, but it was Sam he was watching. Sam said in a low voice, "So now you call her *darling*."

Burt was not quick enough. There was no warning of the blow at all. It landed on the side of Lailey's chin and the sound of it, sickening and brutal, filled a second of appalling silence before

213

Lailey crashed backward into the side of the stage steps and Willoughby said, "Oh, God."

Burt and Dubinsky made a barricade of themselves in front of Sam. Willoughby went back into the dressing room. Dubinsky said to Sam, "That's enough. Now get out!" Lailey was holding his hand against his chin. When he took it away there was some blood on it. Now Burt was watching *him*. The light eyes were almost white with the heat of his anger. Lailey turned the white-hot look on Sam. Burt braced himself. He caught Lailey's lunge on his forearm and Lailey's back hit the wall of the steps again.

Sam scarcely noticed Lailey. He seemed to be coming to himself slowly, as though he only now realized what was going on. He looked first at Dubinsky and then into the dressing room where Willoughby was sitting on the bench, staring resentfully at them.

Dubinsky said, "I'd go now, if I were you—if you think you've done harm enough. Lailey is going, too, I assure you."

Burt picked Sam's hat off the floor and held it out to him. Sam took it and turned away. Before he left, he glanced once more into the dressing room.

Chapter Fourteen

SAM went to the rehearsal. At breakfast, he and Mike had some angry words when Mike heard that he would not be in the office. Mike was uneasy about the company stock. He couldn't give Sam any real reason for the uneasiness except that, just before the Market had closed the price had jumped around—from seventeen to eighteen and a half, to seventeen and a quarter, to nineteen and back to seventeen. It had felt, as Mike put it, like a fish nibbling a line. Mike had been troubled by it, but not Sam. At breakfast, Sam said in his big, confident way, "Nothing's going to happen, fella. What could happen, anyway?" He didn't tell Mike where he was going and Mike left before he did.

Sam was not sure that Dubinsky would welcome his presence after his fight with Lailey and he did not care particularly to see the rehearsal but he wanted to be at the theater in case Lailey tried to come near Willoughby again. He thought that, if he found Lailey there, he would probably beat hell out of him because, whether he loved her or not, Willoughby was still his wife. He found one of the front doors of the theater open and went through the lobby and quietly into the house. Here he concealed himself in the shadows and looked around.

Dubinsky said, "Yes, full lights of course." Mac looked up, startled, rose from his squatting position and crossed the stage at a dog-trot. "Let's get going, Burt," Dubinsky said. He was lounging, relaxed in his chair, but his voice sounded irritable.

Hadley found all this astonishingly interesting. These people seemed completely at home in a world that was wholly unreal to him. The light on the stage was growing brighter by jerks. Burt said, addressing himself to the wings, "All right, son. Places." A cheerful young voice rang out, "*Pla*-ces." Burt said, "Gimme a copy of the script, will you? I'm taking John." "Why?" Dubinsky asked. "Couldn't locate him, Ike." Far off and faintly the boy called "*Pla*-ces" again. The youth wedged in behind the drawing board stood up with difficulty and threw a brown pamphlet across the foots. It opened up and sailed like a bird past Burt's hands. "For Christ sake," Burt said without passion. One of the stagehands picked it up and handed it to him, and he slapped it against the seat of his pants.

Then suddenly the stage was empty and there was tension in the air. The books had become real books once more; the paneling was oak. The youth was leaning over his board and Dubinsky was sitting forward with one hand on the back of the seat in front of him. Sam found that he had begun to breathe more quickly. For a second nothing happened, and then a rustling sound filled the air. Sam heard it before he saw that it was the curtain coming down. It went up almost immediately. The actors were in their places and the play began. Then Sam remembered that Willoughby did not come on at once. He sat back, mildly astonished that he, too, had been holding himself tense.

Dubinsky had sidled out of his seat with the rapid, practiced motion all theater people acquire. He walked up the aisle with his head bowed, and Sam knew by the set of his shoulders that the scene was going all right and that Dubinsky was bored. Presently he lost track of the little producer and the treadmill of his own thoughts superseded the action on the stage. If, as Dubinsky claimed, there was more to this life than show-off and bohemian excitement, it certainly was not apparent to him. In fact, what he had just seen made it seem more unattractive and cheap than ever, though he was now willing to concede the inherent excitement, having himself just become a victim of it with no more to cause it than an empty stage.

He had meant to watch for Willow's entrance but, in the midst of these thoughts, he forgot. There she was, saying, *It was so good of you all to come and visit me for this weekend,* and with her coming the whole scene heightened perceptibly. That quality, whatever it was, he could see plainly any star must have. It had been there on opening night and there was, as far as he could see, no difference in the way she was playing the part now. Dubinsky was standing in the aisle with his hand on the back of a seat, and he seemed tense and very attentive. Presently he made a slight gesture with his hands, palms out, and it was full of weariness and discouragement. He threw himself into a seat and began to beat with his clenched fist on the arm.

Just then Willoughby stopped in the middle of a sentence and said, "Ike, I want to take it over from my entrance, please."

The sudden break in the illusion of the play was a shock and Sam guessed that a convention, which kept the actors from volunteering remarks or ever speaking out of their parts, had been violated.

"All right." Dubinsky did not seem to mind, but his voice sounded strained, and when he had spoken, he pulled out a handkerchief and patted his face all over. He seemed to be expending a great deal of emotion and Sam wondered why that was necessary. Willoughby left the stage. The youth behind the drawing board read a line in a sing-song voice, one of the actors repeated it with expression, and there she was again. Sam thought, how odd—she's different now—she isn't sure of herself. Then, with a sudden flare of interest, no, by God, it's *Hester* who isn't sure of herself. He leaned forward in his seat to watch intently.

Hester now, not Willoughby. Willoughby was gone and this arrogant, patronizing—and unsure—woman was in her place. On

218

opening night it had been Willoughby all the time, but now her familiar personality had simply vanished. How had she brought that about? Sam saw that Dubinsky was on his feet. Something electric was in the air. The other actors were working with intensity, trying, obviously, to adapt themselves to this new condition, nor minding, since this was a rehearsal, if their concentration was apparent. Burt in his work clothes looked odd among the actors. He was reading the part of John from the script in a flat, self-conscious way, and going through the stage business competently but without putting anything of John in it. Whenever he finished speaking his lines, he scratched his ear or hitched up his trousers, but once Sam saw him watching Willoughby with alert eyes.

When, suddenly, Dubinsky threw his arms in the air and shouted, "Hold it, hold it," Sam felt a sense of outrage. The action stopped and Sam had his first experience of the actor's lightning change back into himself. A whole set of different people, and Willoughby—not Hester, but Willoughby—stood there, and all of them showed signs of their exertion which had not been visible before. Sam was suddenly convinced that this was one of the most absorbing experiences he had ever had in his life. He was not even aware that he had forgotten his own problems.

Dubinsky said, "Willow," dropping the single word into the stillness. She stepped forward, and as he walked down the slope of the aisle to the orchestra rail, she came to the edge of the stage.

"Yes, Ike?"

"Do you think you've got it now?"

They were looking at each other as though there were no one else in the theater and speaking in low voices that Sam could barely hear. All the waiting people on the stage were watching them.

"Yes, I've got it."

"Sure?"

"Sure."

"All right, then."

There was a quality in Dubinsky's tone which Sam found moving. It was gentle, but there was a teacher's satisfaction in it and there was confidence. Strangely, the short passage of commonplace words held real beauty and Sam thought, I'm going to have an open mind. If the fellow thinks I've made a mistake, I'm going to give him a fair chance to show me. The resolution made him feel better than he had for a long time.

Willoughby was going to her place, but she turned back abruptly.

"Ike."

"Yes, darling."

"You know that part where I say, *I used to be shy and afraid of everybody and self-conscious. You wouldn't believe it now, would you? I made up my mind one day not to be, that life was too short to care what people thought of you, and from that day I haven't been self-conscious any more.* Couldn't we play that up, Ike—because, of course, it isn't true. Not a word of it, but it's the key to Hester."

"Yes, I think we could. It means more now, doesn't it?"

"And John says, *You couldn't find a better equipment for success than a feeling of inferiority—a feeling that you have to show people —if, at the same time, you have a fighting nature like yours, Hester.* It's almost the key to the whole play, Ike. And I was thinking—after he's said it, could John laugh—because, of course, he sees through Hester?"

"Yes, that's good. Take it, will you, Burt?"

"*Me?*"

"Yes, laugh. You can do it." Dubinsky was smiling, and some of the others smiled too. Burt looked miserable and resigned. Dubinsky went on, "There's nothing important in between. Let's take it now. Give us a cue, will you?"

The youth at the drawing board scrabbled papers and Willoughby said, "We ought to change my business a little, hadn't we, Ike? It isn't a casual remark if we do it that way. How if I get up from the tea table . . ."

"Have you something in mind?"

"Yes."

"All right. Let's see it. Cue."

There was a hurried regaining of places and the cue was given. Dubinsky sat down.

I used to be shy and afraid of everybody and self-conscious . . .

Willoughby rose and clasped her hands on her breast.

You wouldn't believe it now, would you?

Her hands still clasped, she turned her body to left and right.

"No! Holy Moses, no!"

Dubinsky was on his feet shouting. Everybody froze like statues. After the last explosive "no" the silence was absolute.

"Of all the ridiculous . . ."

Willoughby lowered her arms. Dubinsky was deep in thought, hunched over, gripping the back of the seat in front of him. After a minute he raised his head.

"Try not getting up. Turn your chair so you aren't crowded by the table. Sit sidewise and make a sort of sweeping gesture, like this." Dubinsky waved his arm and Willoughby strained to see him. Burt, who had caught the gesture, reproduced it for her and Sam smiled. Dubinsky said, "Cue," and sat down.

This time he let the speech run to the end. Burt read John's lines, paused and then got out a sepulchral, graveyard laugh. Sam smiled again and saw that most of the actors were having a hard time not to laugh. Sam knew that Dubinsky was smiling too, for the atmosphere was suddenly relaxed and easy.

Dubinsky said in a mild tone, "No, that won't do either," and Sam, annoyed, thought when it's *his* mistake he doesn't shout.

They went over it again and then again and again. They repeated it, in all, more than a dozen times, punctuated always by Burt's unnatural laugh. Sometimes Dubinsky shouted, sometimes he was quiet and sad, and Sam, twisting and turning in his seat, grew angry long before they were through. Then his anger dissolved in admiration of Willoughby's calmness and patience. *He* couldn't do it, and the fellow shouldn't ask *her* to. It must be hot up there under those lights and he could smell the gas way back where he sat. Up on the stage they were breathing it.

"No, that won't do. Take it again."

Sam began to suffer for her. She ought to protest.

"Take it again."

He was all on Willoughby's side now, hating Dubinsky.

"Take it again."

Damn the fellow.

"Take it again."

Now his admiration for her was unbounded. She was standing this ordeal with dignity and patience, making of herself a kind of instrument to transmit the fellow's muddled ideas. She showed no trace of fatigue, nor did the others, for that matter, though Sam himself was tired and strained from merely watching them.

Dubinsky seemed to have come to the end of his resources. Willoughby had just tried the speech standing in the window with her back to the stage, and Burt had laughed his hollow laugh. There was general silence, everybody waiting for Dubinsky, and he seemed to have nothing to offer. Finally he said slowly, "That's nearly right, but it needs some little thing. She ought to speak that speech as though every word were true, but indicate somehow, without emphasizing it too much, that it isn't true."

Silence.

"Willow, if this were real life, if you were really Hester, what would you do?"

She came slowly and thoughtfully back to the tea table and sat down. The other actors, who had relapsed into being themselves, did not put on their stage personalities. It seemed to be understood, by means of one of those mysterious, wordless communications which interested and awed Sam, that this time the scene was a matter between Willoughby and the director. She rose again and walked slowly to the window. It was Hester, showing unconsciously by the way she walked that she was aware she was the focal point of the others' emotions. She clutched her tea napkin in her hand. Sam sat forward on his seat.

I used to be shy and afraid of everybody and self-conscious. Her back was toward the others. She turned around and faced them.

beam to her feet, he turned to face her. She was sitting with her arms thrown out along the tops of the cushions in the bold, provocative pose he disliked. Her knees were crossed and she was swinging her foot in quick jerks.

"Shall we go up?" he said quietly, hoping to head off the storm.

The foot stopped swinging. "Sam, how much longer do we have to stay in this nasty little house?"

In the first place, he thought, planning his reply but not speaking aloud, it isn't a nasty little house. He decided not to put it that way. He stood staring at the pattern of the silk across her knees, and he must have looked discouraged. He certainly felt it. For a moment he let go of everything in his mind and thought about nothing at all but the smell of the extinguished candles. Then he sighed and sat down beside her.

"Willoughby, I've told you so many times. We need to put the money back in the plant. We've just come out of the longest business revulsion in history, and I'm using all the money I can lay hands on to convert one hundred percent to steel, and to expand."

"That's ridiculous. We've got to live!"

"We're living better than most of your friends right now."

She leaped to her feet and walked rapidly across the room. "I won't stand it. I won't be laughed at and looked down on!"

"Have you lost your mind? Nobody's looking down on you."

"Everybody is. That little cat. Everybody."

Suddenly all his patience had deserted him.

"You'll live as I like!"

"I will *not!* I didn't marry you to live like *this.*" She swept her hand in a half-circle to indicate the smallness of the exquisite room. "I ought to leave you. You're president of the company—you own the mills. You must be rich. I'll leave you if you make me go on living this way."

"So you've said it at last! That's all you married me for—money. And passion. What a Goddamn fool I was."

He covered his face with his hands and when he took them away again she was standing there looking at him. In her evening dress, standing so still in the half light, scarcely breathing, there was something unreal, something shimmering about her. It made him quiet, and it made his heart beat faster. Then he saw that there were tears in her eyes. He got up slowly. He didn't know what he was going to do.

She came right up to him then and put her arms around his neck. He let her do that without moving.

"Sam, you don't understand." She was speaking quietly but with a fierce intensity behind the words. "You don't understand. I *want* things. I want them terribly. But sometimes I don't know what it is I want. Sam, love me, please. Love me!"

He pushed the beer mug away from him. He couldn't think about that night calmly even now and he guessed his emotions showed in his face, for he was aware that the bartender was watching him. He shifted his chair around so that his back was toward the bar. In this new place the sawdust on the floor was undisturbed and he felt it crunch under his feet.

At least he had had sense enough to realize that she was miserably unhappy, and generosity enough to be sorry, though he had no sympathy for the cause. She had used a curious phrase. "I *need* a beautiful house, can't you see I *need* it?" You didn't need a bigger or more magnificent house if the one you had was perfectly adequate. But if what she had really needed was more scope for a talent that was bursting its bonds, then the agonized cry had meaning. The house was just a symbol. It was a way of life she wanted, a chance to play a more important role—but that had not been evident to him.

"Sam, love me." She clung to him as she seldom did, and there were fire and urgency in her begging. Her hands grasped his shoulders and she strained up to him.

She was unhappy, and penitent too—or so he thought. He kissed her once, and the smell of her perfume was stronger than the smell of the dead candles. They left the room hand in hand.

228

Had she led him or had he led her? He couldn't remember, but it came back to him that they went up the stairs silently, not looking at each other, solemn, both going swiftly toward the same goal. Near the top of the flight he put his arm around her waist. His motions were quick and sure. She came closer to him but she did not turn her head and she kept on mounting the stair. Her train made a soft whispering sound, dragging behind her. They were both breathing quickly and by the time they reached the top his heart was beating in great thumps.

He stopped her. He had to know whether her heart was beating like that too, and with the sureness of touch that had come to him, he put his hand on her brocaded bodice. He felt her heart beat, not slow and thick like his, but light and wild and swift, and it wrung a strange sound out of him but no words. Then he saw her eyes, eager and demanding and not far from anger, and his feelings rose to an intensity that was insupportable. He pulled her toward her door.

She stopped him. "The maid's in there. Wait here and I'll get rid of her."

He went a little way down the hall, by the rail along the stair well, and waited in the shadows. The big clock was ticking, steadily and slow. Its calmness annoyed him. He leaned against the rail, half sitting on it, and put his hands around it because they were shaking. Presently the door opened and her maid came running out, not Suzanne then, but a flighty young thing called Madeleine. The girl ran bent over, the way people run away from burning buildings, and Sam laughed, a deep, hearty, coarse laugh that made him feel good. Then he straightened up because Willoughby was standing in the doorway, and she was laughing too.

If you tried to suppress at talent, put the lid on it, keep it from expressing itself, could you succeed? Unconsciously, he had tried to do just that, though he was scarcely to be blamed since he, no more than she, knew what she wanted or how her nature was trying to fulfill itself. A grander house would not have been the answer—or not for very long. But if, knowingly or otherwise, you did succeed in keeping a talent from its rightful channel, wouldn't it only burst out with force somewhere else? Almost surely the warped direction would be bad, perhaps evil. The force would have to vent itself somehow, creating cravings for things which would not satisfy, prompting actions which would bring no relief.

He had lain on his back with his ankles crossed and his hands under his head, half dozing, not caring whether the sharp angle of his elbow covered most of her pillow. And she, pliant and soft now, lay on her side, one arm thrown across his chest. He felt her hair tickling the fine hairs on his arm, and knew that in a moment it would annoy him and then he would raise himself with an effort and sit on the side of the bed. He wanted to put it off, for when that happened they would be their normal selves again—or perhaps not quite, since they had come so close. He had even wondered if this might not be a new beginning.

She stirred and began to kiss him softly, his cheek, his neck, his shoulder, dozens of tiny kisses, and he lay still, not responding in any way, his thoughts wandering off while she kissed him. Presently she raised herself on her elbow and he turned his head to look at her. The golden hair cascaded over her shoulder and she tipped her head back to make it fall away from her face. She looked very young and serious, and he smiled a little, enjoying the feeling of detachment and peace.

"Sam."

He came a little further back into the real world, and he supposed it must have shown in his eyes because she seemed to know she had his attention.

"Sam, I can have it, can't I? We'll build it?"

"What?" He didn't quite take it in.

"The house, stupid."

He stared at her incredulously. After a minute, he said quietly, "Was that why? . . ."

She laughed, and it sounded throaty and insolent. "I give you what *you* want."

230

He raised himself and sat on the side of the bed and rubbed his face with his hands. He was very tired, and the old weight seemed to have settled back on his shoulders. He didn't want to talk about it. If he went to his own room now before they said any more, he might be able to forget it. He started to get up, but she put an arm on his shoulder from behind, holding him down. She leaned her body against his bent back and put her cheek against the base of his neck. Her cheek felt feverish.

"Sam, please!"

She ran the palm of her hand over his back and he held himself in, hating her touch.

"Sam, I *need* a beautiful house. Can't you see I *need* it?"

"And so to get it, you . . . Christ!"

He was on his feet facing her, and he hated his own nakedness because it made him feel vulnerable. He felt miles away from her, lonely, sorry for himself. She was lying on her side, propped up on one elbow, and she reached down and slowly drew the sheet most of the way over her, but she never took her eyes off his.

"I can't go on in this horrid, disgusting place. I can't, Sam. Let me have the new one, and . . ."

She didn't finish her sentence, but she didn't need to. He drew a fortifying breath so that he could control himself enough to speak reasonably, but suddenly it was all too much for him and he yelled at her. "Goddamn it, no!" He felt the sweat break out all over him.

They had stared at each other for a long time, she with the sheet drawn up to her chin, he trembling in convulsive jerks, their eyes franker than they had ever been. He had the feeling that a great deal was happening between them in that few minutes, but he was past caring. Let it all come out in the open at last.

What a fool she must have thought him—using sex so openly to get her own way. That was what maddened him. He picked up the empty beer mug and began to pound it on the table until he realized what he was doing and shoved it away again. But why shouldn't she use her sex? Hadn't he been taken in that way when he asked her to marry him and she was trying to save herself from the collapse of her father's fortune? And no doubt on countless other occasions . . . His mind shied away from searching them out. He tried to make himself think of her as he had just seen her, working on the stage, a stranger to him in her patience and her intelligence. These qualities must have been in her all along but he had never made any attempt to see them. She gave him just what he demanded—sex and decoration. So why shouldn't she use sex to gain her own ends? Why shouldn't she? Perhaps now, at long last, after the struggles and the hates and the lust, they were growing up, himself as well as she, and in the process they were losing each other.

There had been no tears. She had been the first to lower her eyes, as she began to trace the line of a crease in the sheet with the tip of her finger. He knew that she would say something in a minute and that their life wouldn't be quite the same afterward. He didn't even have to brace himself for it.

"Sam, I think I want to go away for a while. A good long while."

For a minute he thought more about the impression he had that she, too, was relieved now that things were in the open than about the actual purport of her words. Finally he came to himself with a little start. "All right," he said. "All right. Anything you like."

She had started to say all sorts of things then. But he had said, "Never mind that now. It's after two. I have to work tomorrow." He went out and shut the door.

Her preparations for leaving were feverish, though she had the grace to try to hide them from him. She was bright and cheerful to him, and he did his best to behave as though nothing unusual were afoot. He took her to the station, and she cried, and he was sure they were real tears. They waved at each other through the window until the train pulled out, and then he walked away with his hands in his pockets, feeling free and at loose ends and thoroughly miserable.

232

Looking back on it now, he didn't know whether he had really believed she would be back soon or just assumed it because he didn't want to think about it more than he had to.

So now this was the end. He could feel that it was the end, that everything was finished. He looked back on their stormy life together and knew that they could never revive it. He wondered if she knew it too. Of course she did. She had known it, probably, when she lay in his arms—was it only two nights ago? What thoughts had filled her mind then, while he held her? She had used sex again because she still thought it was the only thing he could understand. And she had been right.

After a while he took out his watch. He sat with the watch in his hand without looking at it. Lettie had said he should set her free— give her a divorce, was what she meant. He wondered how people went about getting a divorce. Plenty of them did it on the quiet and it was only talked about guardedly afterward, the way any scandal is. Then he realized he was not thinking about two strangers getting a divorce, but about himself and Willoughby, and the realization gave him a shock, as though it were actually the first time he had had such a thought. He dropped his watch back in his pocket and fished out money for the beer. He didn't want to face Mike and the office just now. He'd find a place to eat some lunch, maybe walk a while and not go back to the brownstone until he had had time to calm down a little. He threw the money on the table, stood up, looked around for his coat and found he still had it on. He crossed the sawdust-covered floor with his old lightness of step, struck one of the short, swinging doors a blow with his fist and went out, leaving the door snapping back and forth on its thick spring. It wasn't until he stood outside, looking at the theater across the street, that he actually said to himself in so many words that he was going to give Willoughby a divorce.

Chapter Fifteen

SAM walked until his big body was tired and his mind purged of thought. Then he went home to the brownstone and let himself in with his key. He entered the dim hall quietly because he wasn't ready yet to face Lettie's understanding eyes.

The coat rack, which also combined a box seat and a looking glass, was, as usual, overloaded. He found space on it with difficulty. Then there was the problem of his hat. He finally deposited it on top of some books and a candy box which had holes punched in the lid, smiling because Lettie's special brand of disorder, though sometimes inconvenient, had a way of making a house seem comfortable. A faint sound of scrabbling came from within the box and Sam, realizing it probably housed Dulcie's chameleon, moved his hat away from the air holes. He turned away and found, now that his mind would let him think about it, that he was very tired. He glanced around him at various objects in the hall, the vase of cattails, the Japanese fans stuck in the velvet frame of a dark oil painting, the butterflies painted on the glass shade of the light which had to be kept burning here, even in the daytime, and at the decorated drain pipe crammed with umbrellas. These homelike things seemed to take the ache from his tiredness. He would have liked to linger among them.

Upstairs, the living room door opened and Mike's voice called, "That you, Sam?"

"Yeah, be right up."

The dog Shamrock came from the back regions of the house, swinging a feathered tail, and Sam stooped to pat him, half thinking, but without his mind taking any alarm from the thought, that it was early for Mike to be back. Sam was still reluctant to let himself be possessed by other people. He had been too far away to come back easily to the everyday world, and the decision to give Willoughby her freedom had been torn from himself with too much struggle. He was not yet ready to begin relating it, in the many ways which would shortly be necessary, to his everyday life. He said, "Good boy," to Shamrock and started slowly up the stairs.

Lettie was with Mike. They were both leaning over the banisters, and when he saw their expressions, he moved faster.

"Is anything the matter?"

"Yes," said Michael.

Lettie said, "It isn't Claire."

Claire! He had not known that she was anywhere in his mind but now, hurrying up the last steps, she seemed suddenly to flood his thoughts, like opening a door on the morning. For the first time he realized that he could, if he wanted to, think of Claire in a new way. He wanted to be alone with this discovery, but instead he heard himself saying, "What's wrong, Mike?"

In the living room, Mike turned angrily to face him.

"By God, if you don't pay attention to your own company's business I'm through."

"Tell him what's happened," Lettie said quietly.

But Michael began to pace up and down the pleasant, untidy room. His hands were jammed into his pockets, his stocky shoulders swung as he walked and his black eyes were hard with anger. He stopped pacing and said, "Let's sit down." His voice was controlled but the anger was still back of his words.

They all three found chairs around the fire, and Mike suddenly seemed to have difficulty in saying what it was he wanted to say. The anger wasn't there any more.

"Listen—there's been a push in our stock. It's bad."

"Yeah? What . . ." Suddenly Sam's face was serious. "How bad?" he asked quietly.

Mike was looking down at his hands, measuring one thumb off against the other.

"You've lost control, I guess."

Then his anger got the better of him again.

"By God, it serves you right! I told you something like this could happen. But you're such a Goddamn optimist. And where were you? Not where anybody could reach you. Not . . ."

"Michael," Lettie said.

Sam said, "What happened, fella? Begin at the beginning. How do you know somebody's got control? Who the hell would want to?"

Michael took a deep breath and ran his fingers through his mat-like, graying hair. He fought his anger a moment before answering.

"All right, I'll tell you. Soon as the Market opened the stock started jumping around, like yesterday edging up all the time. So I got hold of Marcus and told him to look into it quick. He's a good broker, by the way—I'm sure of that now. I waited in his office and he went over to the Exchange himself. He kept out of sight and watched, and he found the buying was mostly being done by a broker. He was picking it up fast and easy, and then the small fry around the floor got onto it and the price ran up to twenty-eight and a quarter, closing. You know the fellow—Herrick. And . . ."

"Herrick! That's the man I told you about I met at . . ."

Sam stopped. Lettie, watching him with a worried frown on her plain, quiet face, saw Sam's sudden angry light of understanding.

"Lailey, Goddamn him! It's Lailey who's behind this!" He was shouting. "It's just the kind of thing . . ."

Lettie thought Sam looked startled by his own violence. She could see he was trying hard to master himself. He managed to say in a fairly normal voice, "We had a fight yesterday noon."

236

Lettie said, "Oh *Sam*. Claire's uncle?"

He glanced at her, took in her words and looked suddenly beset.

Mike said, "Let me finish, will you? It isn't Lailey—it's Herrick himself."

"*Herrick* hasn't any money—unless his wife . . ."

"Will you for God's sake *listen*?"

"You're sure we did lose control? This soon, it would be hard . . ."

"Marcus is sure—and Herrick told me . . ."

"Herrick!"

"Toward closing I left Marcus to come here myself and try to find you. He was doing what he could but he was pretty sure, even then . . . Evidently he was right because Herrick didn't wait till closing either. He came here."

"*Here?*"

"Went to the office, found I wasn't there, and got this address. He's just gone. You missed him by minutes."

"What did *he* want? Seems like a queer thing to do!"

"He wanted to sell out his old friend Lailey. You're perfectly right—Lailey was behind the thing but he didn't want to appear in it."

"He'd know I'd guess."

"Yeah, but probably nobody else would. I gather Herrick isn't his regular man and never handles floor trading for him."

"Never mind that. What do you mean, he wanted to sell Lailey out?"

"Well, the stock was acquired by Herrick in his own name, to keep Lailey's name out of it. Technically, he's the owner—until Lailey takes over, or the rules of the Exchange catch up with him. Anyway, he's sore at Lailey about something—I didn't ask what. He came to offer you the stock."

"I'll be damned. It's a way out—if we really have lost working control."

"We have, all right. What Herrick has doesn't constitute working control but, added to what you told me yourself Lailey has, it does—or it would give you sure control if it were added to what you have. But his offering it to us isn't much of a solution."

"Why not? He wants a hold-up price for it, I suppose?"

"Three hundred thousand over the price the stock was acquired at, which he claims was seven hundred and fifty. A million and fifty thousand. It isn't a solution because you haven't got it."

"It's too damn much!"

"Of course it's too much, but he's got us."

"I don't even see that."

"He said if we didn't pay it, Lailey would. He seemed sure about that. Said Lailey would go to any lengths . . ."

Lettie said, "Oh, it's *Willoughby!*" and they both looked at her.

When Mike went on, he looked faintly embarrassed. "Herrick seemed confident."

Sam merely said, "Yeah."

"Herrick made it clear he was going to get his price from one or the other of you. He'd rather it were you because he seems to think he's got some kind of score to settle with Lailey. I pointed out to him, of course, that if it got around that he was trying to do a thing like this, he'd be ruined. He'd lose what little reputation he has and have to quit entirely. That seemed to be the general idea. He *wants* to quit. He didn't come right out with it but I gathered that he wants to get out—go abroad somewhere. Domestic troubles, probably—or just bored. That type . . . Anyway, he's figured that he could do it nicely on a stake of three hundred thousand."

Sam wasn't listening. He said, "What did you tell him?"

"That the price was too high."

"Sure, but is he going to Lailey? Did you turn him down?"

"No."

"That's good." Sam relaxed and seemed to expand. "Why didn't you tell him to wait until I got here?"

"I did, and he wouldn't. Said he had to go home and dress to go out, but I think he was afraid to face you. He was jumpy, kept touching that little moustache, and he never meets your eyes. He

238

on my nerves sometimes—they were on fire. I said, 'For God's sake, what happened to *you*? Runaway?' He didn't answer that. He said he wanted to start moving in on a new steel stock we've got on the Exchange. Company belongs to that fellow Hadley we met at Stu's, remember? He said—Stu, that is—that he wanted to get control, which shouldn't be too hard because he already had a big block of stock. I could see Stu was mad as hell, so I figured that cut on his chin maybe meant they'd had a fight."

"Does this story have any point?"

"Just wait till you hear! Well, I told Stu I'd look into the stock and let him know what the score was. I was pretty pleased, you understand, that he'd brought this piece of business to me instead of Mandel, so I took it to mean he was getting set for something pretty hot, the sort of thing Mandel wouldn't ordinarily take on."

"And *you* would."

"Now, Vee, you don't know about these things. Just listen, will you? Well, Stu said, 'Look into it, hell! Get over on the floor and get going. Let somebody in your office do the looking. I want the buying started now, not next week.' Then he gave me a few general instructions and I put a man on finding out every last thing about the company and its financing, sent a couple of wires to Cleveland and went right over to the Exchange to start the fireworks. This man I put on is good. He looked me up at the Exchange this morning to tell me what he'd found out. This is where the story gets good. This is a Cleveland outfit, remember. Cleveland. Fenno and Company. Hadley took the Company away from old man Fenno in the panic of '73, and married his daughter, and the combination killed the old man."

"He certainly didn't *say* anything about a wife. Why, at Delmonico's . . ."

"You just listen."

Vera was still buffing her nails, sitting facing him now, her knees crossed and her black beaded slipper swinging.

"You just listen to this, Vee." Maurice rolled over on his side, fished a stick of pomade out of his pocket, applied it to the ends of his moustache, put the paper cap back on the stick and dropped it among the innumerable knick-knacks on the marble-topped table at his elbow. He gave his moustache a couple of twirls, and the expression in Vera's eyes showed she understood perfectly that there was a direct relation between the stiffness of the points of Maurice's moustache and the zest he found in life at the moment.

"Listen to this. He's married all right. About a year ago his wife left him. Left him flat."

"What's this got to do with a stock deal?"

"You have to know all about things to handle the kind of job Stu has in mind. You never know when some little thing's going to be important as hell."

"You just like gossip."

"You don't understand. Why, I could tell you . . ."

"Well, don't. Get to the point of your story, if it has any."

"Wait till you hear. It's *something*. This man of mine said this Fenno girl that Hadley married had a funny name but he couldn't remember it. He said the old man named her after a railroad station near Cleveland—of all crazy things. He said it began with Willow. Willow something. Get it? Willow Cleveland, by God!"

"Oh, no—that's impossible. That's . . ." Vera stared at him. "*Impossible!*"

"Not a bit of it. Stage name, of course."

"Stuyvesant wouldn't be giving dinners for her if . . ."

"You want to bet Stu doesn't know a thing about it?"

"But Mr. Hadley was right there, and . . ."

"And did you hear them telling anybody they were married? No. But think back at how mad he looked, both at Delmonico's and Stu's place. I tell you . . ."

"They must be divorced."

"Maybe so. It's still a juicy piece of steak."

"I just don't believe it!"

Maurice laughed. It was obvious that his wife's sharp brain was checking impressions and that her own words carried no conviction.

244

"There's certainly something wrong somewhere," he said, sliding down further on the chaise and dropping one foot on the floor. His slipper came off and he felt for it with his toe, not taking the trouble to look down. Not finding it easily, he gave it up and, putting his hands behind his head, burrowed into the big round pillow that matched the pearl-gray throw. He liked this room of Vee's. It was the very essence of woman, and it gave him the sensation of being closed in, like being between scented sheets, but Vee never co-operated very well with the feelings it aroused.

After a moment Vera nodded and the speculative look went out of her eyes. In the last few seconds she seemed to have grown several degrees more alive.

Maurice said, "My God, the story of the century. Makes your friend Stuyvesant Lailey look like a fine fool . . ."

Something in Vera seemed to flare. For a moment they looked straight at each other, her black eyes and his hazel ones—and then her heart began to beat fast so that she had to part her lips to breathe. He knows, she thought. He's known all along. Nevertheless, it was the hazel eyes which were lowered first. The contempt came back into hers. Money, she thought. From the first week we were married you'd have thought it was his. Money! Because of it she could do anything with him she wanted. She looked down at him and he rolled over on his side away from the look. He took the stopper out of one the scent bottles beside him, held it under his nose and sniffed. Without saying anything more she turned her back on him and crossed the room to her desk. Maurice watched her, but without really taking in what she was doing.

When Vera lowered the lid of her desk its contents displayed another side of herself. The pigeonholes were full of papers, all neatly fastened together and labeled, and the center section held a row of leather-bound account books. The desk was small and delicate, but a great deal more real business was performed at it than at Maurice's cumbersome one. Vera handled her own affairs. She pulled out a piece of letter paper and a pair of scissors, cut the monogram from the top of the paper and began to write rapidly.

245

Maurice frowned at her back. Not only would she go to Stu and tell him but the effect on Stu would be disastrous. The deeper Maurice's mind dug into this thing, the worse it seemed, because why the hell would a man want to revenge himself on a fellow who was acting like a rival if it turned out that the girl was married to the fellow all along? Not that a thing like a woman's being married would stop Stu Lailey. But if Stu knew about the marriage, there wouldn't be any reason for this angry attack of his. So, obviously, Stu didn't know. It was all damn complicated. Mentally, Maurice brushed the complications aside, which was what he always did with complications. Only two things were really clear to him, first, that Stu mustn't find out the gal was married until Maurice had had time to cash in, and second, that Vera would tell him at the earliest possible moment.

Vera had finished her writing and pulled out an envelope, but before she addressed it she got up and went to the bedside table where that morning's paper still lay. Vera was always a careful newspaper reader because she believed that the men she saw at parties liked a woman who knew what was going on in the world. She brought the paper back to the desk and folded it so she could see the masthead, but before she began to copy the address on the envelope, she glanced swiftly at Maurice. He had sunk back on the pillows again, lying just as she had seen him last. There was a smile of secretive contentment on his face. It lay on him like a kind of glaze. She copied the address on the masthead without bothering to hide from him what she was doing.

Maurice had just remembered that the whole deal would be closed up in the morning and either Hadley or Stu would be handing him enough to get the hell out of this, once and for all. Then Vera could do what she damn pleased. *He* wouldn't care. She'd probably go straight to Lailey with the story he'd been fool enough to tell her, but by that time it wouldn't matter. With three hundred thousand of his own money and a chance to get out, nothing would matter.

Then, for the first time, he took in the fact that Vera was writing

246

a letter. He shoved himself up on one elbow and said sharply, "What are you doing?"

"You can see what I'm doing—I'm writing."

"What's it about?"

"My notes are my own business. It's something I want Thompson to deliver tonight, after he's driven us to dinner."

"Are you writing Lailey what I told you just now?"

She leaned back in her spindly gilt chair and laughed. It was a tinkly laugh and he didn't like it. Then she looped her arm across the back of the chair and faced him over it.

"Do you think I'm such a fool as that? Have him hate *me* because *I* broke the bad news? I should say not! I'm not a fool! You can be sure *I* won't be the one to tell him."

For a moment, they just stared at each other. Then Maurice lowered his eyes, and moved one shoulder in a shrug. He believed her and he wanted to cut off the current which was flowing between them. He rolled to the edge of the chaise as though it involved a great deal of effort, and got to his feet. He shoved his toe into the lost slipper, ran his hand over the back of his head, and shuffled slowly from the room. Vera sighed and turned back to the desk. She lit a candle and gave her whole attention to twirling a stick of sealing wax in the flame. A strong perfume rose from the wax. Then she smeared some on the flap of the letter, stamped it with her seal and rubbed the seal around so the crest couldn't be read. The wax was pink, but the candle flame always streaked the color with smoke.

Up on the stage the last-act curtain had just come down and Willoughby pushed her way through the actors who were crowding into the wings and picked up her skirts in both hands, ready to run down the stairs. Burt caught her by the wrist.

"Wait a minute, sister. Recalls."

He kept hold of her wrist but he was bent forward, listening intently. The applause was a steady roar. The whole cast was spilling out on to the stage, talking to each other excitedly in loud voices. The applause had a solid, hard sound in it, and Burt nodded. It was that he was listening for. The actors were strung out in a line. Burt let go of her wrist and gave her a push.

"Go on. Take it."

They made a gap for her in the center of the line. She was still Hester. The sound on the other side of the curtain appalled her. She tried to remember what it had been like the night before and could remember nothing at all.

"Take it *up!*"

The cast stopped talking and the line tensed suddenly. She wasn't able to think very clearly but her mind photographed irrelevant details, like the dirty-white, crackled inside of the curtain. A blast of heat from the footlights struck her ankles and she knew that the curtain was going up. A streak of brilliance blinded her as the lights sparkled and danced in the current of air from the curtain. The applause swelled.

She was facing the audience. The people made the slope of the theater look light, instead of dark, as it did at rehearsal. The whole mass was in motion—that was all she could see. She bowed gravely, felt and heard a response, and bowed again. The line of actors had receded from her, leaving her out in front. She bowed again and tried to shake Hester off and be herself. The moving air stirred the curls on her forehead, and then she was staring at the crackled, whitish back of the curtain again.

It went up and down and the last time it came down she remembered to move back from the eddy of dust that arose when the curtain hit the stage. She saw the backs of the others as they crowded into the wings. She turned to follow.

"*Hold it! Hold it!*"

The curtain. With the blinding flare of the foots in her face she made a last effort to shake Hester off. She tried to smile, made a gesture of helpless apology, and the applause mounted suddenly. The audience seemed to understand. Then she was facing the blank inside of the curtain again. She turned and ran. Burt caught her in the crook of his arm.

248

"You were better tonight." He was still listening. "Hand's better, too."

She was panting, and she leaned against him. His thin body was tense. She looked up at him in surprise and discovered that he was concentrating on judging the exact moment for the next recall. There were a lot of stagehands standing about now and Mac passed by. He was moving the heavy standard of a big floodlight, "walking" it, and kicking its green gas tube ahead of him, utterly indifferent, as usual, to anything but his own job.

Burt held out his arm, hand flat, palm up, and raised it slowly. His other arm was still around her. She saw the curtain begin to rise on the empty stage. He took his arm away, *"Walk on slow,"* he said.

She walked on. The stagehands were already beginning to kick out the props from behind the set. Through the open stage door she could hear the loud voices of the actors calling to each other as they went to their dressing rooms. She walked on smiling, much more herself now, and the applause rose to meet her.

Flowers. The procession of ushers was already half way down the aisle and the footlights were going down so that she could lean out over them. When they were down, she could see the house easily. People here and there were getting up and putting on their coats, but the applause continued. Her arms were full of roses now, two huge bouquets on each arm. Stuyvesant, of course. The orchestra men were helping to hoist the baskets up on the stage, careful to keep them back so that the curtain would not strike them. They hit the stage with a thump. A tiny bell in the orchestra pit was ringing, signal that the curtain would not rise again. She backed up, smiling. The rose thorns were pricking her arms. The curtain was down.

Suzanne was waiting near the bottom of the stage steps. Burt never let her nearer the stage than that. She had begun to get the yellow look she always had late at night when she was tired. Dubinsky was coming toward them down the corridor. Willoughby dumped the bouquets she was carrying into Suzanne's outstretched arms without bothering about the thorns, and held out her hands to him.

She said, "Oh, Isaac, it went better, didn't it? I'm not just imagining it?"

He squeezed her hand. "Yes, dear, it did. But I don't think it can affect the run."

"I know, I know, but I don't care. It's better—that's something."

He was smiling at her but she thought that you always felt a sort of sadness back of his smile. It was the first time she had realized it, and she wondered about it and about the sense that you had of his aloneness. Then she was surprised at herself because she had never thought about these things before. Isaac as a person was beginning to mean something to her. She opened her eyes wide and looked at him, and his smile deepened as though he had read her thoughts.

"Why," she said, "you're in evening dress." The discovery surprised her. She said, "I suppose you were the other nights too—I didn't notice."

"That's not astonishing."

Behind them, stagehands were carrying the baskets of flowers down the steps and Suzanne was directing them loudly, in French. Willoughby broke off a rosebud from the nearest basket and put it in the buttonhole of Dubinsky's lapel. It hung crookedly and she tried to straighten it. Isaac in his evening clothes with the rosebud that wouldn't stay straight, so different from everyone, so much by himself. She took his hand again.

She said, "Rehearsal at ten?"

"You want to rehearse?"

"Of course."

He wasn't smiling, and he looked tired and troubled.

"And Isaac, if I don't do what you want, you'll scold me?"

"Yes, dear. I'll scold you."

Chapter Sixteen

LETTIE, always an early riser, came downstairs the next morning before anyone else was dressed. In the hall she paused to listen for sounds from the kitchen, heard the banging of stove lids and guessed that Katie was in her usual morning temper. Shamrock came out of the dining room, yawned, stretched in a deep bow in front of her and she went to the front door to let him out. She stood a minute sniffing the chill fresh air, then bent to pick up two newspapers from the stoop—Sam's and Michael's.

A few minutes later Sam heard her calling him from outside his bedroom door. Surprised, he opened it a crack and looked out. She was holding out an open newspaper to him.

"Sam, I thought you'd better see this right away. There's a story here about you and Willoughby—about you being married. I thought from the way you and Michael talked last night, that it might make a difference, Sam."

He opened the door wider and took it, and she stood there watching him read it. He was in his stocking feet and he had no collar on. Sam had never learned to read fast and he gave it his whole attention, frowning at it and smoothing back his hair with his free hand. Minor headlines said:

Is Willow Cleveland Wife of Steel Magnate?

Sam glanced up at Lettie and quickly back to the paper. The story went on:

The wires have been humming all night checking the rumor that Willow Cleveland, newest Broadway star, is the secret wife of Sam Hadley, Cleveland steel man. Stuyvesant Lailey, rival steel man, is said to be backing Miss Cleveland's play, but he could not be reached at a late hour last night and our reporter was turned away from Miss Cleveland's hotel. Reliable sources in Cleveland, however . . .

Sam read no further. He lowered the paper and they stood silently looking at each other. Then Lettie said, "You go downtown first, Sam. I'll go to see Claire. You can't very well go to the Lailey house, anyway. I'll try to bring her here."

An hour later Sam was in a hansom, sitting as he always did, in the exact middle of the seat, his hands on his knees, impatiently letting himself be jolted and bumped downtown. Lailey was in his office. When Sam burst in, having brushed aside a young man in striped trousers who would have restrained him, Lailey was sitting behind a table-desk. He hadn't, Sam thought, been doing anything but staring into space. He jumped to his feet.

"Hadley!"

An angry flush rose to his face and the strange eyes began to blaze. *"Get out of here!"* He was so choked with anger that it didn't sound like his voice.

Hadley came farther into the room and tossed his hat on a table. "Not till I've said what I have to say."

Lailey was leaning his weight on the top of his desk, bending forward toward Hadley.

"I'm all through talking to you about anything."

"Oh, no you're not. Sit down."

Lailey started to come out from behind his desk and Sam hunched his shoulders. "Listen, if you want another fight, you can have that too, but you know what'll happen to you!"

Lailey took another step and stopped, and for a moment his heavy breathing was the only sound in the room.

Sam said, "Go back and sit down, for Christ sake." He closed his hand over the back of a chair, swung it around so it faced Lailey's desk and set it down with a thump. With his hand still on the back of it, he said, "If you want to waste a lotta time having a row about it, it's all right with me, but that isn't what I came for."

"I suppose you came because you know I've got enough of your stock to give me working control of your company. Well, I don't propose to deal with you personally. There'll be a third party appointed by me . . ."

"Will you, for Christ sake, sit down?"

Lailey came slowly back to his swivel chair, fingering the cut on his chin. The skin around it was bluish. His eyes were still on fire but Sam, whose anger was beginning to cool a little, noticed for the first time that they looked sunken and full of strain. He thought that the guy had probably seen the story in the paper. He seemed to be taking it hard. Sam sat down and crossed his knees, his hands on the chair arms, his elbows stuck out at right angles.

Lailey said, "There's no point whatever to this. You'll hear from me when the formalities connected with the stock are concluded."

"Technically, the stock isn't in your name."

"That's one of the formalities I spoke of."

"And so long as it isn't in your name, you don't own control."

"That doesn't signify anything. I don't know how you found out —or maybe you're guessing, but the stock wasn't acquired in my name for reasons of my own. It's unimportant. Now that the buying is finished, it will be transferred to me in the course of the day. Stock is often bought . . ."

"It's a lot more important than you think." Sam pulled in his elbows and tipped his chair up on its back legs. "Herrick was in to see me yesterday."

"*Herrick* was? He was certainly exceeding his authority . . ."

"I wasn't there, matter of fact. He saw Brodi. You know who Mike Brodi is?"

Lailey nodded impatiently. Sam could see he was angry about Herrick.

"He offered us the block of stock he bought for you—for a consideration."

"What do you mean?"

"Just that. He seemed to want to sell you out."

"I don't believe it!"

"It's true. Brodi's probably at Herrick's office at this minute. He was going to wait there until he heard from me."

"I tell you, I don't believe it. Do you know what you're saying? We went to *college* together."

"Just the same, that's the way it is."

Lailey studied Sam silently. Not many people, after such a scrutiny as Lailey gave him, doubted Sam's word. Lailey didn't. Presently he lowered his eyes and, picking up a paper knife, turned it over and over in his hands. He was, Sam knew, thinking about Maurice, and then it dawned on Sam that the fellow was feeling sorry. Have an affair with the wife of an old friend and then, when he turns on you, feel sorry! Incomprehensible! Sam brought the front legs of his chair down to the floor with a bang and said, "You can see what I'm getting at, can't you?"

"Certainly I can. I assume you accepted his offer and paid his consideration, whatever it was. What I can't understand is, why didn't he come to me? I've advanced him money before, when he needed it."

"I imagine he had his reasons."

Lailey looked at him sharply, and Sam had the swift thought that he really did look as if he'd had about all he could take. Beat up. Sam said, "Let me tell you how things stand. I didn't take up his offer."

254

holding her close to him, and she leaned against him and put her head down on his shoulder. The way she did it made him think again how young she was. He mustn't hurry her—must give her time and enough freedom from himself to be sure. There was the long business of the divorce to be gotten through—best not to bind her by any promises until that was over.

These thoughts brought him no unrest. He could wait in calmness for the kind of peace she would bring him. In this love, where passion would play no more than its proper part, there was no restless urgency, no violent craving out of normal. He thought for a while how different his feelings for her were from those which Willoughby had aroused, so different that, with her, he seemed to himself scarcely the same person.

Then the thought came to him that Willoughby, too, might be different with someone she really loved. Someone else might find in her feelings he had never aroused. The thought did not disturb his peace. He was free. He looked down on the bright head resting so quietly on his shoulder.

Claire opened her eyes. Out of their depths she looked straight up at him, and again a strong, warm tide of color flooded her cheeks. She turned quickly and hid her face against him. After a minute she slid her hand up over his shoulder until it rested against his cheek, and she stroked it. The gesture was tenderly possessive and very womanly. In it, she was both submitting to him and comforting him because she loved him. The womanliness of it moved him so that he couldn't see her very clearly. He knew that she had found herself completely. She stirred in his arms and held up her face to be kissed. He said, "My Claire," and knew that it was true.

Chapter Seventeen

THE rehearsal lasted late that morning and most of the cast, feeling that the play should be allowed to die its inevitable death, were resentful. They had never liked Willoughby and they blamed her now for this extra work. And for the first time their dislike troubled her. She tried to ignore her own feeling and concentrate on the subtle changes which Isaac was making in Hester, but some of the fervor, some of the high resolve which had followed her talk in Dubinsky's office had worn off. The work was exacting, Dubinsky's demands unremitting and the hostility of the cast pressed on her until her nerves were keyed to such a tension that she wanted to cry out.

Then, toward the end, when everyone knew Dubinsky would not keep them much longer, something happened off stage. Willoughby didn't know what it was but, before very long, everyone else seemed to know. She was kept continually on the stage, with no chance to ask anyone about it, but, in her hypersensitive state, she felt the excitement in the air. She heard it, too, in the whisperings in the wings. Once, when she glanced that way, everyone was looking at her. That she was herself somehow the center of it, she read in the looks which passed between the actors on the stage. It had tightened their unity against her. She felt this and it upset her, and her voice grew a little strident so that Dubinsky stopped her.

Before she began again, she pressed her hands hard against her eyes until stars wheeled in front of them. After that she lost Hester completely. No one, not even Dubinsky, seemed to care. She felt the indifference everywhere. Everyone was restless, anxious for the act, which was near its end, to run itself out. It made her feel that, to all of them but herself, *The Rungs of the Ladder* wasn't important any more. She had a deeply disturbing feeling that, for them, the play was already dead, that from now on it would be just words. They would play it tonight and other nights and they might rehearse again, but that would make no difference. The life of the theater, the vitality and the interest no longer focused on it and so it was finished. This was how a play died—not at the final curtain but when the creative fire, the united effort are withdrawn and move on to some new play.

Suddenly she didn't want the act to end because, to her, *The Rungs of the Ladder* was the most important thing in the world. Because she couldn't let the play die, she threw herself into it, trying to give it her own vitality. She was Hester again, more truly Hester than she had ever been. Behind the lines of the play she cried out to Imogene, the friend she had deserted, not to leave her but to stay with her and help her in her fight against herself. Down in the house, Dubinsky sat, quiet. It was the new Hester, a Hester torn by her own nature, fighting it, losing the fight.

The chances for happiness are so few.

It was a cry of despair out of the loneliness she had brought on herself. And then the final line, and Hester crushed by dismay and heartbreak because she had destroyed the things which now, too late, she wanted to keep alive. She spoke the words in a kind of hushed horror at herself.

We were married this morning, John and I.

For a few minutes she had brought the play alive, brought Hester alive. She didn't follow the others from the stage. As soon as she had spoken the last lines she walked quickly, not waiting for anything, into the shadows behind the set. She wanted to be where no one could see her. There were tears in her eyes, Hester's hard-wrung, bitter tears. People were calling her. Dubinsky was calling her too, and there was a different sound in his voice. She leaned against the cold brick wall, in the dark, and let the tears run down her cheeks, crying because she was Hester and because she was herself and the play was dead.

The actors were gone now, and the stage was full of noise. They'd given up trying to find her. Mac was shouting, metal stanchions were banging. The gas lights blinked out and a flood of the arc's white light took their place. She pulled out her handkerchief and wiped her eyes. She wasn't Hester any more. She crossed the stage back of the scenery where the light was dim, stepping over ropes and pipes, skirting the angles of the braces.

When she came out on the landing at the top of the stairs which led down from the stage, she was at once aware again of the atmosphere of excitement which had filled the stage. The whole cast of *The Rungs of the Ladder* was in a noisy group at the end of the corridor, gathered around the call-board where theater notices were posted. They were shouting and laughing like children at recess. And then she knew, as clearly as though she herself could see the call-board, what the excitement was about. The assignments of parts for the new play had been posted, and that play was now the focal point to which already had been transferred the theater's complex of talents and emotions.

They had, she knew, found her name there—not as the lead, but somewhere down the list in a small part, once more at the bottom of the rungs of the ladder. That was what the excitement had been about and that was why they had all looked at her. She leaned her weight on the blackened wood railing and tried to steady the beating of her heart. Her knees felt weak. She'd told Isaac she'd be content with that. She hadn't believed it would really happen—she hadn't prepared herself. Now they all knew, and they were jeering at her, enjoying themselves. She clung to the railing.

The youth called Cam turned his head and, seeing her, he stared. She let go of the railing and straightened up. Cam whispered to the others and they all turned to look at her. They were silent. She went down the steps carefully and along the corridor toward them. She didn't hurry. She made herself look grave and pleasant and gracious, with a little smile on her lips that was meant to tell them she already knew what they had found there.

They moved to either side of the board as she came up, leaving a way for her. Russ, a lad more sensitive to the feelings of others than theater youth is apt to be, left the group and went into his dressing room and shut the door. Two more did the same. Cam and the rest stayed and watched her openly.

The notice was in the center of the board. She went right up to it, smiling.

The title of the new play was *The Scamp*. It was lettered in crude capitals at the top of the notice and the characters were listed below, beginning with Amabelle. To the right of each character's name had been written the name of the actor who was assigned to the part. The cast was large and a few of the spaces had not yet been filled in. Someone had drawn a rough star in front of Amabelle's name, but the space to the right was empty.

Willoughby read the list all the way to the bottom, including the line of writing which said that the first reading of *The Scamp* would take place that same afternoon at two o'clock. They were all watching her, almost holding their breaths, but she didn't need to read it again. Her name was not on it. She turned away, her smile grown a little stiff. They all watched her as she went back along the corridor. Cam, the theater's self-appointed funny man, started to whistle, just audibly—it was the "Dead March" from *Saul*, and he whistled it in perfect time with her retreating steps. She heard him. She wanted to run away or turn and shout at them, but she didn't even change the tempo of her walk. No one laughed at Cam and his whistle died. She wanted more than anything on earth to be alone.

267

She could keep herself rigid just until then. She started to go into her dressing room, but she heard Suzanne inside talking to someone. She turned away and went back up the steps and onto the stage.

She thought she had left it a long time ago, but Mac was still shouting. There was a great deal of noise, furniture being dragged, stagehands tramping, the brittle crash of props being knocked out from behind the scenery. Burt was shouting, too. It was dark behind the wings where she stood. She backed up until she felt one of the black barrels of dusty water behind her.

The side wall of the set just in front of her, the one with the door through which she made her last entrance, shook, leaned a little, and rose slowly upward out of sight. She slid around the rain barrel farther into the shadows and put the back of her hand against her mouth. The noise increased. It sounded as though it were inside her own head. The swaying canvas wall now high above her hit something, and dirt rained down. She backed farther away. It was like watching the ending of the world. The opposite side of Hester's drawing room shook like a piece of paper and began to rise. She shut her eyes.

When she opened them again, the stage was clear and all traces of *The Rungs of the Ladder* had disappeared. Her knees felt weak again. Something beside her looked in the dim light like a pile of folded curtains, and she sat down on them. The dust which rose from them felt dry in her nostrils. Everyone had gone now but Burt. He was dragging a deal table to one side of the empty stage. The pile of sides she had seen in Dubinsky's office was on the table. The noise seemed to jar through all her nerves. She put her hands down and clutched the folds of dusty curtain. Somewhere you reached the end of your endurance. At some point you couldn't stand any more. Burt was opening folding chairs now, setting them in a semicircle in the center of the stage for the reading of *The Scamp*. Each chair, as he opened it, made a small bang. Then the sound of his heels on the stage, and then another bang.

Burt completed the semicircle and, sitting down behind the deal table, pulled a thick manuscript toward him and began to study it. The strange, alive quiet took possession of the empty stage. A great wave of weariness washed over Willoughby. She felt the first beginnings of self-pity, which is the narcotic for defeat. There was something hypnotic about it, as though, now that she was faced with defeat, it no longer seemed intolerable. Home with Sam—or somewhere with Stuyvesant—it didn't matter. She was too tired to care.

Then she roused herself. She felt as though she had been standing on the edge of a precipice and, lured by it, had nearly thrown herself over. Her hands were cold and her heart was beating in light, quick thumps.

Burt shuffled his feet and turned some pages, rattling them. Then the quiet settled back. Small, quick sounds were all around her. Some seemed far away, the other side of the brick wall, softly pattering. Some seemed to tap on the boards at her feet. A drop struck her hand, cold and sudden. Rain through the ventilators. She looked up into the blackness over her head.

She could hear it coming faster now, like a spring rain. It gave her life. Strange stage, limitless, beautiful, awesome. She was nowhere near the edge of the precipice now. She was filled with excitement, but at the same time she felt her own aloneness. The stage —this or another, there was no real difference. And if she could keep what she felt now, the change wouldn't be hard, or the new beginning. She stood up solemnly, as though she had been asked to rise. She went quietly toward the door. She knew that Burt, startled, had turned to watch her, but she kept her head bent and went on her way.

She pushed open the stage door and stepped out on the landing. The corridor was empty now, except for Dubinsky, who was walking slowly toward the stairs which led to his office. His shoulders were bent and he was so deep in thought that he hadn't heard the opening of the stage door behind him. At sight of him her normal self came flooding back, and she felt anger at him because he had broken faith with her and given her no part. She almost called to him. She didn't know what stopped her but, instead of calling out, she watched him as he went away from her down the corridor, and her anger drained slowly out of her.

She stood there, with her hands on the railing, watching him. He looked, as he always did, alone. But now, for the first time, she felt that she was seeing him clearly. The things she and the others saw in him—his weariness, his sudden rages—were, she knew now, only surface things. Behind his bursts of anger when his actors failed to reach the heights he had imagined for them, he hid a deep disappointment. The weariness was not real weariness but the outward sign of discouragement, and his aloneness the product of his own sense of failure to reach his ideal.

This momentary understanding of him moved her. She watched him disappear around the turn in the corridor, the great Dubinsky, the lonely man striving to catch up with his own dream. He and she were both alone, but she felt comforted. She felt she knew now the value of his support and the quality of his inexorable purpose, and even though she was to have them no longer, she was comforted. She went slowly down the steps.

In her dressing room she found Suzanne, with the eternal ironing board slung across the backs of two chairs. When Suzanne saw Willoughby she slid the two irons on the gas ring to one side and put a coffee pot beside them. She said, "It's hot, Madame. I keep it hot this long time."

Willoughby sat down on the bench in front of the looking glass. Suzanne cleared a space among the bottles and jars on the shelf to make room for a plate with a napkin-wrapped sandwich on it. She went over to the gas ring and poured coffee into a cup. When she started back across the room with it, their eyes met. Suzanne's were flat and expressionless, but the skin at the corners looked tight and the tiny fan-shaped wrinkles looked deeper. Willoughby thought, she knows. Like everyone else, she's heard about it. She'll get a new place now. She's sorry about me in her own way, but she's ambitious too, and she'll get a new place. That will be just one of many things which will be different from now on.

Suzanne set the steaming cup down carefully. "Monsieur Hadley was here, Madame."

Suzanne waited for her reply like one who has deliberately touched a nerve.

Willoughby picked up her coffee spoon. Suzanne's eyes, watching her with hungry curiosity, the stale smell of last night's roses, the horrid meal on the shelf with the grease paint—each of these things was a trifle, but each was endowed with the power to demand a piece of her and to encroach by that much on her mood. The insatiable demands of the trivial—they were like an enemy.

Suzanne was saying, "He couldn't wait any longer, Madame," and Willoughby had to think who it was who couldn't wait. Sam, of course. Suzanne was still explaining. "He said he had something to say to Madame but that he'd write it in a letter. He said to say 'Good-bye.'"

"All right—thank you. I'll eat my lunch now."

Suzanne left her then and Willoughby sat very still. The first effect of her shock at finding her name was not on the list on the call-board was wearing off and, as though this were a physical injury, the real pain, the pain that would have to be lived with day by day for a long time, began to make itself felt. To deaden it she turned now to those small, commonplace things which she had tried a moment before to put away from her. She pulled the plate toward her, lifted back a corner of the napkin and took out the sandwich. It tasted like flannel. She took a sip of coffee to wash it down, and the heat brought tears to her eyes.

Then she realized that she didn't have to eat this way any more. Not even today. She could dress up and lunch in the most fashionable place in town, go shopping afterward—anything. She saw herself hurrying to do it, calling for Suzanne, dressing in her smartest clothes, quickly, quickly so as to have no time to think—but she sat still.

There was a knock on the door, sudden, urgent. Startled, she looked up. Before she had time to say anything, the door was opened and Lailey stood there. He looked disheveled and his eyes were too bright. She jumped to her feet.

"Stuyvesant!"

Then she remembered the newspaper story, and she had enough detachment to be amazed that she could have forgotten it.

Stuyvesant walked heavily to the settee and threw his hat on it. Then he sat down and buried his face in his hands. She stood looking down at him. She had known all day that this scene was ahead of her and, when there had been time to think about it, she had dreaded it. Now, more than ever, she had no heart for it. She was exhausted and she felt cheated out of her own right to sympathy. She knew, from old experience of scenes like this, that she would have to play it through until his need to release his emotions was satisfied. She was fully aware that he was suffering and she was honestly sorry, but these emotions of his seemed to her a little unreal. She couldn't throw herself into this scene as he would expect. It wasn't, for her, the only thing that mattered.

She sighed with weary acceptance of her task and noticed that the door was standing open. She went to it and shut it, moving softly so that he wouldn't realize she had enough detachment to be concerned about open doors, and then she went to him and knelt in front of him, putting her hands on his knees.

"Stuyvesant, darling—please don't feel so badly. I should have told you . . ."

"*Badly*? How would you feel?"

He took his hands away from his face and looked at her with deep reproach, but she was less aware of that than of the lost look of hopelessness which lay behind it. Her feeling that this was a scene in a play began to vanish.

"Oh, darling—*don't* look like that."

"Why didn't you tell me? Why didn't you have the honesty—or just the decency—to tell me?"

"Because I was afraid if you knew, I'd *lose* you, Stuyvesant. Can't you see that?"

"Yes, I can see that, all right. You were afraid you'd lose my

272

backing. You were afraid if I knew you were secretly married, I wouldn't put money in the show. You're Goddamn right—I wouldn't!"

"Darling, please . . ."

He pushed her hands off his knees and jumped up. He stood facing her, his shoulders hunched, bending toward her. The light eyes burned with an inward fire.

"It's no use, Willow—I'm all through. That's what I came to tell you. I've found out what you really are—you're utterly selfish—you're out for what you can get. That's all that matters to you—what you can get for yourself."

"Stuyvesant, stop it!" She struggled to rise, but her heel caught in the hem of her skirt. She sat where she was, looking up at him.

"It's true. You know it's true."

"It *isn't* true . . ."

He turned away from her and went to the bench, where he sat on the edge, bent over, his hands twisted together. She freed herself and got to her feet, but the hardness of his anger kept her from going to him. She stood there, her breath coming fast, waiting for what he would say next, ready to ward it off. Then he struck the heels of his hands together and made a small, outward motion which was strangely expressive, as though he were letting something escape. She thought she had never noticed before that his hands could look sensitive. She saw that despair was beginning to overcome his anger.

He said, "There's no use shouting at each other like this. It won't do any good. I'm going to leave you. I've made up my mind. I'm going away—abroad somewhere."

"Oh, darling, *don't. Don't.* I need you now more than ever. Darling, I've just found out I've got to begin all over again in a small part in some other theater. I need you . . ."

He raised his eyes and looked at her and the look said, 'It's what I thought—it's all true. You want me to buy you into another show. I was right about you.'

273

She cried out. "No, no—I don't mean it that way. I want *you*—you yourself. I want to be the friends we've been. I *need* you, Stuyvesant. I don't want your help. I have to do it myself this time—the other way's no good in the long run. I know that now. But I need you, Stuyvesant. I need what we've been to each other."

He ran his fingers through his hair, then rested his forehead on his hands. He said in a different voice, "It meant so much to me, after the kind of life I've led and the sorts of women I've known, to meet a woman like *you*, Willow—like what I thought you were. Someone who was in earnest, someone who had an ideal and knew how to work for it—someone who didn't have the petty, frivolous, mean traits so many women have. Someone with intelligence and fortitude. I'd never met anyone like you. It was something new in life. And even the work you were doing. I never knew anyone before who was driven to work by some inner urge the way you are. I never knew people like these here in the theater—like Dubinsky—creative people. It's a new world. And the theater itself—the stage and all about it fascinated me. I began to catch a glimpse of what the creative life means to the people who live it. My own life began to seem shallow and dull and, compared to *yours*, nothing in it seemed worthwhile. I loved you, Willow. I loved you as much as any man could love a woman. And when the play failed, I wanted to marry you. I was going to try to make it up to you in any way I could. I loved you."

He stopped, staring at his clasped hands again. She stood looking down at him. She wasn't thinking about what he had said but about the odd feeling which she had that he had changed. Or perhaps what they had been through together had changed her, so that she saw and felt qualities in other people—in Dubinsky and now in Stuyvesant—which she hadn't known were there, hadn't perhaps been capable of knowing. She remembered that Dubinsky had once said to her—a long time ago, it seemed—that an artist must be reborn. She had thought it a stock phrase, without meaning. Was this what he meant—this new understanding of others, this new sensitiveness to life?

274

Stuyvesant, still holding his forehead in his hands, said in a dull, tired voice, "Your name isn't even Willow, is it?" And it brought sudden tears to her eyes.

"Stuyvesant . . ."

He glanced up at her inquiringly, the way he might look at a stranger.

"Since I've got to begin all over again, Stuyvesant, I'm going to make it a real beginning. I'm going to do things as nearly *right* as I can. Maybe I won't succeed in the end, maybe it will turn out that I don't have the ability in me, as I think I have, but if I *don't* succeed it won't be because there's something wrong with my attitude toward my work. I think it's going to be hard to change, but I'm going to do it. And you're part of it, Stuyvesant. We started wrong, you and I, just as I started wrong in the theater. I'm going to begin over with you, too. I'm going to tell you the truth. Perhaps you won't like it. Perhaps it will make you want to go away from me all the more, though God knows I hope it won't."

Stuyvesant looked up, his attention caught, not so much by what she was saying as by some quality he felt in her. He did not know what it was but it seemed to him that she was speaking with a new sureness, and saying with a new simplicity the things which were on her mind. He didn't interrupt her because he found he no longer wanted to say the things he had come to say and he was not yet sure of the new thoughts and feelings which were struggling in him. She went on.

"The truth is that at first I *did* want to use you, and that's why I didn't tell you I was married. Then—suddenly I seemed to know you so well that I didn't know *how* to tell you. I knew you'd have to find out sometime, but I was so much involved in the play that I didn't think as much about you as I should have. I only thought about myself. But I *was* afraid of losing you, Stuyvesant. Perhaps, if I hadn't been working so hard . . . No, I'm not going to make excuses. But I *was* afraid of losing you, and I don't want to lose you now."

He turned away and began to walk around the little room, his head down. He was thinking about the discovery, which he had just made about himself, that the jealousy and possessiveness which had made him suffer so much didn't matter any more. She had grown beyond their reach. The change in her seemed to him more and more apparent. Could her failure in the play do that to her—and in so brief a time? If so, he thought she was changing in the right way. He thought she wasn't yet aware herself of the forces which were awakening in her. Perhaps that was why she still clung to him, because she didn't yet know that she had found herself.

He reached the end of the room and turned back. She was standing quietly, as though she had talked herself out. Her quietness, after the high-strung feverishness of the last weeks, was strangely moving and it made him feel a great gentleness toward her. He went back to her and took her hands. She let them lie in his and he looked into her eyes, not knowing what it was he was trying to find there but feeling that it was important to find it. She looked back at him with a calm steadiness and an affection which he could not mistake. He tightened his hold on her hands.

Always, before, there had been something secret in her eyes, but now she let him look right into them. At first he saw nothing but the calm. Then he saw her tremendous vitality of spirit begin to kindle. Once more she was vibrantly alive. She seemed to fill more space than her own physical boundaries. He felt himself swept away.

She herself had said this was her real beginning. Nothing could hold her back. What more could he do for her now? Nothing that mattered. In the long run, she would need no one but herself. She would leave them all behind. If he stayed with her, she would lean on him for a little while. Then, needing him no longer, she would be kind, but from a greater and greater distance, while he himself stood still. He had come here thinking that he was about to leave her, but now he knew that, though it would be some time before she realized it, in reality it was she who was leaving him.

He was still holding her hands. He raised them, first one and then the other, and kissed them. "Good-bye," he said. "Good-bye."

Upstairs, in his small office, Dubinsky took a letter out of a drawer and laid it on his blotter, then he took out his watch and laid it beside the letter. His desk had the preternaturally neat appearance it always had at the beginning of a new production, and the first reading of *The Scamp* was about to take place.

It seemed to Dubinsky that he had never faced a new play in such a state of indecision. He pulled the letter toward him but he was already so familiar with it that he did not need to read it again. In Rita's big, erratic hand, it began,

Isaac darling: I am quite well again in just this short time—the ocean air here in the south has done that already for Rita. Quite well, and anxious to be back at work . . .

What, he wondered, really was her condition now? He studied the handwriting as though the lines themselves could tell him what he wanted to know. They did not waver exactly—the dashing form was still there, but he had the impression that they had been written with care rather than sureness. Why did he long for her so much, for her competence and her technique? She wasn't sailing just yet, the letter said. There was time to call her back if he wanted her. If he did not, would she ever again leave that little seaside village in the south of France, where she was going? He might some time visit her there, and the visit would surely be painful to them both. But if he called her back, would it accomplish more than the staving off, for just one more production, of the ultimate end?

He shut his eyes and tried to imagine her in the part of Amabelle, and instantly she was there before him in his mind, moving with her own peculiar grace in Amabelle's great crinoline. Then he tried to put the picture of Willow in her place and found that his mind would create no image at all. The time had come when he must choose between them and he was no nearer than before to making up his mind. He sighed. His choice had to be between Rita's failing power on the one hand and Willow's inadequacy on the other.

No, inadequacy wasn't the word, and he knew he wasn't being fair to her because, in his own mind, he was expecting more of her than when she had first come to him. He had raised his own standards for her. She had the divine fire in her. The trouble was that neither he nor she had yet discovered how to draw it out. There had been a brief time at the end of today's rehearsal when something had released this fire and, for an exciting few minutes, the play had lived. During them she was more than adequate—she was superb, and she had filled him with tremendous hope. But he knew a flash such as that one was accident, set off by God knew what emotional disturbance. It had revealed her potentialities, true, but could she do as much with other scenes in other plays? Could she even reproduce the fire which had been in her during that same scene?

He picked up Rita's letter and put it back in the drawer. He looked at it lying there and wondered whether his longing for her was real or whether it might not be the first sign that he was reaching a time of life when the mind was beginning to rebel against all change. Then he shut the drawer and turned the key. He pocketed his watch and stood up. He looked slowly all around the office, at everything in it, and then he went out.

There was no hurry. Fifteen minutes to spare, and the only respite he was likely to have before the new production caught him up in its inevitable progress. The theater was quiet and the corridors empty. The gas lights in their round wire cages hissed softly.

New plays were new beginnings. You carried the fatigue over from the old one, and you began in a subdued kind of way, dreading it in a sense, feeling stale, wondering where you would find the strength for a fresh start. Somewhere you did find strength. Not all at once—you worked into it gradually, gaining momentum, discovering, as you went along, that the capacity was there. But it was lonely work. Odd that it should be. Probably that was because the whole complicated structure depended, in the last analysis, on you alone.

At the bottom of the stairs he paused in front of the call-board and stared thoughtfully at the list of names of those summoned to the reading of *The Scamp*. The problem was, experience versus the

278

new, the strong, the vital. In the long run, there was no question which would prevail. He slowly took a pencil out of his pocket and wrote Willow Cleveland's name at the top of the list. Burt would find it there. Then he sighed again, but this time the sigh gave expression to a feeling of relief and of having made the right decision.

He went through the corridors and into the house from the darkened lobby. The stage was empty. He stood still a minute, with his hands on the back of one of the seats, leaning his weight on it, looking at the half circle of empty chairs and at the wooden table waiting on the stage. In the white light of the arc lamp they had a clarity of outline sharper than reality. The brick wall at the back vanished upward in the shadows and a rope end, hanging from the flies, swung slowly. The empty stage had a strange, stirring aliveness. It was limitless. It made him believe, as always, that anything could be made to happen there. When the actors came they would reduce it, for awhile, to their own dimensions. His mission would be to recapture, if he could, some of this great illusion, but he knew, and the knowledge made him deeply sad, that the play as a reality would lack the quality of his dream.

He went down to the front row and took a place in the center. He pulled out a handkerchief and mopped his face, and after that he merely waited. Once Burt put his head out of the wings, saw him, and went away without speaking. He sat quietly on through the last minutes of his respite. After a while, off in the distance, faintly, he heard the call-boy's cry. "Places, please. Act One, Scene One places. Places, please. Places . . ."